TRAVELS O

Also by Sasscer Hill

TRAVELS OF QUINN
A Quinn O'Neill Mystery

Sasscer Hill

COVER PHOTO OF SOUTH Boundary by Larry Gleason

Sasscer Hill

Praise for *Travels of Quinn*

"Award-winner Sasscer Hill knows horses and people. Put these together and you've got a heart-stopping thriller of a murder mystery as Quinn O'Neill runs for her life!" –*Charles Todd, best-selling Inspector Rutledge and the Bess Crawford series. Winner of Anthony, Edgar, and Barry Awards.*

Praise for Hill's Agatha and Macavity Nominated "Nikki Latrelle" Series

"... you'll be intrigued by Sasscer Hill's Racing from Death"– *The Washington Post*

" . . smooth and vivid descriptive prose about racetrack characters and backstretch ambiance that reeks authenticity."– *John L. Breen, Ellery Queen's Mystery Magazine*

" . . . an utterly unique take on racetrack thrillers." - *Betty Webb, Mystery Scene Magazine*

"A page-turner, the book's sentences are short and crisp. The action comes off as authentic."- *Sandra McKee, Baltimore Sun*

" . . a major new talent and the comparisons to Dick Francis are not hyperbole."—*Margaret Maron, New York Times Bestselling author and winner of the Edgar, Agatha, Anthony, and Macavity awards.*

"'Racing from Death' is an exciting thriller set in the world of horse racing, very much recommended."– *Carl Logan, Midwest Book Review*

Praise for Hill's Multiple Award Winning "Fia Mckee" Series
Flamingo Road

Flamingo Road, winner of the $10,000 Dr. Tony Ryan Award for Best Book in Horse Racing Literature

"Hill shows her . . . knowledge of horses and the very real problems in horse racing that fill this sound mystery with thrills and hair-raising action from first to last."—*Kirkus*

"A fast pace and a feisty heroine put FLAMINGO ROAD in the winner's circle. Sasscer Hill is off to the races with her new character, Fia McKee, and I'm on board for that ride!"—*Tami Hoag, NYT Bestselling author*

"Flamingo Road, an intelligent and thrilling book."—*David Housewright, Edgar Award-winning author*

The Dark Side of Town

"Filled with sense-laden descriptions and ever tightening suspense, this is gripping mystery fare and a terrific successor to the racecourse mystery world first carved out by Dick Francis." — *Booklist, Starred Review*

"Fans of horse racing and everyone else will find this tale of love, lust, greed, and family ties an enjoyable ride."–*Publishers Weekly*

"Sound racing lore mixes with sex and murder to provide a blood-soaked edge-of-your-seat thriller"–*Kirkus.*

"The nifty plot includes a murder at the track and other surprising narrative twists. ."–*The Toronto Star, an Editor's Pick.*

Travels of Quinn

1

THE SCAM BEGAN BEFORE dawn when we crossed the Savannah River from South Carolina into Georgia.

Though most people called us gypsies, we were Irish American Travellers, descendants of the Irish tinkers who traveled in colorful, horse-drawn caravans. In the 1800s we'd fled to the US during the 1845 potato famine and these days, we traveled in shiny new American-made trucks.

For the next week, my name would be Katie Smith. Though born as Quinn O'Neill nineteen years earlier, using an alias had become second nature. Whatever doubts my life gave me, I buried, because this was how my family operated.

We purchased expensive new items, like Uncle Paddy's Dodge truck and the Airstream towed behind it, whenever we raked in fat surpluses of cash. On those flush days, we bought whatever we wanted. On leaner days, we still enjoyed our luxury homes, vehicles and the wealth we'd squirreled away during years of successful con jobs and scams.

Approaching that first Georgia rest stop, Uncle Paddy shot a warning glance from the driver's seat. "Today you're Katie. You'll not forget, will ye, lass?"

"No," I said.

Coming to America as children, after a 1960s influx of Irish tinkers, my Uncle Paddy and my da still had the lilt of the Irish in their voices, a sound I loved.

Behind our rig, my half-brother, Connor, rode with my father. Their truck towed a flatbed, loaded with an asphalt paver and a steamroller, equipment that would pave the suburban driveways of the folks we'd swindle later that day.

It was just past 5:00 a.m. when Paddy parked his rig at the far end of the rest stop. There were no cars here and no one to watch as we changed the tags on the vehicles and trailers. When I emerged from the truck, the clean scent of the Georgia longleaf pine filled my nostrils. Riding a cool breeze, it moistened the skin on my face.

I fastened my new lambskin jacket against the chill. I wore it over a white, low-necked sweater with rhinestone detailed jeans and fancy cowgirl boots. Not willing to risk ostracism from my close-knit clan, I dressed like a Traveller girl was expected to dress—sexy, with lots of bling. I didn't like it that much, but this is what my people did.

After a quick scan of the lot, I walked to where Connor was toweling away road grime from the side of Paddy's truck.

He pointed at me. "Don't hang around like a leftover Christmas ornament. Give me a hand with the signs."

"Sure," I said, feeling a flush of anger heat my cheeks.

I took the key Connor thrust at me, dropped the truck's tailgate, and crawled to the locked metal box behind the cab. Rummaging through the magnetic signs inside, I grasped one marked Smith Paving Company.

I held it up. "He wants this one, right?"

Connor rolled his eyes. "You learn to be that smart from those books you read?"

Da stopped my angry retort with a sharp, "Give it to me, Quinn, and grab the other one."

Hiding my irritation, I pulled out the matching sign. Though the advertisement for the Smith Paving Company appeared genuine, it was as fake as our phone and Georgia DOT permit numbers. Everything in that box was phony.

Back in Tinkers Town, where we lived, Da's safe hid a dozen or more counterfeit driver's licenses, permits, credit, and Social Security cards. The bogus credentials provided numerous identities during our road trips to make money off the "country folk," our name for non-Travellers.

After Da and Connor smoothed the flexible signs to the sides of the truck, they stood back and admired their handiwork. Glancing at me, my thirty-nine-year-old father tipped his Notre Dame cap.

"Top of the morning to you, Katie Smith, my dear."

I rolled my eyes. "That brogue is so lame, Da."

"Ah, that might be, but remember, it works." His even white teeth flashed in the early gray light beneath blue eyes that were filled with mischief. He was a total scoundrel, but I adored him. Unlike Connor and my stepmother Maeve, Da loved me.

"Don't lay it on too thick," I said. "Some people aren't as dumb as you think."

"Ah, Katie, my love, you know how they fall for our good looks and silver tongues. They're eager to pay us their cash."

I often wished he'd show a twinge of guilt, but he never did.

"Don't give me that look. A man must make a living. If those folks want to part with their money, I'm delighted to take it."

Couldn't we earn money without hurting people? I thought of Paddy's latest sale of faulty Korean tools and Taiwanese equipment from South Carolina's crooked Dixie Tool Company. The products were stamped, "Made in America!" Paddy thought the exclamation point added a nice touch of authenticity.

Forcing these thoughts aside, I watched the April sun break open the horizon to the east as the early mist began to dissolve. The roar of eighteen-wheeler engines and heavy-duty tires grew increasingly loud as the traffic thickened on Interstate 20.

Next to me, Da unzipped his leather jacket and rubbed a hand through his dark, thick mane. He and his brother, Paddy, were both fit, handsome men with the fair skin, blue eyes, and black hair of their Celtic heritage. Da was more handsome, with his large eyes and irresistible smile.

Uncle Paddy had a sharp, hawk-like face, but its intensity seemed to attract the women as much as Da's charm and charisma.

A year younger than me, my stepbrother Connor had inherited his share of magnetism. Except when he slipped up and dropped his act. Then his duplicity was as unmistakable as the fangs on a snake.

"No last-minute word from Mr. Olverson, then?" Paddy asked.

"Not a one," Da said. The three men smiled.

Unbeknownst to Olverson, he had provided us with an introduction to our quarry. He'd phoned a week earlier, saying several of his neighbors were requesting our "excellent" paving work. It should be a prosperous journey for the family.

"Let's make some money," Paddy said.

We climbed into the trucks, and accelerated onto the highway, heading for a Georgia neighborhood halfway to Atlanta.

Paddy glanced at me as he rolled his Dodge down the highway. "You see the advantages, Quinn, of doing the occasional first-class job?"

"Of course, I do. If you hadn't, Olverson would hardly promote you, would he?"

"Right you are. We removed his broken pavement, graded the gravel bed beneath, and lay down a three-inch layer of asphalt. A grand job it was, too."

"I know," I said. "I was there, remember?"

As we'd known it would, the driveway had held up through the following winter. Now, Olverson's unsuspecting neighbors assumed they'd get the same quality work, with DOT approved asphalt. What they'd really get was a shoddy surface job. When their driveways started breaking up, the "Smiths" would be long gone. Good luck finding us then. Despite my feelings of guilt, there was a part of me that loved a good con.

About seventy miles east of Atlanta, we turned into an RV park, our home base while working for Olverson's neighbors.

I went with Da while he checked into the office as "Michael Smith." The woman behind the counter had beady eyes and a sharp nose that reminded me of a chicken.

Frowning, she said, "I saw the paving equipment you brought in. You're not gypsies, are you?"

"No, ma'am." Da said, with a flash of white teeth. "We're Irish American Travellers. And I'm one of the good ones." He gave her a wink and laid a wad of cash on the counter.

The woman's frown dissolved into a grin. "I guess any man that pays cash up front is okay with me."

I gave her my delighted-to-know-you smile, and when we left her office, Da was whistling "When Irish Eyes are Smiling."

After Paddy backed the Airstream into our assigned spot, we got busy hooking up the electric, water, and septic lines. When we were done, I glanced around the RV park.

A stream-fed pond, scraggly lawn, picnic tables, and two green buildings with showers and toilets completed my visual inventory. Paddy's Airstream had a shower, but why would we deplete our propane when we could use someone else's hot water?

At eight a.m., we drove through the stone gateposts of Golden Meadows, the upscale development where Olverson lived. With the machinery laden flatbed rattling behind us, we clattered past the expensive landscaping planted outside the gate and along the short double drive leading in.

Single family brick homes sat on about an acre of ground apiece. Azaleas, crepe myrtles, evergreen bushes, and young live oaks had been carefully planted and nurtured on front lawns. There was money here.

Da parked our rig before a house I recognized as Olverson's. He and two men I hadn't seen before emerged from inside. They carried hot cups of coffee that sent swirls of steam into the cool morning air.

"Right then," Uncle Paddy said. "Is the Smith family ready?"

Connor said, "Sure," and stifling a sigh, I said, "Yeah."

"We'll be ready," Da said, "as soon as our Katie Smith wipes that frown off her face."

Connor's lips twisted into a sneer. "Get over yourself, Quinn. This is what we do. What do you think paid for your leather jacket?"

"I know what paid for it! But sometimes I feel bad for these people. Sorry if that offends you, Connor."

After making a rude scoffing noise, he ignored me.

Not all Travellers were con artists, but I'd been born into one of the most notorious families living in South Carolina's Tinkers Town. The only family worse than us was the O'Carroll's, and unfortunately, they figured largely in my future.

Squeezing my eyes shut a second, I said, "I'm fine. Let's do this."

Da nodded. I put on my best eager-to-please face, and we opened the truck doors and got out smiling.

2

The roar of the steamroller filled my ears as the stink of hot tar burned my nostrils. The smell contrasted sharply with the tangy, fresh scent of the Georgia pines that surrounded us.

Da had finished laying a three-inch layer of hot asphalt on Mr. Semington's driveway, a few houses down from Olverson's, and Paddy was working the steamroller to smooth and compact the new surface.

Meanwhile, the self-appointed paving experts, Olverson, Semington, and the third man, Mr. Huston, were drinking a fresh round of coffee as they scrutinized and discussed the job. Their thinning gray hair, along with wrinkled faces and sagging paunches, suggested they were well over sixty.

It amazed me that they failed to notice the advertised three-inch layer was quickly being rolled into a thin, unstable surface. There was a big difference between three inches of compacted asphalt like Olverson had received and what Semington and Huston were receiving.

Da wiped his hands and face with a clean rag and joined them. I followed. "You're a lucky man," he said to Semington, cheerfully. "Your drive was in such good shape, we didn't need to remove your pavement or grade underneath. Saved you a bundle."

Didn't need to remove and grade? What a big fat lie. But I'd been taught to exude confidence when Da spoke. If I didn't, I'd regret it.

I forced a smile. "It's looking really good."

Huston stared at my heavily mascaraed eyes, red lips, and low-necked top before his eyes slid to my tight jeans. No wonder he didn't see the lousy job he was getting. I turned and walked away across the yard.

Normally, unmarried Traveller girls traveled in packs during the school year. It was a way to protect ourselves when we left the insulated village of Tinkers Town. Oddly, though we liked to dress sexy, and the country folk thought we were skanks, most Travellers' girls, myself included, were still virgins, and planned to be when they married. Travellers' boys didn't like to marry used goods, and most girls were afraid to marry outsiders. Better the devil you knew.

As I wandered through Semington's landscaped yard, thoughts of life in Tinkers Town swarmed after me like a cloud of biting mosquitoes.

My Aunt Mary, Paddy's wife, didn't like me working with the men. Like many of the middle-aged women in Tinkers Town, she had a stout chest and body. She dyed her hair black and probably used a can of mousse a day to keep it big and poufy. Like her Tinkers Town buddies, she loved wearing expensive jewelry, fashionable clothing, and big hair.

Then there was Maeve, my stepmother. She was the queen of excess. I forced my thoughts away from the woman I hated and pushed them back to Aunt Mary.

A respected woman in town, I'd heard Mary complain about me to Da. "She should stay here with her friends. Stay with her family, not live in a trailer with the three of you men."

Truth be told, I didn't mind being away from the other girls. We weren't that close, which was something Mary observed with foreboding. She didn't like my tendency to be a loner.

I'd overheard her once, "She's too much like that mother of hers. It worries me."

My mother had run off when I was two, so she wasn't around to hear Mary's complaints. My stepmother, Maeve, didn't care what I did, and the other town women were too intimidated by Maeve and Da to say anything.

The one time I'd heard a naysayer speak up, Da had said, "But our Quinn is a silver-tongued devil and a clever thief. And how do you expect her to use her talents sitting in Tinkers Town?"

As I circled back to the job, the memory of Da's words made me smile. As I approached, Semington and Olverson were exchanging a high five.

Glancing at me, Semington said, "Katie here's right. This drive is looking good. A terrific job for a terrific price!"

"Hey, Smith," Huston said, "you still think you'll be able to get to my drive today?"

Da gave him a wink. "Sure, and you know it."

He'd loaded enough asphalt that morning to continue paving after he finished Semington's drive. The heated hopper in his machine could keep the asphalt simmering for hours. He worked long days, and he liked to keep the work rolling. Da's motto was, "Get the money and get out!"

Sure enough, moving closer, in a low voice, he said, "You and Connor need to get to work."

I glanced at my half-brother, he nodded, and a moment later we were walking the streets of Golden Meadows to do our sales pitch. After I pulled one of the glossy Smith brochures out of my tote bag and handed it to him, I opened the little notepad I kept. I was supposed to quiz him, and make sure he was on top of his game.

"So, who do we have?" I asked, glancing at the notes I'd made.

"Olverson at 1520 Westfield Way, Semington at 1524 Westfield Way, and the unsuspecting Huston at 1315 Green Meadows Road."

"Okay," I said. "And the people Olverson's already talked to are . . .?"

He shot me his derisive "duh" look. "The Franklins, the Jessups, and the Richardsons. I've got their addresses right here," he said, tapping his temple.

"Of course, you do."

"You gettin' smart with me, Quinn?"

"No," I said, backpedaling quickly. I was a little afraid of my half-brother and sick of having to tread lightly around him. With a sud-

den flash of anger, I swore that someday, he'd regret the way he treated me.

Putting the notebook away, I trailed after him. "Look," I said,
"you don't have to tell me to let you do the talking, okay?" Even if I
am smarter than you.

"Quinn," he said in the annoyingly patient voice of an adult talking to a small child, "I've been out of school for years traveling with
Da and Paddy. Since I was seven and you were playing with dolls,
I've been with the men when they dress driveways, prune trees, paint
barns—all that shit."

I hated it when he lectured me like that. He wasn't finished.

"By the time I was thirteen, I'd already had five summers learning
how to take the money, while you were at home reading your stupid
books. I'm a master of confusion and illusion.

I know, because you've told me a hundred times.

"You might be able to steal stuff, Quinn, but you don't have a
clue how to run a serious con."

I swallowed my retort and followed him down the street. Most
of us Traveller's kids never made it past fifth grade. Our parents kept
us apart from the outside world, a way to protect and insulate the
clan's culture.

"Hey, moron," he said impatiently. "You're, like, a million miles
away. Start listening!"

"Sorry, what did you say?"

"Forget it."

We'd reached the end of Olverson's block, and took a right onto
Clover Lane, where the Franklins lived. Connor paused, his eyes
skimming over the closest driveway. "This one's desperate for work,
but it's too big a job."

I could see the owners had allowed the roots of a big oak to buck-
le and break up their concrete drive. To fix it, the tree and much of

the pavement would have to be removed, the dirt underneath graded, and a new surface laid.

A good con is a clever mixture of truth and lies. Connor wasn't about to bet the owners were dumb enough to go for a simple overlay of asphalt. Saying the driveway only needed a little dressing would be such a big fat lie, it would explode in his face.

But at the next house, he smiled and rubbed his thumb and index finger together. "Now here's some real cash."

A handsome brick home stood at the end of the drive. It had an expensive metal roof, copper gutters and drainpipes. The Mercedes out front didn't impress me as much as the pride and money the owners had put into the home.

"Lookey there," I said. "The drive has some ugly cracks and a lovely pothole."

Connor's smiled at me, more of a smirk, really. I followed him to the front door, straightened my shoulders, and acted like Connor and I were the most honest, wonderful people these folks would ever be lucky enough to meet.

The doorbell was answered by a gray-haired woman in an oversized knit outfit that didn't quite succeed at hiding her large stomach and hips.

She looked us over, her gaze finally settling on Connor's earnest looking expression.

"Good day to you, ma'am. My name is Connor Smith and this is my sister Katie."

I nodded and smiled at the woman.

Connor continued. "And you would be?"

If the woman's better judgement warned her to keep her distance, apparently Connor's handsome face and sweet expression convinced her to answer.

"Emma Bunting."

He immediately shook her hand with a practiced grip I knew was cool to the touch and just strong enough.

"Our company's in the neighborhood today helping your neighbors, the Semingtons and Hustons. We're dressing their driveways with top quality asphalt and we use the best equipment money can buy."

There might have been a spark of mischief in Emma's eyes as she said, "And I suppose you noticed our pothole?"

"Yes, Ma'am, I did."

Tinkers Town girls thought Connor was dangerously cute. His dark hair was about two inches long and spiked with gel on top. Though we'd both received Da's blue eyes, Connor had inherited the thin, sharp face of my stepmother, Maeve. Apparently, the ladies thought he had an irresistible "bad boy" look.

"Fred," Emma called over her shoulder.

From somewhere beyond the hallway's plush wall-to-wall carpeting, a man's crabby voice answered, "What! What do you want?"

"Get out here and talk to this young man about our driveway."

Fred, a tall gray-haired man with a curved spine and a jutting jaw, emerged around a corner. His malformed spine had caused his upper body to hunch forward. I wondered if it caused him pain. Don't get soft about some old man, Quinn. You're here to line up work.

Fred stared at Connor. "Are you one of those traveling gypsies?"

"Yes, sir," Connor said proudly, his erect stance dripping with confidence. "But were American-Irish, and one of the good families."

He winked at Emma Bunting.

Fred lips flattened. "I've heard a lot about you people. You have a bad reputation."

"Mr. Bunting, if we catch your driveway right now, it will stop further damage from happening. Besides, we're already in the neighborhood. Saves you money right off the top. I don't blame you for questioning the quality of our work. But you might owe it to yourself and Mrs. Bunting here to ask your neighbor Ollie Olverson about us." Connor waited.

A light flicked on in the eyes beneath Fred's sagging lids. "Hey, are you the outfit that did Ollie's driveway last summer?"

"The very one." Like his mother, Maeve, Connor could turn on the fake charm with ridiculous ease.

"Well, that's different." The old man smiled. "Indeed, it's quite different."

Hook, line, and sinker. I kept the pleasant expression on my face, glad for Connor's ability to control his smirk that would give us away. I knew it was just under the surface, straining to appear.

"Where are you people working now?"

"Semington's," Connor said, handing a glossy, four-color Smith brochure to Fred.

Fred studied it a moment. "Emma, you wanna take a walk over there and check it out?"

"Yes. Oh, could I have one of–"

I had a brochure in her hands before she finished the sentence, and when I left with Connor a few minutes later, I gave the Buntings my "I'm an angel" smile before we moved on to troll the neighborhood for more unwary homeowners.

As we hustled down Clover Lane, a breeze came up and gently shook the crepe myrtles planted along the sidewalk. A few remnants of last year's blossoms dropped shriveled seed pods on my hair and on my shoulders. I tried not to compare them with old Mr. Bunting. I didn't want to think about him.

Sometimes I thought too much. One of my cousins had been arrested and jailed earlier that week, caught in a house painting scam. He'd taken an upfront payment and left the house after painting only one side. But they'd caught him before he got out of state, and his attempt to pay off the owners hadn't worked.

They hadn't wanted restitution, they'd wanted retribution.

When Connor had seen how much the arrest frightened me, he'd tried to dismiss its seriousness.

When that hadn't worked, he'd said, "That Vincent Sherlock wasn't the brightest rock on the block, Quinn. Only a fool travels with a single set of fake plates. Remember," he'd said with a confident smile, "Me and Da are the smartest guys in Tinkers Town."

Still, I dreaded the day the prey might turn on the predators.

3

Four days later, just before dawn, Da awakened me with a gentle shake.

I'd been asleep on the lounge bed in the Airstream's kitchen, curled up beneath a comforter. Connor, still fast asleep on the larger dinette bed, never stirred as I sat up rubbing the sleep from my eyes. From the other end of the Airstream, I could hear my uncle snoring where he slept in the king bed, he shared with Da.

After a quick wash, makeup, and a hair volumizer, I emerged from the bathroom. Da handed me a cup of hot coffee, richly laced with cream and sugar. At the first sip, I groaned with pleasure.

Outside, the sun was still below the horizon and the air was chilly. Walking across the damp, bedraggled grass, I watched an RV rumble out of the park. We'd be gone soon, too, and I was glad it was our last day in Golden Meadows. I only wished I could avoid what I had to do later that day.

After settling in the truck with our coffee, Da fired up the engine, and hit the highway. Twenty miles later, he took the exit to Greensboro Hot Mix, the plant that supplied us asphalt for Golden Meadows. I'd gone with Da every morning when he loaded the hopper for the day's work.

As usual, my tight, rhinestone jeans, and low-cut top did not go unnoticed by the plant owner's son, Steve. In his early twenties, already working on a beer belly, the guy had some interesting tattoos on his arms. The ink suggested he identified himself with a jackhammer, a sledgehammer, a drill, and a welding rod. Maybe it was compensation for a lack of equipment behind his zipper.

Since he managed the office during the early morning shift, I'd seen more of him than I'd wanted. Still, I'd done my best to stroke his ego, encouraging him to talk about himself while I hung on his every word as if mesmerized.

People said I was pretty because of my mother's high cheekbones and blond hair. They said she was beautiful. But when she'd left, Da had burned her pictures. If anyone had kept her photo, I'd never seen it. Nonetheless, I used my inherited looks to help bring in the money.

That morning, Steve stared hard at me from behind the counter. I returned his stare with a brilliant smile.

Da told Steve how many tons he needed, and Steve wrote up a ticket for Da to show the plant worker who supplied the load. I stayed behind to pay the cash.

"Okay, babe," Steve said, "that'll be fourteen hundred for today."

I grinned and pulled the money pouch from my tote bag. I set both the pouch and my elbows on the counter, making sure to lean forward far enough that my breasts pressed into the counter until my cleavage swelled above my neckline. Then I pulled my remaining cash out and let my face fall with dismay.

"Damn, I forgot we bought those new tires yesterday!" I let my eyes grow big and pleading. "I've only got five hundred. But we're getting cash for three jobs today, and I can give you the nine-hundred when we come in for tomorrow's load. There'll be plenty left over for the new load, too."

Steve's lips compressed into a thin line. "We don't do that, Katie."

"I know, but we've been good clients, paying cash up front every day. You know we're good for it, and we have another half-dozen jobs lined up for the rest of the week. *Please?*"

His response seemed to be directed at my breasts. "Dad will have my head if I do that."

"I tell you what," I said, "why don't you come over to our RV camp tonight? I'll give you the cash then, maybe a beer, too." I wasn't sure how to make my face do seductive, but I gave it my best shot.

"Tonight?"

I raised one brow and nodded. "Yeah, tonight. Let me write down the address of our camp." The writing of the address involved more leaning over the office counter.

Steve grinned. "This sounds like a winner. I'll bring the beer."

Hook, line, and sinker. I'd just shorted him nine-hundred bucks. When he showed up at the RV park with his beer, we'd be long gone.

I felt the little thrill that came when I pulled off a con like this, especially on someone I didn't like. The tingle of excitement had the added benefit of shutting out the rheumy eyes and twisted spine of Mr. Bunting. But it was stupid to feel guilty about the Buntings. It was just business, right?

At the office door, I turned back to Steve. "I'll see you later, Sledge." He flushed with color, and I fled the office, jumping into Da's truck as it pulled up with the hot asphalt.

"What'd you pay him?" Da asked.

"Five hundred."

"Good girl. See what magic you can work later today at the Buntings."

Like a bucket of cold water, the words doused my good spirits. What was wrong with me? Fred was just a cranky old guy who yelled at his wife. I repeated the mantra I'd used so often. Our way's too cool for school. Today, it didn't seem to work.

But it wasn't the long hot summer of tar, oily machinery, or the Buntings that truly eroded my spirits. It was something much worse. I'd soon be launched into a life that my years of denial couldn't stop.

My future was controlled by a contract Da and Maeve had signed years ago.

The truck jolted me back to the present as it hit a bump on the ramp to Interstate 20. I tried to think of something fun to look forward to, but my thoughts spun right back to that same, unpleasant place. I closed my eyes tight. It didn't help

If Mom had stayed, would she have fought against the pact that was about to take over my life?

"Where you at, girl?"

Da's intense eyes stared at my face. Whatever he saw there had caused his brows to draw so tightly together, the line between them resembled a ditch.

"I'm fine," I said. "Just planning the moves for later."

"Looked to me more like you'd lost your last friend."

"Nah." I flashed what I hoped was a reassuring smile. "I'm good." To keep him from asking more, I said, "So three more jobs today, right?"

"Yeah, three more and then our time in Golden Meadows will be a pleasant memory."

The last job would be the Buntings. While Da had signed the contract in Fred and Emma's kitchen, Connor had made sure, that like him, I took a visual inventory between the front door and the kitchen. I'd asked to use their bathroom and made a brief prowl through several rooms I had no business in. I'd quickly learned the Buntings had more to offer than the other clients and knew their house should be saved for last.

"After the Buntings," I said, "We'll beat it out of Georgia."

"That's exactly right, Katie. Never stay in one place too long."

The Travellers lived by this rule. Da couldn't chance someone who'd known known him in the past, hearing about his work in Golden Meadows. He didn't need a surprise visit from an angry former mark.

As the big Dodge engine rolled us forward, the pine bordered highway unreeled ahead like a video loop. Equally vivid, were the unpleasant thoughts of what I'd do to the Buntings that day.

4

By one o'clock, the first two jobs were finished. Da and I drove the paving machinery to the Buntings' house, leaving Connor and Paddy behind to clean up the second job site.

When Emma and Fred stepped out onto their porch, she stayed behind, watching, as Fred hobbled down the drive to talk to Da.

I climbed from the truck and moved up the sidewalk to chat with her. I'd been stopping by her house and visiting the past few days, ostensibly to give progress updates on our other jobs and to re-assure her we'd be getting to her and Fred soon. I'd asked questions about her and her family. I'd cooed over photos of her grandkids like I thought they were the most exceptional children I'd ever seen. I'd listened attentively while she went on about where she was from, how she'd met Fred, and the long story of their marriage.

A few days of this, and our relationship progressed to the sweet-tea and cookies stage, which had led to her showing off some of her prized possessions. Proudly, she trotted out silver that had been in the family for generations, and jewelry she'd inherited from rel-atives who'd lived in New Orleans. They had been, she said, quite "well heeled." When I saw her diamonds and other rocks, I knew she wasn't exaggerating.

When I greeted her, she quickly invited me inside.

"I'm sure you're a help to your father," she said, ushering me past the dining room where the top of a sideboard sparkled with lovingly polished silver. "But do you really belong out there with that heavy equipment all day? You're too pretty and feminine for that."

I shrugged in response as we moved into her kitchen that gleamed with granite counters and expensive appliances like a Viking stove. Being a Travellers' kid, I was well-schooled in recognizing a home's financial tells. I could produce an accurate cost estimate based on its location, size, the type of construction, materials used, the quality of the HVAC, electrical systems, the roof, and the interior surfaces and fixtures.

Reaching for the refrigerator door handle, Emma paused and turned to me. "Katie, do you mind my asking why you aren't in school?"

Yeah, I minded, but I smiled and said, "It's just our way. Travellers go to work early in life and save their money."

"I won't argue with that philosophy, but you strike me as a clever girl. Combine that with your looks, and you should be able to land a nice office job. Wouldn't you rather be doing something else, dear?"

Smiling, I said, "I'm happy enough." Exactly why the clan liked to keep itself and its children away from country folk. They always wanted to change our way of life.

Emma lifted a pitcher of sweet tea from the refrigerator, and after pouring two tall glasses, she set plates of chocolate chip cookies and sliced lemons on the kitchen table. The tang of fresh citrus and the sweetness of chocolate would normally have tempted me, but today, I had no appetite. I hung my tote by its thick straps from the arm of the kitchen chair, and we sat, sipped, and munched on the cookies.

I heard the front door open, then Fred's voice. "Emma could you come out here a minute? You need to talk to Mr. Smith and me."

As she stood to leave the kitchen, I asked, "May I use your bathroom, Emma?"

"Of course, dear. And then you should stay here and finish those cookies. You're way too skinny."

I grinned. "Thanks."

Adrenalin jetted into my veins when I heard the front door close. I sped from the kitchen to the master bedroom. Previously, I'd investigated the mahogany chests and night tables, and now, made a beeline for Emma's top dresser drawer. I opened it and removed her plastic tray of costume jewelry, revealing a suede-covered box beneath.

I set the plastic tray on top of the dresser and grabbed the suede jewelry case. After raising the lid, I withdrew several huge diamond rings, three large eighteen-karat gold necklaces, a diamond brooch and the two sets of earrings studded with lavish jewels. I folded the stuff into thin pieces of bubble wrap I kept in my tote bag, then shoved the whole lot inside.

Once I'd put the box and tray exactly where I'd found them, I glanced around the room. Their only other valuable piece of jewelry was Fred's Rolex, but he wore it every day. I scooted from the bedroom, stopping outside the bath to listen. I didn't hear anyone in the house. Da was supposed to be keeping the Buntings occupied, but I couldn't be too careful.

In the dining room, I parted the curtains, and peeked through. As expected, Da had the Buntings in conversation near the street. They were looking at the pothole and cracked pavement. Emma was laughing, and Fred was talking.

With a rush to the sideboard, I yanked open the silverware drawer. By now my hands were shaking.

Emma kept a large velvet-covered box shoved into the back of the drawer that held a heavy set of sterling silverware. She'd said it had belonged to her great Aunt Lucida and the sentimental value meant more than the financial, which, she said, was significant.

The stuff would bring some real money when Uncle Paddy sold it by weight in Atlanta. I felt a stab of guilt and tried to shrug it off. I mean, it wasn't like she could take it with her, right?

I opened the drawer, heaved the velvet covered box out, and set it on the sideboard. When I ran to the window for a last peek, Da still had the Buntings busy at the end of the drive. I began grabbing silver knives, forks and spoons, rolling them into additional bubble wrap. Rattling tote bags were not recommended in the Travellers' Guide to Successful Thievery.

I grabbed a steadying breath before clutching the weighty bag with both hands. Returning to the kitchen, I bit into one of the cookies for show, wrapping the others in bubble wrap and slipping them into the tote. When Emma came back inside, it would be best if she thought I'd been eating cookies. I waited, resisting an urge to pick at my cuticles. Instead, I twisted a lock of blond hair around a finger, tugging hard at my scalp.

When I couldn't sit still any longer, I grabbed the rest of the bitten cookie and slung my tote over my shoulder. It took a few staggering steps before I got my balance and could walk normally under the weight. Damn, the bag was heavy.

Out the front door, maintaining a steady pace along the sidewalk, I casually munched on the last cookie. At the end of the drive, Paddy was parking his truck behind Da's rig.

The distraction gave Da time to send me a questioning look without the Buntings noticing. I gave him a nod, and he returned a wink.

"It's getting late," he said to Paddy. "Let's get started on this job."

I saw a look pass between them, and as I knew they would, they went to work on the Buntings drive as if speed would save the world from disaster. We wouldn't be here much longer, but for me, it was the hardest time. I would have preferred to steal moments before we left, but I grab the opportunity to get inside a home when it presents itself.

"Katie," said Connor, "give me a hand for a minute, will you?"

I gritted my teeth and followed as he went to the far side of Paddy's truck. He opened the driver door and pretended to fool with something on the front seat. When I reached the passenger side and leaned in, he gave me a sharp look.

"Your girly nerves are showing, Quinn. Here," he said, and pulled a silver flask from between the front seats. When I shook my head, he said, "Drink it."

I was sick of my brother acting like I worked for him, but I'd learned it was easier to comply.

When I was sure the Buntings weren't looking, I took a large swig. The Irish whiskey burned all the way down, and I shuddered.

Most people didn't realize that Travellers don't, as a rule, drink alcohol. It can play havoc with a good con–a bad habit that doesn't lead to wealth. But in this case, Connor had a point. The warm glow produced by the Jameson's eased the edge off my tension.

Looking back, I was relieved to see the Buntings had decided to turn the repair of their driveway into the afternoon's entertainment. Fred had grabbed two chairs off the front porch, planted them on the grass nearby, and they'd settled in to watch.

"So,' Connor whispered, "how much did you get?"

"Enough." I didn't want to talk about it and quickly laid my heavy tote onto the floor on the passenger side.

Connor was about to grab my arm and leave his nasty, trademark bruises. As he'd gotten older the bruise marks had become more vicious looking. Before he could touch me, I scuttled back to the Buntings and sat on the grass next to Emma. Somehow, I managed to talk to her in a normal voice, but it was impossible to meet her gaze.

Time crawled by, and I grew increasingly anxious to make tracks before I got caught. Finally, Paddy finished rolling the new asphalt, and loaded the steamroller onto the flatbed trailer behind Da's paver. Moments later, we got our cash payment from Fred, and were ready to leave, but Emma asked us to wait.

While she walked to the house and disappeared inside, I waited with Paddy in his truck as Da fired up his rig and pulled out of sight around the corner. When Fred said a last good bye to us and his crippled frame headed for the house, for some reason, a sense of foreboding blossomed.

"I don't like this," I said. "We should get out of here."

"What's the matter with you Quinn. Everything is–"

My head jerked back as Emma burst through the front door, her face white with anger and pain.

"Fred! Stop them! We've been robbed!"

Fred turned and hobbled back to our truck faster than I would have thought possible. Paddy had already locked the door, cranked the ignition, and released the parking brake, but Fred grabbed the truck's door handle.

"Stop," he yelled and started banging on Paddy's closed window with his other hand.

"Let go," Paddy shouted at him. "You don't want me dragging you down the street, do you?"

"Paddy, just drive," I said, my voice so unsteady, I hardly recognized it.

"You son of a bitch," Fred cried. "Stop this truck!"

By now Emma was close and she stared at me through the glass like I was a poisonous snake in a terrarium.

"You little bitch! How could you? I was going to give you a silver spoon." Her furious gaze switched to her husband. "My God, Fred, she took all the silver!"

A sour smell had begun to ooze from my pores. I hadn't realized shame could sicken me.

Fred pounded even harder on the window. Suddenly, Emma's face turned a fainter shade of white.

"My God! The jewelry." With a crablike gait, she tried to run back to the house.

"Call the police," Fred yelled after her. He was still clinging to the truck's door handle.

Paddy put the truck in gear and eased forward, but Fred held on. Paddy gave the truck a little gas, but Fred's gnarled hand continued to clutch the handle.

"Let go, you fool," Paddy yelled, as he pumped more gas into the engine.

Physical pain twisted Fred's face. With aging lungs and decrepit joints, he fought to keep up with the truck. With a look of desperation, he finally let go and fell to the pavement. Paddy gunned the engine, and as we fled from Golden Meadows, he whooped with excitement.

My nerves were so raw, my intestines became twisting snakes. I wrapped my arms around my stomach, hoping the burn would stop.

5

We slammed into the RV camp, and gravel spewed from Paddy's tires, leaving a cloud of dust behind us. When we pulled up to the Airstream, Da and Connor were furiously unhooking water and electric lines. They'd already changed the tags on the sleek RV, and as Paddy braked to a stop, I jumped out to remove his license plates.

Connor, who'd set our replacement tags on the ground, shoved a screwdriver at me, and I got to work. Within minutes, we'd exchanged four sets of tags, and the Airstream was hitched to Da's red truck. The flatbed loaded with equipment was switched over to Paddy's Dodge. New signs were pasted on Paddy's truck, new registrations and licenses were stuffed into glove boxes and wallets.

Noticing our flurry, the camp owner hurried toward Da, no doubt anxious to get their final payment. I walked away from the trucks for a moment, trying to get a grip on my nerves.

A large multi-horse trailer with quarters for humans was parked close by. Glancing back at Da and the RV camp owner, I trotted over to the big horse rig. When I looked through the open side door at the occupant inside, a horsey smell wafted my way. I liked it. More surprising was how strongly I was drawn to the horse with his large liquid eyes and finely made head.

I'd always thought horses were cool, but I'd never seen one like this before.

He was black with bright white patches, a white blaze, and white bangs that streamed down his face and fell below his nose. His mane was a froth of white that hung below his neck and shoulders. At the bottom of his shiny black legs, fluffy white hair that looked like feathers covered his hooves. A sudden desire to touch him overwhelmed me.

As anxious as I was to leave, a glance back showed Da still involved with the camp owner, and I stepped inside the trailer near the horse's head. He turned to me and pressed a velvet nose against my outstretched palm. I felt like I'd come home.

"Hey, what do you think you're doing?"

Startled, I turned, ready to bolt, but a guy standing outside the trailer blocked my retreat. The first thing that hit me was how good looking he was. An English tweed cap covered long wavy blond hair, setting off his intense green eyes. His accent was British.

"Sorry," I said, "he's so beautiful I had to get closer."

The guy didn't say a word, just stared at me.

"Jaysus, Katie, what are you after?" Da called. "Come on. Time to go!"

I turned sideways and slid past the guy in the tweed cap.

"What kind of horse is he?" I asked.

The guys expression softened. "Gypsy Vanner. He's a champion." There was pride in his voice.

Gypsy? What were the chances of that? I raced back to Da, climbing into the front seat next to him. Looking back, I could see the horse had stretched his neck out to stare at us. The blond guy also watched us, his face expressionless.

Da fired the engine and rolled forward. Stealing a last look at the horse, I saw another man had emerged from the RV and was standing by the horse trailer. Slick-backed, black hair, a pompadour, and sideburns, he looked like Elvis Presley.

Da's foot on the accelerator soon left the two men, the horse, and the RV park behind. It was time to get the hell out of Georgia.

On Interstate 20, I rode with Da in the white truck. Connor had switched to ride with Paddy, and they traveled somewhere to our south on the back roads. If the police were looking for a man and a blond girl in a red truck, towing Smith paving equipment, they wouldn't find them.

Though I'd started to relax, and my stomach cramps had eased, I was depressed when I should have been on a high. We'd completed eight jobs, hauled in almost twenty thousand dollars in cash for cheap jobs, and I'd successfully ripped nine-hundred dollars off the asphalt company.

That stuff I could handle, but the stash of stolen family heirlooms in the tote bag at my feet seemed to vibrate with accusation. I kept hearing police sirens in the distance that weren't there.

Da, on the other hand, was whistling "When Irish Eyes are Smiling," and I knew that Connor and Paddy were probably still slapping palms as they traveled home on their southern route. I wished I had their hard shells, but I didn't.

I kept seeing Emma's betrayed eyes and the desperate look on Fred's face as he fell to the pavement.

6

We slipped into Tinkers Town just before dark, and I let out a mental sigh of relief. One thing about our neighborhood, I felt safe here, secure among the people I'd grown up with. People who would applaud me for what I'd done.

But after the attractively planned streets and conservative homes of Golden Meadows, the peculiarities of our neighborhood struck me. Driving down Shamrock, the main street, we passed trailer homes squatting to the side of, or behind the huge McMansions on the one to two-acre lots. Tall light poles were planted squarely in front of some of these big houses, slicing in half the view of elaborate front doors and arched windows. Square, metal boxes perched atop these big poles. Why had I never realized how ugly these things were?

As we rolled past, Da pointed to a lot. "Looks like the Sherwoods started building their new house while we were gone."

I could see they'd broken ground and laid a foundation. The house was going to be huge. Probably, they wanted their house to be as big as the other Sherwood home, that was almost finished in the adjacent lot. Like Da and Paddy, the patriarchs of these houses were brothers.

The almost finished Sherwood house boasted a huge portico with stone columns. Plywood and plastic covered the large space where the wooden front door would hang. For now, both families lived in double-wide trailer homes behind the houses. Delaying completion was a Traveller method used to postpone the unwanted increase in property taxes.

The country folk thought our homes were tacky. But Travellers believed the grander the house, the better the family. Da hooked a left onto Dublin Street, where we lived. About three houses later, on a side street, one of the Murphy families was holding a beauty pageant. They'd erected the obligatory stage and carpeted it in red in front of their McMansion.

Party lights glittered around the façade's tall windows and front door. Floodlights illuminated the young contestants, their faces painted with bright make-up. Their hair was big, teased and enhanced with hairspray and extensions. The dozen or so little girls wore professionally designed costumes and pranced coquettishly before an enthusiastic crowd of family members and relatives.

Da turned toward the house, slowed the truck and lowered his window.

One of the Murphy men saluted him and approached. "Nice to have you home, Rory O'Neill. Successful trip?"

"Ay, and you know it, Red Paddy."

Many of the men in Tinkers Town had the same names—there were four Paddy Murphy's and thirteen John O'Carroll's. The clan used nicknames like Black Pete, Red Paddy, or Mikey Boy to differentiate.

"Showing off your young beauties tonight?" Da asked.

"We've got a dozen little Murphy gals in this town. They'll need husbands before you can say Christ-on-a-stick. Might as well start showing their stuff now."

Strutting their stuff was more like it. Beneath clouds of hair spray and sparkling tiaras, their tiny lipsticked mouths revealed dazzling white teeth and movie star smiles as they minced about the stage.

We left the truck to watch. As the girls sashayed in time to rock and roll music, my feet, with a mind of their own, began moving with the beat. Travellers' girls were taught to dance early and to dance sexy. Any conflict I harbored about this practice was erased by the delighted faces of the girls. They were so cute and having so much fun.

The music shifted to slower pace, and the dancers stopped and faced the audience. With shoulders thrown back, and a hand on a their hips, each girl thrust her opposite hip forward. The move was provocative, and the audience whooped and applauded.

Outsiders called this behavior trashy. They didn't understand it was just part of the ceremonies leading to our marriage contracts, an arrangement that kept our town together and safely isolated from outsiders. Though I never admitted it, I had doubts about this custom. Still, these parties were a tradition everyone enjoyed, especially the young girls.

One of them had a pile of fake blond curls fastened to the top of her head. She'd been squeezed into a tight, strapless dress with a flouncy crinoline that ended just above her chubby little knees. It brought back memories of the night I turned five.

Maeve had dolled me up with lipstick. She'd applied blush and mascara, before using half a can of hair spray to tease my blond hair into high waves. Then she'd encased me in a frilly, gown as tight as a spandex glove. Aunt Mary had added shoulder straps of stitched-together silk roses, and I'd thought I was quite the superstar. That first night had been fun, maybe because I hadn't realized what was happening. But when I was eleven, that changed.

For as long as possible, I'd let my ability for denial keep me from obsessing about it. Now, as I stared at the little girl in the white dress, I remembered that pivotal moment with brutal clarity.

There'd been a mob of us kids, the girls dressed to kill. I'd ended up dancing with my cousin Tommy O'Carroll. He had big ears that stuck out too far. It was hard not to stare at them. In the meantime, our fathers, Maeve, and Tommy's mother looked on with beaming smiles of approval. I remember thinking, what are they so happy about?

Next thing I knew the four of them were in our kitchen, signing a document. A marriage contract. Though I'd known most Travellers marry by contract, it was an unpleasant shock when it happened to me.

The rock music seemed to grow louder. The glitter of sequined costumes and party lights almost hurt my eyes as reality boiled over my wall of denial. I had a wild desire to grab the blond child before me, throw her over my shoulder, and escape our futures.

But my family had already made the choice for me and paid money. I would share my life with Tommy, share his bed and his family that was even more crooked than mine. Live with his bristly hair and big ears. Have his babies. Would my babies have big ears?

I closed my eyes for a second, trying to get a grip. *You're just messed up from the thing with the Buntings. The contract is our way. It will work out.*

But fear and anger had gained momentum and was flattening my denial like a steam roller over hot tar. My family was forcing me into a union I didn't want. My jaw tightened. My hands curled into fists.

Forget it. I was not going to do this!

7

The children still danced on the stage. Unable to watch any longer, I turned away, and Da caught sight of my face.

"What's wrong?"

I tried to smile and failed. "Nothing. I'm going to walk home."

"I'll drive you."

"I feel like walking."

He stared at me. "Jaysus, girl. You're in a mood." Then he shrugged. "Suit yourself."

Night was full on as I turned my back on the crowd. The air held a chill, but when I wrapped my arms around my stomach, it was more to comfort myself than to stay warm.

When I turned onto our street, the first house I passed was dark, its huge arched windows unlit by interior lights. The family was probably at the beauty pageant. In the dark, the ambient light gleamed off a marble statue of the Madonna, standing ghostlike in the front yard.

I picked up my pace. I could see lights blazing from our house, the high wattage reflecting off Maeve's plastic yard statues of Jesus and the Virgin Mary. As I drew closer, I almost had to shade my eyes from the bright light blasting from the windows and crystal fixtures on either side of the front door. Maeve refused to follow the Traveller custom of blinding the windows with shades. She liked to show off what she had.

Though I'd grown up surrounded by Traveller's architecture and décor, my stepmother's taste struck me as over the top tacky.

Through the arched window above the front door, I could see her six-foot-high arrangement of pink and white artificial flowers. Trimmed with tiny gold angels, the apparition dwelled on the staircase-landing beneath a huge crystal chandelier that appeared to burn with a thousand watts of power.

Maeve was not a conservative woman.

I'd watched her work to be neighborhood queen of the biggest and best. It was something she lived for. No doubt her display of wealth was why Tommy's mother was so thrilled with our union. It would cement her family's status.

Digging into my tote, I found my key, and opened the massive front door. Inside, another crystal chandelier blazed over Maeve's pink and black fake marble tile. Did other people need dark-glasses in their own home?

Wanting only to avoid her and escape to my room, I hurried toward the staircase.

"So, you're home." My stepmother walked toward me from the kitchen.

Her tall, bony figure loomed over me as she drew closer. She was wearing her signature platform shoes with five-inch heels. Tonight, it was the purple pair.

"Where's Rory?" she asked.

"Thank you," I said. "I'm fine. We're all safely home, and the job went well."

"Don't get smart with me, miss prima donna. Where is Rory?"

Mentally, I counted to ten. "He'll be here in a minute. He stopped to watch the show for the Murphy girls.

She tilted her head to one side. "How was it, then?"

"Really terrific," I said, knowing how she hated to be outdone. "Their stage was fabulous, and the rock music was the best I've heard in this town. They must have paid some big money for that band."

Beneath her heavy brows and long nose, her lips curled with disdain They'd been thin and cruel looking until she'd had them plumped with injections. Tonight, she'd painted purple lipstick beyond their natural outline. But she'd left one half of her cupid's bow higher than the other.

"You listen to me, miss priss, they haven't seen anything until they see the wedding I put on for you and Tommy."

"Of course, they haven't," I said, hoping to placate her and flee to my room.

"You've been putting off your wedding plans for too long. I want you to sit down and *listen* to me."

"Sure," I said, turning away and taking another step toward the staircase. "Maybe tomorrow."

"We'll do it now. Just you, me, and the Blessed Mary."

Ah, the Blessed Mary. I was sure the whole religious thing was an act with her. And a control method. She used religion to paint herself and Connor as saints, while convincing Da I was the sinner.

Gritting my teeth, I marched back to where the hall opened onto two large living rooms. Inside them, pink leather couches reflected the brilliance of additional chandeliers on the ceilings. Pairs of black leather arm chairs squatted before matching pink-and-black-checkered ottomans.

The room was stuffed with carved-wood coffee and side-tables. They were lavishly gilded in eighteen to 22 karat gold, depending on the cash available when Maeve had placed the orders.

I entered the room with Maeve's most prized possession. A plastic statue of the Madonna holding the baby Jesus. The Virgin's head and shoulders were covered with a shawl of real leopard, dyed a garish pink. I called this room "The Sanctuary."

With a mental sigh, I marched to the most distant pink armchair and sat. The odor of spray-can incense assaulted my nose.

Maeve seated herself close to the statue and tossed her black mane. As much as I hated the woman, I had to admit she'd been blessed with a beautiful head of jet-black hair and a fine set of blue eyes. She had a wildness about her that I suspected men found sexy. They noticed her. God knows Da had.

"Time for you to stop dicking around and get married. Rory's way too lenient with you. The O'Carroll's are impatient."

I traced my fingers along the sleek, pink leather of my chair. "Don't you want me working with Da to earn money, so you can shop? I pulled in quite a haul this trip."

Maeve's lips flattened and with a voice as cold as a snake's hiss, she said, "Working with the men isn't your place. You belong here in this town with Tommy . . . and the babies you should be raising."

Yet her words were quiet and measured. Her patience-of-a-saint act might work on the rest of Tinkers Town, but I knew better. I'd seen the evil bitch that emerged when she dropped the façade. Sadly, Da never had. Or maybe he just refused to.

She assessed me with a prolonged stare. "You have the gypsy talent; I'll give you that. But I know exactly what you're doing. You're only working to put off the wedding."

She hesitated, staring at the ceiling as if seeking the Lord's help. "You're nineteen. Most of our girls start marrying at eleven. You're becoming an old maid. You're an embarrassment to me! You should be raising babies with Tommy."

If Maeve had her way, in a few years, she'd have all those little Sherwood girls married and producing babies like bunnies. I refused to respond to her anger. She'd taught me to hide my feelings by remaining expressionless. It drove her crazy. I did it now.

"People are starting to talk, Quinn. You're disgracing the family!"

"God forbid people should talk," I said.

"Do not take the name of our Lord in vain."

I gave her my best eye roll.

"Listen, you little bitch. I may have gotten this contract for you with Tommy, but it cost this family a lot of money. Don't you care that Rory signed the contract and gave his word?"

By now her face was red. Her lips spat with disgust. "I'm not giving money back to the O'Carroll family because of *you*!"

She seemed to realize her façade had slipped. Badly. She took a breath and arranged her face to look more pleasant.

"Rory and Desmond O'Carroll have worked for years to gather wealth. This marriage will keep the families strong and protected. That's how we've survived since our people came to America. Anyways, we can't afford to get on the wrong side of the O'Carroll family."

"What about what I want?"

"You selfish bitch! You lose the money and so help me—"

"All right, all right!" I shouted. "I'll marry him." It was a big fat lie, but at that moment I'd do anything to shut her up. Except the lie didn't solve the problem of escaping my future with a husband so practiced in the art of deception.

"That's better then," she said. The pink leather squeaked as she settled back in her chair and smiled at the statue of the Madonna.

Despite my effort to control them, my fingers grabbed a lock of blond hair and twisted it into a tight knot. Usually Maeve would snap at me for this, but she was so pleased with her perceived victory, she didn't bother.

"This will be so much fun, Quinn. You need to think about your gown. We'll go to Boston to see Ciara. She's the best designer, and of course, you'll have the best, whether you appreciate it or not. And then, we'll need to . . ."

Her voice muted as my thoughts turned inward to the past. Not all Travellers got stuck with a signed contract. There'd been no such document when Da married my mother, Jennifer Smith. What little information I'd been able to pry out of Aunt Mary painted a picture of Da marrying a total outsider.

The one-time Aunt Mary had spoken about my mother had been when Da and Paddy were out of town. We'd been alone in her house, safely away from Maeve's ears.

"Your mother," she'd said, "called herself a 'sociocultural anthropologist[1],' whatever that means. All I know is she had a Ph.D. from Yale and came to Tinkers Town to study our culture. Then she fell for your da. He shocked the compound when he married her, let me tell you."

Mary had grimaced at the memory, but I'd swear I'd seen a flash of amusement in her eyes. "There were a lot of young ladies not too happy about that! Your Da was rich and good looking. The best catch in town. Maeve had her panties in a nasty knot."

Mary had broken into such a satisfied smile, I'd realized she might be an ally against my stepmother.

"Jennifer knew what your Da did for a living, but she thought she could change him. But by the time you were born, poor little tyke, she'd given up on Rory and just up and abandoned the both of you."

"Didn't she try to take me with her?" Anyone could have heard the anguish in my voice.

"No, she left one night, and no one's heard from her since."

"Didn't Da go after her?"

"You know better than that, Quinn O'Neill. His heart hardened the night she left, and he's refused to mention her name since. And no one else dares mention it either." She'd rubbed her arms as if chilled by her thoughts.

For a moment, I surfaced from my reverie. Maeve still droned on about her plans for my wedding. Tuning her out, I let my thoughts drift back to my mother.

Why did you leave me? I can't even remember you. For a moment, my eyes squeezed shut, blotting out Maeve's pink room. Da must have really loved my mother to have turned so bitter. Was I a constant reminder of the love he'd lost? Was that why Maeve hated me so much?

---

1.   https://en.wikipedia.org/wiki/Sociocultural_anthropology

A sudden thought gripped my heart. All that anger against my mother. No word from her in seventeen years. Had someone killed her?

8

The sound of the front door opening snapped me back to the present. Connor entered the living room, his eyes narrowing as they slid over me before focusing on Maeve.

"There's my darling boy!" Maeve rose and wrapped her son in a hug. "Did you make a killing in Golden Meadows?"

"We did all right and then some." His lips curled into a satisfied smirk. His eyes were cold as they stared at me from his mother's arms. He disentangled himself from her embrace. "I'm not a baby."

"Ah, but you'll always be my baby."

I stifled a smart comment, allowing myself an eye roll instead.

"You settling the wedding plans for Quinn?" Connor asked. "She's been such a mule about it."

I was used to them talking about me in the third person. Like I wasn't even there. Of course, they didn't do it when Da was around.

Maeve flipped her dark hair back and smoothed her short leopard-print skirt over her thighs. "I'm taking her to Boston to get her dress the day after tomorrow."

That soon? Had she told me this while I was lost in the past? The thought of spending a night in a hotel room with this woman made my skin crawl.

"Quinn," she said. "I want to get Connor something to eat. We can talk about your wedding in the kitchen."

I stared at her as she left the room with Connor. Her animal print skirt had a purple cast to it. It went with the shoes and lipstick. If there was a site called hooker.com, that had to be where she shopped. She favored cut out lace dresses, where the solid fabric panels covered just enough to avoid arrest, and the see-through lace revealed everything else.

With a long mental sigh, I followed them into the kitchen. It was even larger and more lavish than Emma Buntings, but less attractive.

Maeve's purple heels clattered across the pink and black tiled floor on her way to the refrigerator. Connor slouched against the kitchen's island with his elbows resting on its pink granite top. I stood against the set of black cabinets near the door.

"What would you like, baby?" Maeve asked. "I have a lovely piece of beef filet from last night?"

"Sure," he said. "Earning all that cash gives a man an appetite."

Fortunately, Da and I had stopped at a Subway just outside town. Maeve wasn't about to ask if I was hungry, and I wouldn't have wanted to fix something with them in the room, anyway. I'd rather not eat.

"You ask me," Connor said, "Quinn's lucky the O'Carroll's even want her. Good thing you sealed the deal for her."

Raising a heavy brow, Maeve said, "I do have my ways."

"Yeah, Mom, you're awesome."

They were so full of shit. I'd been a highly sought-after candidate. Not only because the O'Neill family was good at making money, but my mother was an outsider, making me an outcross to the inbreeding that plagued many of the village families.

Maeve smiled at Connor, then opened the big refrigerator and pulled out the leftover steak and a casserole of macaroni and cheese. After dishing it all into a skillet, she set the pan on a gas burner to heat.

"So," she said, "we'll have a fancy engagement soiree for you and Tommy. Between it and the wedding, people will talk for years."

And you'll go down in history as the Diva of Tinkers Town. Only Maeve could use words like "soiree" and "fete" while owning a closet full of platform, high-heeled tennis shoes.

"What's wrong with you, Quinn?" she said. "You should see your high and mighty expression."

Connor stared at me, a nasty smile on his face. "Ma says you're just like your mother. She thought she was too good for Tinkers Town, too."

There was a moment of alarmed silence as Maeve glanced quickly into the hallway to make sure Rory hadn't come in. My mother was not to be mentioned in this house.

Satisfied he was still absent, she gave Connor a sorrowful glance. "Your poor father was duped by that bitch. It's a shame he ever knocked her up. That woman with all her fancy talk and education thought she was better than the rest of us."

She turned on me with narrowed eyes. "And you're just like her."

The smell of smoke and burning steak rose in the air. I pushed away from the cabinet and folded my arms over my diaphragm.

"Well guess what? The O'Carroll's don't have a problem with me, and I can't wait to marry Tommy and get out of here!"

"And you can thank me for that." She puffed out her chest, which only accentuated her meagre breasts and pushup bra. "Connor is the real prize in this family. The O'Rileys forked over more than two-hundred thousand so their Brigit can marry him."

"Yes, I think I've heard that before."

"You got a smart mouth on you, Quinn," Connor said.

I ignored his comment. He was lucky. Brigit was pretty and sweet. She didn't suffer from chimpanzee ears like Tommy. She didn't have a police record, either.

"Don't you think she's got a smart mouth, Ma?"

Maeve nodded, her mouth flattening to a tight line

"Well, maybe we should do something about it," Connor said.

A look of shared malice passed between them, and a sudden chill filled the room. My bravado vanished. I was acutely aware that Maeve's long, sharp kitchen knives were in the drawer next to Connor. I mean—he wouldn't, but . . ..

I let my breath out when Maeve broke the tension with a don't-worry-about-it wave of her hand. "Her marriage to Tommy will take care of everything."

Connor grinned with satisfaction. "And I get her room. We'll tear down her wall and make a master suite for Brigit and me, right?"

Maeve looked at him fondly. "Of course, we will."

Typical that the discussion of my wedding had turned into an "everyone loves Connor" session. This was fine with me since the last thing I wanted to talk about was marriage.

His mouth stuffed with steak, Connor began his tale about the Golden Meadows adventure. Listening to him, you'd think his shrewdness and daring had singlehandedly won the stockpile of cash, silver, and jewelry.

When he paused to shove in more steak, I said, "Excuse me," and tried to ease out of the kitchen.

The sound of the door beyond the laundry room and Da's voice calling my name, halted my retreat.

Maeve hurried to him as he entered the rear of the kitchen. Arms open, she said, "Sweetheart, I missed you so much." She hugged him, and kissed him on the lips, emitting a little moan. Then she turned and smiled at me and Connor.

"Quinn and I have been talking about the wedding plans and Connor's been telling me about your trip to Georgia." She put an arm around Da's waist. "You are something else, Rory O'Neill. My honey always makes the money!"

Da gave her a squeeze, and with a frown, shifted his gaze to me. "Glad to hear you're moving on with the wedding."

"You don't have to worry about our Quinn," Maeve said. "She's a Traveller girl, through and through." She was smiling like I was the pride of Tinkers Town.

The frown still darkened Da's face. "Jaysus, girl, you did have me worried. I didn't like you hesitating with Tommy. You seemed to forget I'm a man of my word. We will honor the contract! Besides, the O'Carrolls are not people you want to piss off."

And you wonder why I hesitate?

As if reading my thoughts, Da said, "Tommy's a good man. You should see him in action. In fact, his da and I have a little job in Aiken and I want you both to come with us. You'll appreciate seeing Tommy at work. He's fierce on the job."

If it meant delaying my trip to Boston with Maeve, I was all for it. "I'd love to do another job with you, Da."

Maeve's lips tightened, but she didn't say anything.

"And after that," Da said, "we'll get you two married."

Connor exchanged a glance with Maeve who still stood with her arm around Da. A spark of triumph lit her eyes.

I forced a smile for Da, and finally escaped from the kitchen.

Heading up the wide staircase, I crossed the landing, passing Maeve's six-foot-high arrangement of fake flowers and gold-foil angels. Hurrying up the last half of the staircase, I reached the upstairs hall and made a beeline for my room, where I closed the door behind me and locked it.

In my safe place at last. The room held the rich scent of leather. I'd left my closet door open and inside were leather boots, shoes, jackets, and a long sheepskin coat.

"You're such a Traveller girl," I chided myself out loud. "You spend too much of Da's money on clothes." Yeah, but if I didn't, Maeve would spend it all.

I sank into my dark, burgundy leather chair. Its subdued color and my moss-green and burgundy carpet were such a relief. I loved the room and the pale moss-green walls I'd painted myself. No pink, black and gold in my room. Ever.

Maeve hated my color choices. "I don't know how you stay awake in here," she'd said. "It's so dull."

I'd found a framed horse print by this guy named Munnings in an antique store in Augusta. After I'd hung it over my bed, Da told me about my great grandfather in Ireland and how he'd been a famous horseman.

"Trained race horses, he did. They say with his gypsy ways he could get a horse to do anything. It's in your blood Quinn, but these days we don't have time for the horses."

Rising from my chair, I crossed the room to my laptop. It sat on a carved wood desk Aunt Mary and I'd found in the fashionable town of Aiken. Powering up the computer, I made yet another pointless attempt to find my mother. I'd tried so many times.

As usual, I started on Facebook and other sites, looking for a new Jennifer Smith or Jennifer Smith O'Neill, hoping to find one I hadn't come across before. There weren't any. I moved to one of my people finder sites and tried again. God knows how much money I'd spent on fees to look at photos and information on an endless number of Jennifer Smiths, and Jennifer O'Neills.

Why did my mother have to have such a common name? Did she even live in the US anymore? Had she changed her name? Did she really look as much like me as people said? Sighing, I shut the computer down and collapsed back into my leather chair. Had my mother ever searched for me?

I lowered my head into my hands, wishing Maeve would drop dead. I wouldn't cry if I never saw my half-brother again, either. But I loved Da. Thank God for him, Paddy, and Mary.

Gazing at the rich leather items in my closet and realizing I had family that loved me, I gave myself a mental head slap.

Count your blessings, Quinn. Things could be worse.

9

The next morning, a shaft of sunlight crept through a gap in my curtains. Pouring light across my closed eyelids, the warm glow awakened me.

Stretching, I climbed from bed, padded across the carpet and pulled the curtains back. My room looked over our backyard and the old doublewide trailer still parked there, even though our house was finished several years earlier.

Not much about Maeve made me happy, but for once I was grateful, she'd been so desperate for her gold furniture and pink-leather chairs that she'd refused to waste time in a trailer. Not when she could live in what she considered the grandest house in Tinkers Town. Sharing the confines of that trailer with Maeve and Connor had not been fun.

Checking my phone, I found a message from Tommy's cousin, Anna O'Carroll. The O'Carroll girls were going to dinner at Salvatore's in Augusta that evening and wanted me to join them as I was about to be part of their family.

Of course, everyone in Tinkers Town was related to everyone else, so essentially, I was already part of the family. But the thought was nice, and I could use some female company after a week with the guys in Georgia. At this point, any diversion was welcome.

"We're wearing matching outfits tonight," her message informed me, "so come by my house first." Below that, was a list of things I was expected to wear.

Early that evening, I walked the three blocks to the cluster of O'Carroll homes. As instructed, I wore a short skirt, high heeled ankle boots and a fur vest.

When I reached the O'Carroll enclave, it was apparent they'd been busy planting palm trees. Tommy's parents had even added brick gateposts with newly planted shrubs on either side. Rose bushes were planted around their statue of the Madonna. This was a step up for Tinkers Town, a community that, for the most part, paid little attention to landscaping.

No doubt Maeve would be jealous. Probably launch a landscaping war.

The house belonging to my future father-in law, Desmond O'Carroll, was the grandest of the lot. Much like ours, it had a recessed front door. Large arched windows decorated the walls on either side, but here, and in the other O'Carroll homes, the window shades were pulled down and seemed to stare at me with empty eyes. Travellers liked their privacy.

Desmond had added two-story brick columns at each end that rose like castle towers. He'd built these twin monuments to remind us his ancestors had once lived in an Irish castle, or so he claimed.

Maeve got all fluffed up when she told people I was marrying into Irish royalty. More likely, Irish thugs.

I reached Anna's house, and when I rang the bell, she flung the door open and pulled me inside.

"There's eight of us tonight and you have to wear these!" Anna was short and thin, with piles of brown hair down to the shoulders of her fur vest. She thrust a new package of what looked like plaid tights into my hand. "Our colors."

"Okay," I said, taking the tights. They were green, orange, and white, like the Irish flag.

I followed Anna into the living room. Beneath its vaulted ceiling, a gang of young women were sitting on a grouping of brown leather couches and chairs. Beneath their fur vests, their sweaters and blouses revealed a lot of cleavage. They wore very short skirts, heels, and their long manes were puffed up by mammoth amounts of hair spray and backcombing.

Trying to fit in with my soon-to-be relatives, I'd sprayed half a can of volumizing mousse into the long layers of my hair before I'd left home. But these women hung out together all the time and I had a sharp sense of being the outsider, especially when I saw Lara O'Carroll, a first-class skank.

One of Tommy's many cousins, she was holding court with three or four women who leaned toward her, devouring every loud, authoritative word spilling from her heavily-painted lips.

Since the group was ignoring me, I was free to study her a moment. The last time I'd seen her, she'd been shimmying on the dance floor with a provocative expression of sexual ecstasy. Her movements had suggested a woman ready to lie down for any man in the room. I suspected it was a come-on without a reward. Despite appearances, she was probably a proud virgin and smug about it, knowing she could use it to marry well.

Turning away from Lara and her group of sycophants, I saw one of the O'Carroll girls was immensely pregnant. She didn't look more than fifteen, but Traveller girls married early. Another young O'Carroll mother had brought her five-year-old daughter with her, and a pair of six-year-old Sherwood twins giggled together in a wide armchair. Like the rest of us, the children were dressed in plaid tights and short skirts. They wore eye makeup, jewelry, and carried shiny little leather purses.

I'd always been different from these gals. I was a loner, and this trait didn't sit well with the tightknit Travellers' girls. Instead of makeup, hair, clothes and the opposite sex, I'd immersed myself in books. I'd read some of the literary classics, delved into books about art, history, and even had a subscription to *National Geographic*. The world outside Tinkers Town fascinated me.

Once, when the *Geographic* was delivered, I'd overheard Maeve whispering to Connor. "She's just like that mother of hers. Stuck up because she reads this stupid magazine and has all those books in her room. And then she uses those big words. Probably doesn't even know what they mean."

Lara's loud laugh drew me back to the present. Tall, maybe five-nine, she had the wide shoulders and narrow hips of a swimmer, or runner. I'd never realized how large boned and powerful looking she was.

For whatever reason, she despised me. That was okay, because I couldn't stand her, or her over-bleached white-blond hair and boat-load of black eye makeup. Today, she was wearing extensions, and some of the other young women wore wigs.

Turning my attention to Anna, who had always been nice to me, I was pleased to see she'd included my friend, Kayla Riley, in the group. Kayla and I had met when we were five, and now, she rushed over and gave me a hug. She had blue eyes, strawberry blond hair, and a ruddy complexion, a combination not usually found in Tinkers Town. Most of the Travellers had dark hair and dark eyes.

Since I was a natural blond like my mother, with blue eyes like Da, Kayla and I had been drawn to each other the day we met.

Her mother was an outsider, too, one more thing that brought us together. Except her mother was far more acceptable than mine. She'd come to Tinkers Town from distant relatives in Ireland. And she hadn't run off.

"Go put your tights on, Quinn," Kayla said. "We'll be in the kitchen doing our faces."

Emerging from the bathroom with the addition of plaid tights, I walked into the kitchen, where everyone was applying glitter to their eyelids and sparkly paste-on shamrocks to their cheeks. After Anna spiffed me up, we piled into two Lexus SUVs and headed for Salvatore's in Augusta.

When we entered the restaurant, we got a lot of stares. That was the point, wasn't it? A pack of young women in short skirts with big hair and a lot of makeup tend to get that kind of reaction. The children were icing on our gaudy cake.

But I had to admit, it was fun. I felt a sense of comradery and realized that after marrying Tommy, I'd belong. Maybe my loner ways weren't such a good thing.

Once we were seated at a table, everyone, including the children, set their cell phones on the tabletop, right beneath their faces. They switched them on and the LED lights hit the glitter on our faces, producing an eerie, almost ethereal effect.

Comments sputtered around the room. "It's those Traveller people."

"Do they always run in packs like that?"

"With those outfits? Safety in numbers."

A male voice said, "That one might as well take it all off."

He had to be referring to Lara, whose tight blouse was unbuttoned enough to display the top of her very low-cut pushup bra. She'd added glitter to the swell of her breasts.

She glared at the guy who'd spoken, "Why don't you put your eyes back in your head before you lose 'em?"

"You're not worth the time, honey," he said, his voice carrying through the entire restaurant.

He was sitting with three other guys in their early twenties. One of them had a jackhammer and a welding iron tattooed on his biceps. A surge of panic shot through me. With a sharp intake of breath, I looked away, trying to hide my face.

"Hey, I know you!" he said. Steve, from the Georgia paving supply company, stood and strode toward me. "You're the bitch who ripped me off!"

10

"I have no idea what you're talking about," I said to Steve as his stout figure loomed over me.

"Don't give me that crap." His lips curled in anger, his eyes loaded with menace. "You're Katie Smith, at least that's who you said you were. Whoever the hell you are, you stole 900 bucks from my family!"

I was surprised to see Lara throw me an approving glance. In a smug, nasty tone, she said, "Obviously, you've never met this woman before. You don't even know her name."

Giving her a dismissive wave, he said, "Like I don't know that! This bitch was in my shop last Wednesday and ripped me and my dad off for $900."

"Sorry about that, dude," Lara said. "This lady was with us all day last Wednesday. We were in Columbia helping her pick out a wedding registry. Weren't we?"

A chorus of female voices erupted from the table, "That's right. She was with us all day."

The six year-old-twins nodded solemnly, and one said, "All day." Then they both gave Steve the most innocent little smiles you've ever seen.

Sal, the restaurant's owner, appeared at our table. We knew him well, as we often used Salvatore's to cater dances and weddings. He was one of those rare outsiders accepted by the Travellers. Probably because everyone loved his restaurant and his excellent Italian cuisine, almost as much as he did. His large, happy belly attested to his love of food.

He gave Steve a narrow-eyed stare. "Is there a problem?"

"Yes. I'm surprised you'd let these skanks in here." His two friends laughed while Steve curled his upper lip with disdain.

Sal drew himself up. "Sir, I'm going to have to ask you to go back to your table and leave my customers alone."

"Or what? You gonna beat me with your belly?"

One of Steve's friends snorted so hard, he spit red wine onto Sal's white table cloth.

"Antonio!" Sal called. The kitchen door swung open, and a huge guy with long arms and a baseball bat emerged. A smaller man with a rolling pin grasped in his sinewy hand appeared behind him.

Steve moved two steps back from our table. "Yeah, yeah, I'll sit down."

But under his breath, I heard him say, "For now." He looked right at me when he said it.

When Steve retreated to his table, we ordered from Sal. Everyone but me seemed to forget about Steve and his buddies. Maybe the girls were used to confrontations. Maybe they liked them.

Me? I was still rattled by the cries and horrified stare of Emma Bunting.

But my veal parmesan, fried eggplant, and salad were delicious, and the food acted like a mild tranquilizer. Not to mention the wine. Feeling more relaxed, I watched Anna hand a fistful of something to Sal on her way to the ladies' room. When she came back, I leaned forward, asking what she'd given him.

She put a finger to her lips. "You'll find out."

After we'd finished our meal, followed by cannoli and gelatos, everyone pulled out cash to pay our bill. When we go to a strange place, we usually stiff the wait staff, and leave without paying. We're not called "damn gypsies" for nothing.

But Sal was a friend, and we tipped him well. Even the Sherwood twins rustled up tip money from their little pink purses.

When we rose to leave the restaurant, so did Steve and his friends. I wouldn't have minded being accompanied by the baseball bat and the rolling pin, but we were on our own.

Except we weren't.

A long Mercedes passenger van idled on Broad Street, immediately outside the restaurant. It had Alabama tags, and when I saw Anna's grandfather, Shane O'Carroll, at the wheel, I knew the tags were fake. One of the twins called to Shane, "Hi, Uncle Paddy." Of course, she knew that wasn't his name, but Traveller girls learn the game early.

Two Sherwood men stood on the sidewalk wearing leather jackets. One of the kitchen help stepped out and handed them what I now realized were the sets of keys to the vehicles we'd driven to the restaurant.

Giggling and joking, we clambered into the van and slid the doors shut. Lara waved at Steve, who promptly gave her the finger. He and his buddies hotfooted it down Broad street, climbed into a pickup truck, and quickly pulled in behind the van.

Shane turned the van into the alley alongside the restaurant, and Steve's friend steered his pickup in behind us. When Shane reached the end of the alley, we were facing the road that ran parallel to Broad Street. The right lane was safe from oncoming traffic since a meat and poultry truck idled at the curb to our left. Shane floored the van and made a sharp right. The delivery truck sped forward and careened into the alley, blocking Steve and his friends.

We all cheered and shrieked with delight. I knew the two Sherwood men would drive the cars home after Steve and his friends were long gone. Heck, they'd probably have a late dinner with Sal before returning to Tinkers Town.

Other than Kayla, I'd made little effort to befriend my cousins or the young women of Tinkers Town. But by the time Shane rolled us into town, I was almost starting to like Lara. Maybe my impending marriage to Tommy wasn't such a terrible thing.

Returning home, I found Maeve had left the house for a ladies' night out, and Connor was off with one of his Sherwood buddies. I was glad to find Da alone, especially since he was so pleased I'd spent time with the O'Carroll girls.

A warm evening for early spring, we sat outside in Maeve's over-sized, plastic lawn chairs on a patio surrounded by plastic pink flamingos. The flamingos were so awful, I actually liked them.

I told Da my tale about Steve, and he loved it.

"Look at you there, Quinn, grinning like a leprechaun. Christ on a bike, the man must have been pissed to be stopped by a poultry truck!"

He laughed so hard, he had to wipe a tear from one eye. With him relaxed, I took a chance and released the long-caged question.

"I know you don't like talking about her, but please, have you ever spoken to my mom since she left? Do you know where she is?"

His face darkened, the last traces of laughter shriveling. His nose flared wide. "I'll not talk about her."

"She's my mother! I deserve to know." The suppressed fury rising inside me was powerful, almost frightening.

"She deserves nothing!" His anger matched my own, but it was so quiet and controlled, a spiderlike chill crawled up my spine.

"She's dead to me. Forget about her, Quinn."

"You are so selfish!" I shouted. "I want to know about her, see her, *meet* her. All you care about are your stupid hurt feelings! I'm sorry she left you, but she left me too!"

"That is enough, Quinn!" He stood, glaring at me, before he strode to the side door of the house, jerked it open, and slammed it behind him.

I burst into tears, sobbing with anger and frustration. The stupid son of a bitch. How dare he treat me like that? So, she broke your heart. Do you have to break mine?

I knew long cold silences would divide us the next day. I hated fighting with him, but he was so stubborn, and he should tell me. Shouldn't he?

I jerked to my feet, pacing around the yard until finally collapsing back into the chair, where I tried to breathe evenly.

I'd see Tommy the next day. Maybe it was time to be more open with him. Emotionally, I'd kept him at a distance, always working to keep our conversations light and inconsequential.

Like a good Traveller woman, I'd let him do the talking, never sharing my inner thoughts. Not that he'd ever asked about them. Besides, it wasn't like I could tell him I dreaded our impending marriage.

Like it or not, he was my future.

On the western horizon, the sun was setting, gilding the flamingos to golden-pink. Sitting alone in the plastic lawn chair, I contemplated my future, trying not to feel like Alice, struggling to find her way through Wonderland.

11

I let Tommy in when he rang our bell at eight the next morning.

I hadn't seen him since before the Golden Meadows job, and gazing at him now, I almost smiled at his ears.

When we were little kids, I thought if he could flap them, he'd be able to fly. But really, they were kind of cute. Maybe this marriage thing wasn't so bad.

His da, Desmond, stood next to him, short and stocky, with the same sandy colored hair and ears. Fortunately, Tommy's mother was of average height, had a willowy body, and finer facial features than Desmond. Tommy was a mixture of the two, which is to say, he was taller than his dad, and more slender. Whereas Desmond's eyes crowded close to the bridge of his nose, Tommy's were wider-spaced and a richer shade of blue.

Not a bad looking guy, if you didn't mind the slyness in his eyes—an indication my future husband was a master at separating people from their money.

"Hey, babe" he said, stepping in close and putting his arms around my waist. "How's my Quinny?"

I'd stiffened at his touch but forced myself to relax as I stepped back from him.

Smiling, I said, "I hear we'll be working a job today. Tell me about it."

"A bunch of us will be in Aiken. You and me—we'll work as a team, Quinn. Something I'm looking forward to, especially after we're married." With a knowing wink, he said, "I can teach you a thing or two about the hand being quicker than the eye."

As he spoke, his gaze ran over my body, and he flushed. Probably thinking he wouldn't have to wait much longer. So many Travellers' girls kept their virginity until marriage, it had been easy to put him off. But once we were married, that would change. I wasn't sure I wanted to think about that.

"So, what's the scam?" I asked, trying to shift his focus.

"Pops got a tree trimming and gutter job at a house on the edge of what they call the 'Hitchcock Woods.' People with property on those woods are stinky rich."

"And you know which ones stink the most, right?"

"You bet! The real target is the house next door. That's where you'll come in. Da worked up a clever con for you, Quinny."

We moved down the hall to the kitchen where Maeve was serving up a mess of ham and eggs for the men already seated at the table. She wore a short skirt and high heeled platforms that showed off her long legs.

Judging from the men's' surreptitious glances, her animal attraction was in full force. Maeve had a confidence in her sexual allure that drew certain types of men like moths to a candle. She also had an amazing ability to hide the ugliness inside.

I tried to ignore her, and while I buttered a platter of toast at the counter, Desmond, who had seated himself next to Tommy, told me how I would work my scam.

As Desmond spoke, Da never looked at me. Maeve noticed this, and a satisfied smile settled on her mouth. When Desmond paused to shovel in a forkful of eggs, she leaned close to my ear.

"Trouble in paradise, Quinn?"

I gave her my best impassive stare and buttered more toast. I thought breakfast would never end, but finally, I left with Desmond in his truck. The rest of the men climbed into a four-door Dodge truck that towed Desmond's equipment.

When we neared the job, Desmond turned onto an isolated stretch of road, away from the others. A while later, he dropped me off next to the Hitchcock Woods.

As I climbed from the truck, he said, "March straight away from this road. You'll see a horse trail. Go left and follow it down to a muddy crossing. Can't miss it." Trying to hide his amusement and failing, he continued. "After you finish your mud bath, follow the trail uphill until it turns to the right. You go straight, and you'll be in the target's back yard."

As the truck pulled away, I glanced down at my shiny new riding boots. I'd always thought it would be fun to ride a horse and have the clothes that went with it, but this wasn't how I'd imagined it.

Instead of riding, I was trudging into in the deep pine forest for the sole purpose of messing up the boots, the cool Barbour vest, and other clothes the O'Carrolls had bought for me.

I found the trail and negotiated the steep descent churned with hoof prints. Young pines and laurel bushes grew on either side, and deeper in the woods, I could see tall pines with massive trunks. At the bottom, I found the crossing. With a sigh, I marched into the mud, then carefully lowered myself into the muck to make it look like I'd been tossed from a horse at the crossing.

"Just one side," Desmond had warned. "Wouldn't do to have the mud all over you. Make it look like you landed on your side and then rolled to your knees to stand up. And watch the knee wound!"

Marianne, my future mother-in-law, was gifted with the trickery of makeup. She'd created a nasty looking cut and scrape on my knee to go with the torn fabric on the knee of my breeches. The whole mess was covered with saran wrap so I wouldn't screw up the artwork while wallowing about in the mud. I was also careful not to touch the "wound" on my cheek or the fake dried blood that went with it.

After I'd wallowed long enough to cover one side with muck, I stood, removed the saran wrap, and finger painted the knee area with mud as well as my cheek. Per instructions, I sprinkled a few leaves and twigs into my hair. As I headed uphill, carrying my mud splattered helmet in one hand, I could feel the pre-job tension coursing through my veins.

When the wide path turned right, I went straight, following a narrow horse trail leading through the undergrowth. Ahead, I could see the beginnings of open space. I stopped for a moment looking back at the woods. The ground swept away downhill then rose back up in the distance, revealing a long-leaf pine forest that seemed to stretch forever.

Desmond had said the woods were for horseback riding and contained over two thousand acres. I liked the tangy, clean scent of pine, the rattle of woodpeckers high above me, and the sounds of unseen animals rustling about the forest floor. I was surprised how much the limitless expanse of the woods affected me.

The vastness of the pine forest expanded my head. It was the feeling I got at night, when a star stenciled sky loomed far above me.

It was time to walk to the property ahead. As I followed the trail, the estate came into view. A rock wall separated me from a horse paddock and a stone barn. Beyond that, landscaped gardens allowed broken glimpses of a massive stone home with four chimneys.

What was it about lovely homes belonging to the wealthy that I found so intimidating? Their money? Their air of unquestionable acceptance? My sense of not belonging? Yeah, probably that last thing.

The place wouldn't intimidate Connor. It would only make his mouth water. And I had no doubt Tommy's eyes had glowed when he'd first seen the property.

In the distance ahead, I could hear the reassuring sound of Da's paver and the shouts of the men working. I couldn't smell the asphalt yet, but I would soon enough. The trail took a last turn through a dense patch of laurel and hollies and revealed a wooden gate set in the stone wall.

Adopting a limp as if my "injured" knee was killing me, I opened the gate. Three horses in the paddock spotted me and threw their heads up. They took off, their raised tails waving like flags.

Limping along the edge of the paddock, I called, "Hello," every so often, in case someone was around.

No one answered. The smell of damp earth, pine, and blooming spring flowers formed an earthy potpourri. Following a brick walk that meandered through magnolias, azaleas, and a rose garden, I reached the large back porch of the house.

It had stately columns and a second story veranda accessible from the bedrooms above. Careful to maintain my limp, I hobbled onto the stone floor and rapped the knocker on the wooden door.

12

Inside the home where I would steal a sapphire, a chorus of barking dogs erupted. I could hear a voice shushing them. The door opened to reveal a woman around forty, her hand firmly on the collar of a massive dog with large teeth. Two little fluffy dogs and a Chihuahua spilled past them and milled about my ankles.

She took in my appearance. "Oh, dear. You've been hurt." Looking past me, she asked, "Are you alone?"

When I nodded, she said, "You'd better come in. You had a spill?"

"Yes. We parted company and I landed in the mud."

"Yes, I can see that. I'm Peggy Dearborn." Her handshake was firm and strong. She wore no makeup, and her skin was lined from days in the sun and weather. "And you are?"

"Lizzy Van den Berg," I lied. "I was riding with friends, but we got separated, and then my phone disappeared into the muck. I'm sorry to show up like this." I gave her my practiced apologetic smile, took one lame step, and put an unsteady hand on the top of a wooden chest standing nearby. "I was hoping I could use your phone?"

"Of course. But wouldn't you like to clean those cuts and put something on them?"

"That would be so kind," I said. "Thank you."

"We have everything you need in the guest bathroom."

At her words, my pulse ticked up and a little thrill of impending success shot through me.

The O'Carrolls knew from a friend of the Dearborn's maid that her weekend guest was Meredith Hutchins, of New York. The extremely wealthy Hutchins was staying with the Dearborn's to attend a large charity ball. She would be in the guest room.

The Traveller's network had whispered and then confirmed from an Irish gardener in New York, who knew Hutchins' house maid, that the woman had brought exquisite jewelry with her for the ball. The star piece was a 15-carat Kashmir sapphire ring.

Apparently, Meredith had purchased it at auction for more than a hundred-thousand dollars several years earlier. If Desmond couldn't sell it whole on the black market, his family knew people who could cut it into two or three stones. They had always been into bigger crimes than Da and Uncle Paddy.

Leading the way to the guestroom, Dearborn asked, "Does it hurt to put weight on your knee?"

It's not so bad," I said with a grimace as I hobbled forward while scanning the room.

Unlike the houses in Tinkers Town or those in Golden Meadows, this house was old and worn. Comfortable, with muted colors and beautiful carpets comfortably sprinkled with dog fur. There were real oil paintings—not prints—of horses, dogs, and striking still life scenes of flowers and mountain scenery.

There were bronze statues of horses and dogs on the tables, and shelves filled with worn, leather-bound books. The large furry dog, who'd thankfully put his teeth away, threw himself onto a sofa and stretched out. His fur darkened into an intimidating black mask around his eyes.

Maeve would hate it. She didn't like dogs, and the idea of letting one have the run of her house would horrify her.

We entered a wing, where Dearborn led me into a bedroom with an antique canopy bed and a large fireplace. Had to be the guest room.

A door in one wall opened into a marble bath with fixtures that Maeve would have torn out because they were old and not up to her standard of the latest, gaudiest, most expensive equipment.

I thought the house was the coolest place I'd ever seen. With a mental head slap, I told myself to stop sightseeing and get down to business.

"My guest is out riding," Dearborn said, "so you'll have the bathroom to yourself while you clean up. There's some antibiotic ointment and band aids in the cabinet under the sink. I'll just be in the living room."

"Thank you," I said, and softly closed the bathroom door behind her.

If the information we had about the sapphire ring was wrong, nothing would be lost. I would simply go next door to where the men were working and see what I could take from there.

I didn't like this life, and once I was married to Tommy, I planned to stop stealing, whether he liked it or not. I'd refuse to join in the women's shoplifting schemes, too. Aunt Mary and Maeve no longer stole stuff, so, why should I?

While thinking these things, I quickly washed my face, letting the mud and wound makeup swirl down the drain. I used a wash cloth to clean off my knee. After drying my skin, I found the Band-Aids and covered each "wound" with a large bandage.

Quietly, I opened the door and crept into the bedroom. Right there on the dresser was the jewelry box described by the New York gardener. The initials, MH, for Meredith Hutchins were stamped in red on the black velvet box. I made a beeline for it and tried to open it. Damn. Locked.

Why hadn't we thought of this? I didn't have time to pick or break the lock. I'd have to give the whole box to Tommy. I rushed to the nearest window, looking for the thick azalea hedge Tommy had mentioned. No luck, but when I looked outside the window on the other side of the canopy bed, I spotted the hedge.

Tommy would be hiding in those azaleas.

I darted to the dresser and scooped up the jewelry box. I couldn't drop the jewels into the cloth bag in my pocket as planned. I'd have to toss the whole thing out the window.

With the velvet box under my arm, I zipped back to the window. The old wood rails were stiff but opened enough for me to push the box through. It thumped as it hit the ground. The distant sound of machinery was accompanied by the whiff of tar and motor oil that drifted in through the window.

"Tommy," I whispered as loud as I dared.

No response. Turning away from the window, I listened carefully for the sound of footsteps from within the house and heard nothing.

"Tommy!" I hissed with more volume.

No answer. Where the hell was he? I could hardly retrieve the box and carry it out the front door. I'd have to go through the window, grab the box and run to the house next door. Nervous, I glanced back, listening for Dearborn.

The empty spot on the dresser where the velvet box had been seemed to scream an alarm. Get out, Quinn. Get out now!

My hands were shaking as I shoved the window sash higher. The old wood groaned loudly in protest. I had one leg through the window when I heard Dearborn's voice.

"What are you doing?"

Rushing toward me, she shrieked, "You took Meredith's sapphire!"

The big dog was right behind her, his teeth in full display and gleaming. I got my other leg out and was about to push away from the sill when she grabbed my wrist.

"Where do you think you're going?"

I leaned forward and bit her hand. With a cry, she let go. I dropped the few feet to the ground and looked for the box. It wasn't there. It had to be! Wild with fear, I looked around. Shit.

I took off running and glanced back. The dog was leaping through the window.

"Get her, Runford, get her!" Dearborn shouted.

He was on me in seconds, huge paws on my shoulder blades, knocking me to my side on the ground, one side of my face pressed into in the mulch by the azalea hedge. He straddled me, teeth bared, hackles alive with rage. His mouth clamped down on the boot where it encased my ankle.

I froze. He didn't savage the boot, just held it in the vice grip of his jaws. The needle points of pressure coming through the leather were painful against my skin.

"One move, you little bitch, and he'll tear you to pieces!"

I'd never stayed so still in my life.

After pushing herself through the window, Dearborn stood over me and the dog. As she whipped out a cell phone, Runford continued to hold my leg firmly between his big teeth. Faint and unintelligible, I could hear the dispatcher's voice on Dearborn's phone.

"My emergency? My house has been robbed. My dog is holding the thief. Can you send someone right away? No, I'm not hurt. Just get someone over here before my dog turns this miserable woman into hamburger meat."

More broken words from the phone.

"Yes, I'll keep the line open."

My eyes squeezed shut in defeat. I had no idea where the sapphire was, but it was missing, and I was the thief. I was so busted.

Dearborn put a hand over her phone and glared at me. "You little jerk, did you really think you could waltz into my house and steal my friend's jewelry?"

I didn't respond. My slightest reaction might incite the dog. As if reading my mind, he readjusted his painful hold on my ankle and growled. I was terrified he was working himself into a rage.

Lying there in the dirt and mulch at the edge of the azalea hedge, I forced myself not to stare at the dog. A twig pressed sharply into my cheek. I ignored it and tried to get a handle on my situation.

Tommy hadn't been there. He would have answered me. Had he and Desmond chickened out, thinking the cops would realize the men working next door were Travellers? Put them together with the theft? Except chickening out wasn't an O'Carroll trait.

Had someone else been hiding in that thick hedge, taken the box when I'd turned away from the window to listen for Dearborn?

I would be questioned hard as to how I'd known about the sapphire. I wouldn't talk, wouldn't give up my fiancé and the others. Ratting Tommy out went against my nature, and I'd be charged no matter what happened. Besides, I'd make enemies for life if I betrayed a Traveller.

But where was the fucking jewel box? My mouth had gone dry. I couldn't swallow. It felt like Runford's teeth had pierced my leather boot and drawn blood.

But I suddenly realized that my life had probably changed forever. This frightened me even more than the dog's huge teeth pressing my leg.

13

CUFFED AND COWED, I sat in the back of a county sheriff's car as it drove me away from the Dearborn Estate.

The deputy at the wheel had identified himself as Deputy Tyler. He had a bullet-shaped head, enhanced by one of those high and tight haircuts. I'd never liked those things.

Why are you thinking about the guy's hair? You've been arrested!

The car smelled like stale ashtrays and fear. I'd thought only dogs could scent fear. But in this car, I could smell it. How many had been locked in here like me, permeating the seats with dread?

I wanted Da. Surely, he'd already talked to Tommy who must know what had happened. I mean, he had to, right? Da was probably calling the criminal defense lawyer used by Tinkers Town. Da would take care of me.

Thinking about him, my eyes burned with tears. My nose started to run. I needed a tissue, my sleeve, or even the skin on my wrist, but my hands were cuffed behind me, the metal tight and painful.

We cleared the woods and rolled into a commercial district. Eventually, we left the schools, churches, carwashes and shops behind us as we headed out of Aiken.

Tyler swung his cruiser onto Wire Road and headed farther out of town. I hadn't been on this road before but knew it led to the county detention center.

Da will have me bailed out in no time. Of course, he will! Yet my hands shook from an uncontrollable fear that surged from my core.

We made a sharp left and rolled into a driveway. Ahead was a sliding metal gate crowned with coiled razor wire. Beyond the gate was a solid brick wall, the back of a large building. Deeply inset into the thick wall was a dark metal door with a small black window. It was flanked by gray dumpsters.

If I went inside that door, would I ever come out?

Tyler passed through the gate, hung a left, and instead of driving to that dark entrance, went under a brick columned portico. A white, windowless van was already parked there. Maybe for transporting prisoners?

Deputy Tyler got me out of his car. We stood waiting before the entrance. Someone inside must have given us the onceover, because with a loud click, the heavy glass-and-metal door unlocked and slid open.

Beyond was a large room with a counter. People were seated in chairs. They had the resigned look of people you see waiting at the Department of Motor Vehicles. The look of frustrated, helpless people caught inside the slow-moving wheels of government.

As I was led through the room, the sharp odor of disinfectant hit me. At the counter, a guard removed my cuffs. Tyler left without a word, and I was taken into a cubicle, processed, photographed, and fingerprinted.

When I finally got my one phone call, they told me it had to be collect. Going through an operator, I dialed Da's cell. It rang and went to voice mail. I left a message, my voice hesitant and fearful.

My last words were broken by tears. "Please, Da, get me out of here."

"He's not answering," I said to the officer behind the counter who'd let me use the phone. She was a powerful looking woman. Tall, dark-skinned and muscular, with blond streaks in her hair. "Can I make another call?"

"No, ma'am. Just the one." There was no sympathy in her eyes. It didn't matter if I was young, or cute, or female like her. She'd long since hardened, and no doubt, if she could spare the occasional kindness, it would never go to a Traveller. We were too well known to law enforcement. The O'Carroll's had seen to that.

"How can my da call me back?" My voice sounded strange to me.

"He can't. But if he gets your message, he can call into the system with his questions. You'll probably have your bail hearing tomorrow morning and he can come in for that."

"But what about—"

She turned to another guard who'd come through a locked door behind the counter. "This one's ready to move along." Then she ignored me, turning instead to study a chart spread on the counter before her.

The new guard was lean, with mean eyes. The name on her identification badge read "Flint." Except for the hard eyes, she was expressionless as she snapped my hand cuffs back on. Then, she fastened shackles onto my ankles with a chain stretching between them that left me hobbled like a horse.

My dismay must have shown, for when she glanced at my face, her lips curved into a smirk. "Just be glad you don't have an extra chain between those hands and ankles. 'Course if you misbehave, I'll be happy to fix you up."

I didn't want to antagonize this woman, so I remained silent. After shuffling through a metal door, I was led down a long, windowless hall, encased in solid cinderblock walls. At least they were a soft, yellowish-white and not a dreadful institutional green.

Eventually we arrived at a heavy plate-glass and metal window. On the other side, was a large room where women of various ages sat and talked, some watching a TV that hung from the ceiling. They wore either orange or blue jumpsuits. Near the door was another long counter like the one in the first room. Guards stood behind it.

Once inside, a detention officer removed my hardware. She told me to grab a bedroll from the pile next to the counter, then led me up a staircase to a long gallery overlooking the room below. Gray metal doors with small barred windows peppered the facade of the long cinderblock wall. Must be the cells. Without ceremony, I was put inside one, and the door clanged shut behind me.

Two platform metal beds stood against two of the inside walls. One was empty. A small, skinny black girl sat on the other one. She had desperate eyes that stared at nothing, not even at me. Her body was shaking and if she ground her teeth any harder, something would break.

When I asked her name, she said, "Tania, rhymes with Pennsylvania."

After that, she ignored me. I found it odd she was so concerned about the pronunciation of her name, but maybe it was important to her to hang onto a piece of her identity in this place.

I unrolled my blanket onto the skinny mattress pad covering the hard metal frame and stared at the toilet that sprouted from one wall. There was very little space between me and that toilet, or the sink next to it. Privacy would become a distant memory.

The long night passed slow and sleepless. Every sound that came through the walls was foreign and alarming. Why had Da made no effort to contact me? The question was like a worm in my brain. Morning finally crawled forward to meet me, and when it did, a guard let us out of our cell.

We went down the iron staircase into the TV lounge area, which apparently substituted as a dining room. I lined up, cafeteria style, behind Tania and was served "breakfast." The wet, yellow and brown stuff on my plate vaguely resembled eggs and sausage. To me, it tasted like ground-rat slop with cockroach seasoning. I couldn't eat it. I chewed on a piece of dry toast and managed to swallow it with coffee that might have been brewed during the previous century.

Tania, sat next to me. The girl had never spoken to me throughout the night, except to tell me her name and later beg me for something to stop her shakes. When I told her I couldn't help her, she'd shut down completely.

Sitting beside me now, she was silent. She pushed her breakfast plate away without looking at the food. At least she sipped her coffee.

An older woman in a blue jumpsuit joined us. She had long blond hair that had mostly washed out to gray. She was thin and bony; her hands were veined with blue, her eyes tired, but not without life.

"First time in?" she asked me.

I was desperate to talk to somebody, anybody.

"Yeah. How did you know?"

"Honey, it's written all over your face. And I ain't seen you before."

"How long have you been here?" I asked.

"Girl, you need to learn your prison colors."

"What do you mean?"

"You see, I'm wearing blue. That means I been sentenced already. You got the orange, means you haven't been to trial yet."

"Oh." I knew nothing about prison etiquette and was afraid to ask why she was there. For all I knew the question would anger her.

"Anyways, I'll be here a while yet. But like I said, I ain't seen you before. You come in yesterday?"

When I nodded, she said "You two girls will probably get your bond hearing this morning, but I heard you're gonna get No-Bail-Nancy."

"Shit!" Tania said, startling me. "My momma's gonna be here. Thinks she can take me home. How'd we get Judge No-bail?"

"Just your lucky day in paradise," the older woman said. Then she laughed, until it turned into a long hacking cough.

She had to be wrong. With no prior offense, surely, I'd get bail and be home with Da later that day?

14

At 9:30 that morning, the guards collected me, Tania, and five other women. They outfitted us in cuffs and the now familiar ankle chains, forcing us to shuffle through a maze of the long cinderblock halls.

One of the prisoners had bandages on her head, with a rusty red stain, where apparently blood had seeped through during the night.

Eventually we hobbled into a small room with a dais that held a desk and a microphone. A blond woman in a black robe sat behind the desk. She was protected by thick glass I assumed was bulletproof.

Through more dense glass on our right, I could see a few people staring at us. They were casually dressed, and a couple of them appeared very poor—if limp, dirty hair, bad skin, and threadbare clothing are any indication. I could almost match my bond mates with what I presumed were family members.

Where was Da? No one I knew was there. How could this be?

These desperate thoughts were interrupted when one of the bedraggled visitors stood up and yelled loudly enough that her voice carried through the glass wall.

"What happened to my daughter's head. What did you do to her?"

The judge adjusted her pair of hot pink glasses, then leaned forward and spoke through her microphone. "Sit down and be quiet, or I will have you removed!"

The woman appeared shocked by the sharp, heartless response, but twisting her hands together, she sat. It seemed the judge had decided to settle my fate first. She rustled the papers in front of her, then frowned.

"Miss O'Neill," she said peering over the top of her glasses, "you live at 231 Dublin Street, in Tinkers Town. Is that correct?"

I had to swallow before I could answer. "Yes ma' am."

"You are charged with stealing a sapphire ring valued at $100,015. That's grand larceny, Miss O'Neill."

Had there been no other jewelry in the box? I stared at her, not knowing if I was supposed to respond or not.

"Due to your family connections, you represent a substantial flight risk. Your bail is denied and you're to be detained until your trial."

She never said another word to me. Instead she said, "Miss Tania Lorkins?"

I realized she was addressing my cell mate, Tania, but she pronounced her name as Tawnya.

"You are charged," the judge continued, "with possession of methamphetamine with intent to sell."

"Nuh uh," Tania said. "I wasn't gonna sell it. Was for me. And you pronounced my name wrong, it's Tania, rhymes with Pennsylvania."

The judge continued as if the girl hadn't spoken. "Though this is your first offense, I'm denying bail. Methamphetamine is a serious drug with serious consequences. You will be held over until trial."

Through the glass I saw a scrawny black woman, an older but almost exact duplicate of Tania, drop her head into her hands. The judge's hard eyes moved back to the papers before her. I thought her hot pink glasses were a poor choice with her cold eyes. The court session ground on.

After the hearing and another long shuffle back to the common room, they served us lunch. It was recognizable as a ham and cheese sandwich and I was starving, so I ate it. I ate Tania's too, after she refused to touch hers. She did drink coffee and eat the cellophane-wrapped brownie they'd put on our tray.

With no bail, I was going to be here for at least a couple of days. What was I supposed to do for clean underwear and toiletries beyond the soap, toothbrush and toothpaste supplied with my bedroll?

Unsure who to ask, I spotted the washed-out blonde I'd spoken with before. She was one table over, licking the chocolate brownie icing from her fingers. She sat with some other women I had never spoken to. Unsure of my reception I walked over.

The other women didn't smile, but they nodded at me. Washed-out actually smiled. So, I squatted down next to her. Instinct told me it might be safer than standing over these other women. I had a lot to learn about prison protocol.

"Is there a store here where I can get some stuff I need?"

"There's a commissary," a gaunt woman with missing teeth said. But you gotta have an account with money in it."

"Will they give me back the money that was in my pants pocket?"

"Hell no," Washed-out said. "You ain't allowed to have cash. Somebody, like family, has to put money in for you."

"Oh," I said. Why hadn't Da already done this?

"Thanks," I nodded at the women and walked back to Tania. What I wanted to do, was cry.

Not long after, they put us back in our cells. With no talking, and only cinderblock walls to look at, I experienced the new, sharp pain of smart-phone withdrawal. I would have committed a crime for access to the internet. Not that I'd be able to concentrate, my mind raced so fast, you'd think I'd snorted a hit of Tania's methamphetamine.

Why had no one come? Where was Da? Uncle Paddy? Aunt Mary? Why hadn't I heard from Tommy? Something had to be wrong. They wouldn't abandon me like this, would they?

The sound of the cell door bolt turning woke me up. How had I fallen asleep? I raised up on one elbow and stared at our wall clock. Two p.m. The door pulled open. The tall, muscular guard stood there. The one with the blond-streaked hair. I noticed her nametag read Carson. "O'Neill, you have a visitor."

My heart leapt with gladness. "Is it my da?"

"No. Come with me."

"Who is it?"

"Just come with me, miss."

Did I imagine it, or did she look worried? My hands trembled as I followed her along the gallery and down the iron staircase.

Can't you just tell me who has come to see me?

Without a reply, she took me back to the counter for hand and leg hardware, out the secure door, and down the now familiar cinderblock corridor. We reached the intersecting hallway, where before, we'd turned right. This time, she took me left to a locked door, opened it, and ushered me inside.

A stranger sat on the far side of a metal table. He was thin, maybe forty, with dark receding hair. I got a faint whiff of minty aftershave. Intelligence shone from eyes circled by the gray of exhaustion. If a hint of humor flickered there, it quickly disappeared as he studied me.

Before either of us could speak, the guard pointed to the far side of the table and told me to sit in the metal chair that was bolted to the floor. She hooked my leg iron to a floor ring, then stepped outside and shut the door behind her.

In the meantime, my visitor man had pulled a folder from a black brief case sitting the floor beside him. He swallowed and brushed a piece of lint from the lapel of his black suit. He took a breath, exhaling slowly, like I do when I'm nervous and trying to stay calm.

"Miss O'Neill, my name's Sandy Sanders. I'm an attorney and I've represented your family in the past."

"So, my Da, Rory O'Neill, hired you, right?"

"Actually, it was your uncle, Paddy O'Neill."

"Why? Where's Da?" I wanted to jump over the table and grab the man. My voice had risen, and I didn't care.

Sanders's eyes dropped to his hands, then he took a breath. "I'm sorry to have to tell you this, Miss O'Neill, but your father passed away yesterday."

15

FOR THE LAST TWENTY-four hours, I'd been struggling to control my emotions and fear. Sanders's words shattered my ability to control anything. I leapt at him, but my leg-iron jerked me back to the metal chair.

"You're a fucking liar! Da is—why are you saying this? You're crazy!"

He held a hand up, palm out. "Please, Miss O'Neill. I'm telling you the truth. You need to hear me out."

"But Da isn't dead. You're wrong. He can't be dead!"

Sanders shook his head. Pity clouded his eyes. "I'm very sorry for your loss. It must be a terrible shock."

"How did he die? Did someone kill him?"

"I don't know yet. Your father's body was found behind the house where he'd been working."

His *body*. The fight drained out of me. I sagged in my chair. My head dropped, leaving my eyes to stare blindly at the metal table. The enormity of Sanders's words left me empty, like a shell. It was a while before I could speak. When I did, my voice sounded small and strangled.

"They were working at the house next door to where . . . to where I took the ring. Is that where you mean?"

Sanders nodded.

I could almost hear the machinery, smell the asphalt from Da's paver. He'd been so close. I could have gone to him, told him I was sorry for the things I'd said.

I raised my chin and stared at Sanders. "Please, tell me what happened. Was it an accident?"

"Believe me, I wish I had answers for you. But, I don't. The FBI and county Sheriff's Department are running the investigation.

There'll be an autopsy, of course. But we will be forced to wait for answers."

"So, I have to wait in this place, hoping someone will tell me what happened to my da?

But something Sanders had said made my head snap up. "You said the FBI. What did you mean?" I half stood, wanting to pace, or break something. I could feel my lips curl into a snarl. I probably looked insane. I certainly felt that way.

Sanders hurried on. "A lot has happened in the last twenty-four hours. Please, try to grasp what I'm about to say."

Suddenly, I didn't care what he had to say. What could be worse than Da . . . God. Our last words had been so bitter and unkind. Tears stung my eyes. I tried to control them, but they morphed into loud, wracking sobs.

Sanders fished a white handkerchief from his jacket pocket. As a bearer of terrible news, he'd come prepared. He fidgeted with the papers in his folder, careful not to look at me for a few minutes, giving me time to wipe my face, blow my nose, and try to get a grip.

Eventually, he closed the folder and met my gaze. "Like I said, a lot has happened. There were some arrests yesterday. A number of the folks in Tinkers Town were picked up by the FBI on racketeering charges and—"

"What? I would have heard. I would have—"

"You couldn't have known. It happened almost simultaneously with your arrest at the Dearborn home. Believe me, the feds are masters at gathering evidence and putting an airtight case together—no matter how long it takes. And they don't move forward with arrests until they've proved their case."

He paused a moment, rubbing at his temple, where his hair was going gray. The movement caused his heavy gold wedding band to wink at me in the fluorescent light. He'd probably get more work from the arrested Travellers than he knew what to do with. He could probably buy his wife some nice jewelry.

"Unfortunately, you people are royally screwed on this one. Nobody saw it coming."

"Are you representing some of my people?"

"Yes. And there's something else you should know. They picked up Tommy O'Carroll. He's your fiancé, right?"

No wonder he'd been missing. Maybe I didn't want to marry Tommy, but I sure didn't want him spending his life in prison. Did he have the missing sapphire? "Jesus. How much trouble is he in? Will he be in the same detention center as me?"

"A lot, and no. He and his father are tangled up in interstate fraud. That's a federal offense. He'll be going to court in Columbia and if he's sentenced, he'll go to federal prison."

"If he's sentenced? What if he pleads innocent and gets off?"

"I don't believe that will happen. Tommy is looking at substantial federal charges and he's already indicated he wants to plead guilty. Remember what I said about the FBI having an ironclad case?"

I nodded.

"Quinn, I've already seen the evidence in the case against him. I seriously doubt that Tommy O'Carroll's going anywhere. I wanted to tell you this now because I don't want you blindsided by jailhouse gossip. You have enough troubles."

He paused again, giving me a long look, as if waiting for it all to sink in.

"Right now, there is the matter of your trial. That's what's important, and you need to focus on it."

"Who cares about a stupid trial? I want to see my Uncle Paddy! You've got to get me another phone call. I have to speak to him!"

Sanders put a hand on my arm, his fingers gripping hard enough to get my attention. "I'm going to look out for you, Miss O'Neill. That's what your uncle is paying me to do. Try to stay calm, okay?"

I stared at him like he was a peculiar beast I'd never seen before. "Stay calm?"

"Now listen," he said. "I've arranged for a video phone call with your uncle this afternoon. Fortunately, they don't seem to have anything on him that will stick. He wasn't picked up."

He paused as if to make sure I was keeping up with what he was telling me. "The video call will be like Face Time or Skype. You've done that before, right?"

"Yes, but why can't I see him in here, like this?" I gestured to where he sat close to me.

"Visitors aren't allowed inside the detention center beyond the lobby, Miss O'Neill. But you can talk to him. Just don't say anything you don't want recorded."

He smiled then as if he'd made a little joke.

I stared at him, my situation sinking in like news of terminal cancer.

"Understand," he said, "that the law here is hard on Travellers. You were already denied bail because your people are considered a flight risk. I'm going to do what I can to speed up your trial date. We don't want you incarcerated for weeks, or even months waiting for your trial."

I was stunned. The legal system could keep me incarcerated for that long?

Finally, I realized how important the "stupid" trial was. I was in deep trouble and this legal stuff was way over my head. I had no idea what could happen to me. My mouth had gone dry again. I had to swallow before I could speak.

"Mr. Sanders, what kind of sentence could I be facing?"

"Grand Larceny can carry up to a ten-year prison sentence."

My stomach roiled with nausea. "Ten years?"

As if sensing my rising hysteria, he spoke fast. "That's why I'm here, Miss O'Neill, to come up with options agreeable to a judge so we can get you out of here."

"What do you mean, 'options?'"

"We'll discuss that later. In your favor, you have no previous record. Your father would likely have been detained on the same racketeering and fraud charges facing the others. But with his death, that won't happen. Your family's slate appears clean and that's good."

Clean? I could almost feel the weight of the bag filled with stolen jewelry and silver. If Da's picture and mine were in the newspapers, wouldn't the Buntings recognize us? And then there was Steve from the asphalt plant.

My arms wrapped around my middle, trying to stop the trembling. Dizziness joined the nausea.

"I realize you've had a lot thrown at you today, Miss O'Neill. Try to be strong. Talk to your uncle this afternoon. I believe I can put a good plan together for you."

My hands grasped the edge of the table and I leaned forward. I had so many questions.

Sanders stood quickly and turned away from me. "I'll be in touch, Miss O'Neill."

He rapped on the door. A guard opened it. Sanders went through, and a moment later, my only contact with the outside world was gone. The only evidence he'd been there was a lingering trace of mint aftershave.

16

The guard took me back to my cell, where the cinderblock walls began closing in.

Tania was stretched out on her bed, staring at the ceiling. Without looking at me she said, "So, what happened to you?"

"I . . . something bad happened. I can't talk about it."

"Uh huh, lot of that going around." She rolled away from me and faced the wall.

I sat on the edge of my bed and dropped my head in my hands. My head was a caldron, my thoughts a slow boil of misery. What had happened to Da? He was so healthy, so full of life. He was so—an ugly thought bubbled to the surface. Had someone murdered him? No, it couldn't be. Everyone loved Da.

But, he's dead.

I stared at the wall clock. It was after three. Sanders had said I'd get a video call from Uncle Paddy this afternoon. Damn, I should have asked what time. How would I know if he called? Would the guards take care of this?

So many unanswered questions, and no control over anything!

Footsteps approached, the door lock snapped open, and the female guard with the mean eyes motioned me to stand.

"You got a video call, O'Neill. Come with me."

I did, and followed her downstairs, back to the counter for cuffs and the ankle chain. She walked briskly, and I had to hobble like a crippled rabbit to keep up with her. We went out into the cinderblock hallway, and through a door leading to a set of stairs.

After we climbed up one level, she led me to a room with a small window that looked out into the hall. Probably placed there so the guards could keep an eye on offenders.

Inside, I found a metal box attached to the wall. A video screen took up the bottom half of the box, and an old-fashioned phone receiver hung on one side. A metal chair faced this contraption, so I sat. The guard said something into her radio, and a moment later the screen lit up, and Uncle Paddy was staring at me.

The guard closed the door, locked it, and moved out of sight down the hall. Grateful for the privacy, I looked back at Paddy. He had a phone receiver in his hand, so I grabbed mine.

"Quinn, darlin' are you all right, then?"

It was so wonderful to hear his voice. I felt the sting of tears. I tried to hold them back as I spoke.

"Is it true? Is Da really dead?"

He was unable to speak for a moment, then managed to nod his head.

"Please, Paddy, that lawyer Sanders told me nothing. What happened to Da?"

"A fucking garda shot him." I'd never heard such bitterness in my uncle's voice or seen such intense hatred in his eyes.

"What! Why?"

"Did Sanders tell you about the arrests yesterday?"

"Yeah, but all he said was they found Da behind the house. I don't understand. Why didn't Sanders tell me a cop shot Da? Paddy, what happened? Why would he kill Da?"

I stared at the screen, waiting for my uncle to make sense out of this insanity. Again, he seemed unable to speak, or maybe he was collecting his thoughts. He'd always had darker, more intense eyes than Da. Now, they were black.

"It was a young buck did it. Right out of the academy. He claims Rory went for a gun—"

"But Da doesn't carry a gun!"

"Jaysus, of course not. He knows better. He was pulling out his cell phone, probably to warn Tinkers Town about the arrests, the police, and the feds. That fucking cop shot him in the chest. Rory never had a chance."

I'd never heard Paddy's voice shake before. His jaw muscles were bunched so tight, I thought he might crack his teeth.

We stared at each other through the screen, neither of us able to find the next words. Finally, I said, "Where is he? What have they done with his . . . with him?"

"He's in the county morgue, Quinn. We can't get him back until after they've done their autopsy."

Autopsy. I shivered and moved beyond it. "I want to come to his funeral! Will they let me?"

Paddy's shrug suggested he felt as powerless as I did. "I don't know."

"Can you ask Sanders?"

"I will."

"Is Sanders any kind of a lawyer?" I asked. "Is he any good?"

Paddy leaned forward, apparently on firmer ground. "To be sure. He's a crafty one. Helped keep a bunch of us out of jail over the years. Knows how to work deals."

At his words, my brain speed ticked up. "He said something about finding options for me. What does that mean?"

Paddy thought a moment. "Maybe find a job working for that Mrs. Dearborn or something like that. Pay restitution for the sapphire."

"Restitution? You mean, like pay back a hundred grand? That's crazy. I could never pay back that kind of money."

"If it kept you out of jail . . .?" Paddy's voice trailed off.

I felt like I was suffocating. "I don't want to talk about this anymore!"

Paddy drew back, his hands palm out. "All right, lass. I understand. Your Aunt Mary sends her love. Told me to say if there's anything she can do for you, you just let us know. That goes for me, too."

His tone had changed. He was back pedaling, making ready to leave. And who could blame him?

"Paddy, I'm sorry. You got me that lawyer. You're talking to me, you're . . .." Damn it, I was crying again. I wiped my face with a hand. "I'd be lost without you and Aunt Mary."

"We know that, lass. Don't worry too much, we've got your back."

His words warmed me, but moments later our session ended, and I was in chains heading down the hall with the mean-eyed, indifferent guard.

17

That night my thoughts raced out of control while the minutes crawled forward as slowly as shackled prisoners. Sanders' words about being incarcerated for "weeks, or even months," played loud in my head.

The growing stench from the toilet, so near my bed, mingled with the acrid fumes of disinfectant. The mixture burned my eyes, clinging to my skin and hair like heavy smoke.

Locked up for months? I couldn't bear the thought. If I didn't get out of this place, I'd go insane.

Eventually, mental exhaustion pulled me into a light sleep. But at some point, Tania grew restless, moaning softly and crying out in the dark, startling me back to wakefulness.

Staring into the cell's blackness, I knew that as surely as I'd stolen the sapphire, the cop who'd murdered Da had robbed my heart.

When the lights came on at six, the electronic lock on our cell snapped open, giving us the freedom to traipse downstairs for breakfast. On my way to the cafeteria line, a guard waylaid me, telling me I needed to check in at the desk.

What now? I hurried to the counter. Carson, the guard who'd let me make my one phone call when I arrived a lifetime ago, watched me approach.

"You're O'Neill?"

"Yes, ma'am." I gave her a tentative smile. It was not returned.

"Your uncle deposited money for you. You can use the commissary now."

She handed me a sheet of paper. Reading the form confirmed what Washed-out had said about using the funds for personal items from the commissary. As I continued down the page, my breath sucked in. I could use the money for phone time credits and prepaid phone cards. I could call my friend, Kayla Reilly, or Anna O'Carroll and ask her about Tommy. I clung to this sudden knowledge like a lifeline.

Attached to the page was an account credit for four hundred dollars. When Carson saw me staring at it, she said, "That's the maximum amount allowed a month. You Travellers always got plenty in your accounts. Most folks in here are lucky to get fifty."

I didn't know what to say. Was I supposed to apologize for being a Traveller? I gave her impassive face.

"Thanks for the info," I said, and walked away.

I got breakfast from the cafeteria line and glanced around the room. I saw no point in sitting with Tania and settled one table over with Washed-out.

"What's your name?" I finally asked her.

"Pam. You're Quinn, right?" I didn't remember ever telling her my name, but I guess word gets around in jail.

She stared at the account notice I'd placed on the table next to my tray. I'd been careful to make sure the first page covered the deposit amount.

"You're a Traveller, aren't you." A stated fact, not a question.

When I nodded, she said, "I don't have nothing against you people, but some do. I'd watch my back if I were you."

Her words sent a spider of dread down my spine. "Anyone in particular?" I asked, my eyes scanning the room for hostile faces.

"Yeah, that little blonde over there with the curly hair."

She didn't point, but I knew she referred to a petite, thin-faced young woman, with wild, curly platinum hair. She was three tables away, too far to see her face clearly. She was sitting with a group of hard-looking white women.

I'd noticed the blacks in the room mostly kept to themselves, and in the two days I'd been there, I'd seen no animosity between races.

The scrawny blonde hardly looked threatening. "So, what's the deal with her?" I asked.

"Don't stare at her, Quinn!"

Maybe Pam, who I still thought of as Washed-out, simply liked to stir things up. Then again, it never hurt to be cautious. I set my face into what I hoped was a benign expression and looked away.

"She's awfully puny," I said. "What can she do to me?"

"Listen up. Betty Lou Branson is crazy. You just keep away from her."

"All right." I was starting to feel annoyed. "So, tell me where the commissary is."

"In the far corner over there. Behind that TV?" She referred to one of the ceiling hung monitors. "See that metal door beyond it, near the corner of the cinderblock wall?

"Yeah. Thanks."

Our conversation dried up, and after toast and a few bites of whatever the gruel was they served that morning, I swallowed my coffee and left to check out the store.

When I went inside, I found snack foods, writing paper, stamped envelopes, toiletries and undergarments. Ignoring these last things, I snatched up a package of cheese-and-peanut butter crackers. I wanted other stuff, too, but went to the checkout counter with the crackers first, where a woman behind a computer monitor debited them from my account.

Stepping outside the commissary, I ripped open the cellophane and bit into a cracker. A little moan escaped me. It tasted that good after the crap I'd been eating in this place.

After I devoured the entire package, I went back inside, grabbed a basket, and picked out some nylon underwear of dubious quality, a bottle of shampoo, deodorant, and some body lotion. Then I threw in more crackers, granola bars, and chocolate.

Amazing how the little things can lift your spirits. I think I even smiled as I returned to the main room. Then something smacked the back of my head, hard enough that my knees buckled. I fell. My package of goodies spilled from their plastic bag onto the concrete floor beside me.

I'd always known happiness was fleeting, but in jail, its lifespan must be zero.

"Oops, did I bump into you, sugar?"

Rolling to my hands and knees, I opened my eyes, but closed them as pain stabbed the back of my head where I'd been hit. Stay still, Quinn.

Struggling against the pain, I forced my eyes open and looked up. Betty Lou Branson stood over me, her face lit with a kind of angry glee, one small hand grasping a small piece of metal pipe.

I didn't know if the two guards behind the front counter had seen her hit me or not, but they were ignoring us now. Some of the inmates stared, but no one made a move toward us, and nobody said a word.

One of the tough looking white women walked past, and I saw Betty Lou slip the piece of pipe into her hand. The other woman walked into the canteen with it, where no doubt she'd make it disappear.

A vicious smile formed on Betty Lou's mouth. "I hear all your folks in Tinky Town are in a shit load of trouble. Couldn't happen to a nicer bunch of assholes. Aw, bless your heart, kneeling there on the floor, and me going on like this."

She stepped closer to me. "Are you hurt, sugar? Let Betty Lou help you up." She leaned over as if to offer me a hand, but kicked me in the ribs instead, and when I fell over, she slammed me again. This time, in the side of my head.

I'd never been in a fight, and the power driving her small leg shocked me. She'd hurt me. I was dizzy, my vision blurred, and I seemed to have forgotten how to stand up.

"Why are you doing this?" My words, barely more than a whisper were directed to the floor.

"You're a fucking Traveller, right?"

"And you're a fucking piece of shit!" another voice said.

Betty Lou suddenly fell on the floor next to me. My vision cleared enough to see into her eyes. They were crazy and radiated anger. Insanity must be the fuel driving this slight woman, giving her so much strength. But who had knocked her down?

"Don't fuck with Travellers you piece of shit!"

With a shock, I recognized the voice and made the mistake of jerking my head up to look.

"Lara? Jesus, where did you come from? I didn't know you were here."

"Be glad I got here in time to save your butt." She leaned over and scooped up my supplies and slid them into the plastic bag.

I'd never thought I'd be so glad to see Lara O'Carroll, but God help me, I was. Her appearance wasn't that surprising. She'd been inside before.

Betty Lou's face flushed red and with a snarl, she sprang from the floor and swung at Lara.

Lara ducked the punch and shoved Betty Lou hard. Her larger physique and bone structure caused the smaller woman to stagger, but as she went down, Betty Lou clung to Lara. They hit the floor together in a tangle of arms and legs, screaming curses and yowling like cats. Though small, Betty Lou was quick and nimble, and landed a few good punches until Lara pinned her to the floor.

An electronic alarm sounded. Pounding, steel-toed boots announced the arrival of the counter guards. The electronic door behind them burst open as more ran into the room.

In seconds, they were all over the three of us. I was jerked to my feet by Carson, and handcuffed. Betty Lou cursed and spit as they dragged her away. Lara didn't fight the women that grabbed her, just shrugged, and let them cuff and steer her away toward the stairs that led to our cells.

"Can you get Quinn's bag of stuff," Lara asked Carson.

She did, and glancing at me as she pushed me along after Lara, she said, "Your head's bleeding. Who did that to you?"

"Nobody!" Lara spoke fast. "She fell, didn't you, Quinn?"

Knowing Lara had been here before, I followed her lead.

"That's right, I tripped and fell."

"Sure, you did," said Carson. "And the other two were rolling around on the floor like wildcats because you fell down?"

"It was a misunderstanding, that's all," Lara said.

Not far away, the band of hard-faced women that had sat with Betty Lou were watching us. When Lara said it was a misunderstanding, one of toughest looking smiled. She gave Lara a look that I could only interpret as, "Yeah, bitch, you better say that."

I had a lot to learn about survival in prison, except I didn't want to know any of it. That my survival depended on understanding this foreign land was just another step in this ongoing nightmare.

18

Carson took me to the prison infirmary, where a heavy-set, cocoa-skinned nurse examined the back of my head. She had a nice face and kind hands that were comforting.

"You got quite a lump," she said. "Whoever did it didn't break the skin back there. But they did a job on the side of your face."

Gently, she sponged the blood from my jaw just below ear level. She dabbed it with antiseptic and applied a bandage. Next, she checked my ribs where Betty Lou had landed a vicious blow. When she asked me to take some deep breaths, I did, with only a slight wince.

Carson, who was leaning against the wall, said, "Doesn't look like she broke anything. I'd be more worried about the blow to her head."

"Who hit her, anyway?" the nurse asked Carson.

"Betty Lou Branson."

"Huh." Looking at me, the nurse said, "You're lucky you didn't get hurt worse."

"Lara O'Carroll intervened," Carson said."

The nurse stiffened slightly. "You a Traveller?"

I sighed. "Yes."

"All right, then," the nurse said to Carson. "You can take her back now."

"Don't I need an X-ray or something for my head or ribs?"

"Nope. You don't need anything." She turned her back on me and walked into an adjoining room.

And they wondered why Travellers stuck together so tight.

Carson fastened me back into handcuffs and led me from the infirmary. When she released me in the common room, I avoided looking at anyone. Instead, I climbed the metal staircase, went to my cell, and lay on my bed. Tania wasn't there, which was fine with me.

I thought about booking a call to Anna O'Carroll to ask about Tommy, or calling Paddy, but I was so tired that after I dropped my commissary bag on the bed, I lay down, my head pounding. Why hadn't I asked the nurse for a painkiller? My eyes slid shut.

"Hey, Quinn, don't you know you're not supposed to sleep after a head injury? Wake up." Lara's voice.

When the bed bounced as Lara took a seat, I cracked one eye open. Earlier I hadn't noticed she wore no makeup. Not the kind of thing you keep track of when you've just been beaten up. I realized I'd never seen her without it.

When I raised myself into a sitting position, she said, "That's better," before wrinkling her nose. "It stinks in here. Is your roommate sick or something?"

"Meth addict."

"Oh." Lara stood, and moved closer to the open door.

Without makeup, I noticed that her face was narrow, her nose quite prominent. She usually wore so much gunk, I'd never been sure what she looked like.

I thought of the day Aunt Mary and I had passed her on our street in Tinkers Town. Lara had thrown us such a sullen look of disdain, that Mary had stopped walking and turned to glare at her receding figure.

Under her breath, she'd said, "That black-rooted 'oor is a bitch. And she's neither as gran' nor as smart as you. She's green-eyed jealous is what she is."

How I wished I could hear Mary's melodious, Irish accent now. She'd been born in Ireland and still used a bit of the dialect. Mary could also speak the Travellers' language known as 'Cant,' a mixture of English and Gaelic.

I'd heard our townsfolk and Da use the Cant language when talking in front of the people they were scamming, or for warning about police and law enforcement. It was just another way to keep outsiders at bay. I'd never learned to speak this language, and I knew that some busybodies said it was my mother's blood causing this refusal.

But remembering how I'd snickered at Mary's nasty comments about Lara, I felt bad. You never know a person until the chips are down.

"Why are you staring at me like that?" Lara asked.

"I was just thinking how cool it was that you punched Betty Lou earlier. Thanks."

She waved it away. "Had to. You're one of us." She studied me a moment. "You know, you're more like me than I realized. I thought you were Miss Better-Than-Everybody, like I always heard your mother was. But you got some balls, girl. Liked the way you treated that arse at Salvatore's. And I heard about the jewelry you scored in Georgia, and that big sapphire."

Her last words brought back the mystery that plagued me. "Did you know the sapphire disappeared? Have you heard anything about what happened to it?"

"Disappeared?"

"Yeah, like one minute it was on the ground where I'd tossed it outside a window, and the next I was being attacked by this dog. Someone must have been hiding in an azalea hedge next to where it lay. By the time the cops arrived, and I was out from under the dog, it had vanished."

"You know," Lara said suddenly, "they say Tommy was arrested before you took the sapphire."

"Are you sure."

"Yeah. You know Desmond O'Carroll's brother Shane?"

When I nodded, she said, "You never heard this from me, but he's got an inside with one of the sheriff's deputies and he saw the arrest report. Tommy was one of the first picked up. So, it was before you snatched the stone.

"But if he didn't take it, who did. I'm telling you, it just evaporated!"

"And you looked, right?" Lara asked.

"I couldn't. I was too busy being arrested. But it wasn't loose. It was in a box. I would have seen the box."

"Weird."

"Tell me about it," I said.

Lara thought a moment. "You're right. Someone else must have been hiding in the hedge. Or maybe the woman that had you arrested took it back. She could put in for insurance and still have the sapphire. It's not like she gives a shite about you."

The insurance scam that Lara described was a typical Traveller ploy. But I doubted that insurance fraud was among Mrs. Dearborn's talents, or her New York friend Hutchins, either.

"I don't think so," I said.

"It's got to be somewhere."

"I know." I was quiet a moment before speaking. "Lara, do you know the lawyer Sanders?"

"Everybody knows Sandy. He's our guy. If anyone can keep you out of jail, it's him."

I was glad to hear this, but my knowledge of criminal activities was limited to shoplifting and our fix-it-up scams on the homes of the unwary. What crimes had Tommy and his da, Desmond, committed?

Carefully, I rose from the bed. "I got to get out of this room."

"No problem," Lara said. "Let's go downstairs."

We did and found an empty table where we could sit and talk with as much privacy as the place allowed. Lara went to the canteen and brought back two Cokes and some aspirin. After a few cold sips, the caffeine and aspirin seemed to ease my headache a little.

"Lara," I said, "when I talked to Sanders, he mentioned something about racketeering charges. Tell me about Tommy and

Desmond? Sanders said they would have to plead guilty. But for what?"

"The O'Carrolls always said your da was one of the best at raking in cash from the country folk for driveway, roofing jobs, and stuff like that. But he never wanted in on some of our family's best scams. Said it was too risky."

And apparently, he was right.

But Lara's chin was high, and her mouth carried a proud, knowing smirk as she continued talking about the O'Carroll "enterprises."

"Sure, and your da knew how to avoid paying taxes on his income, but do you have any idea how much we make selling food stamps on the black market? My family knows how to falsify documents to get the stamps, life insurance benefits, and Medicaid money, too."

Sanders was right. Those were federal crimes. No wonder the FBI was involved. The O'Carroll family had to be in a lot of trouble. To me it sounded horrible, but Lara had a gleam in her eye as, in a low voice, she described their scams.

"While you O'Neills are out there breathing tar fumes and nailing shingles on roofs, we're raking it in with the clean white paper of insurance claims. You know, a slip-and-fall here, or a car wreck there. The store or business where we "fall," or the guy that rear-ends us—they don't want an insurance claim on their record. They want to settle with cash. Besides, we never ask for too much, just enough to cover 'medical costs.' And let me tell you, it adds up."

By now, I'd emptied my can of Coke. I didn't want to hear any more about the O'Carroll exploits. But she launched into an explanation about how they fixed their income tax returns.

"We use them as proof of income to finance new cars and we–"

"That's great," I said, "but what kind of charges is Tommy facing?"

The proud gleam in Lara's eye dimmed. "Well, that's the bad news."

"How bad?"

"Um, most of that stuff carries a maximum sentence of twenty years and a two-hundred-and-fifty thousand dollar fine."

"Twenty years all told or for each individual crime?"

Lara's stared down at her hands where they lay on the table. "Each."

"My God. He'll never get out!"

Before this had time to sink in, Lara threw me a warning glance. Turning, I saw the mean-eyed guard walking purposefully toward me.

"O'Neil," she said, "you'd better come with me. You've got a visitor."

19

THE GUARD TOOK ME BACK to the same interview room. I wasn't surprised to see Sanders sitting at the metal table. With family members prohibited from visiting, who else could it have been?

Shuffling past him, I caught the same whiff of mint. After the guard had fastened my leg iron to the floor, I sat and gazed at Sanders. He was fidgeting with papers on the table and didn't look up. The dark circles beneath his eyes hadn't lessened.

Something was eating at him and I hoped it wasn't my case. He must have felt the intensity of my stare because he raised his eyes to meet mine.

"Miss O'Neill. How are you holding up?"

I shrugged, afraid that if I spoke, I'd scream, "What do you think, dimwit?"

His stare sharpened. "What happened to the side of your head?"

"People in here don't seem to like Travellers."

"I'm sorry. Did they remove the woman who did this? They should have taken her out of the general population. Did they?"

"I—I guess they did," I said, realizing I hadn't seen Betty Lou Branson since they dragged her away, spitting and cursing. "Look, Mr. Sanders, I don't care about her. I just want to get out of here!"

He leaned forward on his elbows. "Okay. Here's what's happening. I got you on the docket. Your court date is in two days."

At the word court, a thread of fear tangled inside me.

Noticing me flinch, he straightened and ran a hand across the papers before him as if to smooth them out. He took that same slow breath again, like he was trying to calm himself.

"Quinn, you have to plead guilty."

It was the first time he'd called me Quinn, but it didn't soften his words.

"Guilty? I don't have the stupid sapphire."

"But you attempted to steal it, and the stone is missing. Am I correct?"

"Yes, but I don't have it."

"But you know who does?"

"I don't."

He sighed. Are you protecting someone, Miss O'Neill?"

"No!"

Of course, he thought I knew. He probably realized that even if Tommy had taken the sapphire as planned, I wouldn't have given him up. Except the timeline didn't work and he knew that. If Lara's information was right, Tommy was arrested before the sapphire had vanished.

Sanders made an impatient sound. "That is a hard scenario for a judge or jury to believe. Try to grasp what I'm saying. If you plead not guilty, you will go to trial and will likely be sentenced to hard time in prison. You need to understand how hard I've worked for you, Quinn. Under normal circumstances even if you do plead guilty, your trial would be scheduled for weeks, if not months in the future."

I could feel my eyes widening at the prospect of that much jail time.

He, gave me a look of something like triumph. "There's a way to avoid that. The prosecutor has a huge caseload and the deal I've proposed will expedite and resolve one of her cases. If you agree to plead guilty, the judge has agreed to proceed straight to sentencing without delay. Additionally, since you have no previous charges, the judge will allow you probation depending on restitution."

That word again. "Restitution?" My anxiety brought anger. "How can I pay back a hundred thousand bucks? I don't have any savings. I don't even have a job!"

I didn't realize I'd been trying to stand until my leg chain jerked me back. Frowning, Sanders raised a hand, palm out.

"Just hear me out, okay?"

I slumped into my chair. "Sure."

"There's a man named Presto DuPriest. Owns a nice farm in Aiken. He's a good guy, has hired convicts before. I spoke to him about your situation, and he agreed to take you on. If the judge goes for it, you could get out in two days."

This was happening too fast. "What would I do on a farm?"

"Work, Quinn. Start paying restitution."

I looked away. I'd be on the damn farm for the rest of my life. But I'd be out of this place. Maybe I could figure out who'd taken the stone, get it back somehow.

Sanders broke into my thoughts by rising from his chair. "So that's our plan, okay?"

I nodded. Why bother answering? I had no say in the matter anyway. Like before, he exited the room abruptly, leaving questions buzzing in my head like a swarm of angry bees.

Two days and five suspicious meals later, two sheriff's deputies loaded me into a white county prisoner's van with four other women who, like me, were due to appear in court that day.

The deputies sitting in the front of the panel van had windows and daylight, while the rest of us were left in the dark. An excellent metaphor for my new life.

We bumped and rolled blindly along for about twenty minutes before the van slowed. Outside I heard more traffic sounds and figured we'd reached downtown Aiken. Minutes later, the van stopped. With a snap of a lock, the rear doors cracked open. The deputies swung them wide and ushered us out. It was awkward clambering out since we were chained together. We managed and were soon shuffling toward a set of doors in the rear of a building.

My gaze followed the decorative white stone walls upward to a fancy cupola with a clock perched atop the roof. The Aiken County courthouse. The time was eight a.m., and I imagined we'd have to cool our heels somewhere until the business of the day began.

A couple of men in coats and ties, and a woman in a navy-blue dress gawked at our chains and orange jumpsuits. It was the first time I'd been displayed in public, and the humiliation brought heat to my cheeks. I wanted to crawl in a hole and never come out.

To fend off my feeling of shame, I imagined Maeve being forced to handle this kind of embarrassment. It brought a smile to my lips. Mean-spirited maybe, but I didn't care about being a saint. At least not where she was concerned.

We pushed through a side door into a hall and entered a room with several small tables and chairs. It reminded me of my meeting with Sanders—a place where prisoners probably pow-wowed with their lawyers. Ahead, was a closed wood door with a sign that read "Courtroom." The same thread of fear tangled into knots in my stomach.

Moments later I was stuffed inside a small holding cell with two other women. Cage-wire filled the door's tinted window, and a metal bench lined the wall. We sat.

Time dragged. We took turns staring through the window. Every so often, a guard, a lawyer, or another prisoner passed by before disappearing through the courtroom door.

I was led from the holding cell to speak with Sanders, who prepped me on what to say. I was so nervous, by the time the guard put me back in with the other women, I'd couldn't remember anything he'd said.

Finally, a tall black deputy came to usher me into the courtroom. My knees started shaking, and I stumbled so badly, he all but dragged me to the closed door.

"Get a grip, lady. The judge doesn't like to be kept waiting."

He could have threatened me with a cattle prod, and I still would have balked at going through that door. But with chains binding me and the big man leading me, refusal was impossible.

20

Once inside the courtroom, I was so apprehensive, I shrank away from the spectators seated to my left. My pulse jackhammered in my ears when the deputy steadied me and pushed me toward the bench. A stern looking judge wearing a black robe stared at me.

Trying to stay calm, I looked away from him, taking in my surroundings. But after the suffocating ride to the courthouse and the tiny holding cell, the high vaulted ceiling and bright windows brought a wave of dizziness.

The deputy steered me closer to the judge and positioned me before the bench. I stood with my legs shackled and hands cuffed behind my back. I felt rather than saw the deputy move to stand behind me. Sanders appeared next to me and placed a reassuring hand over my wrist.

Leaning close to speak, he sent an acidic odor of coffee to my nostrils. He gripped my wrist more firmly. "Stop holding your breath, Quinn."

I did, and the room righted itself. A blonde stepped forward to the left of the judge and faced him. She began a long, detailed monolog about my crime. I remembered Sanders saying she'd be the prosecutor. Listening to her, I felt disconnected. Surely, she was talking about someone else?

She progressed through every detail, from when Dearborn had found me on her doorstep, to when she'd set the dog on me and called the police.

By the time the prosecutor's tone signaled she was reaching her conclusion, I felt woozy and realized I was holding my breath again. I was so jittery, I hadn't even heard her recommended punishment. Not that it made any difference. My fate was out of my hands.

Sanders gave me an almost imperceptible nod and whispered, "Here we go."

The judge turned to me. "Miss O'Neill, how do you plead?"

"Guilty, your honor." My voice sounded strangled.

"Speak up, Miss O'Neill, I couldn't hear you."

"Guilty!"

"Miss O'Neill, you realize that by pleading guilty you waive your right to a trial by jury?"

"Yes, sir."

"Are you pleading guilty of your own free will?"

"Yes, sir."

"Were you promised compensation, or any kind of an award for pleading guilty?"

"No, sir." What fool would admit to that, anyway?

"Did your attorney explain everything to you?"

"Yes sir." Can we just get this over with?

He wasn't finished. "Did your attorney answer all your questions?"

"Yes, sir."

"Are you satisfied with your attorney?"

Oh, for God's sake, what difference does it make? "Yes, sir."

My knees were still trembling, and I was glad the deputy stood close behind me, since I was sure I'd sink to the floor at any second. The room started to spin. Once more, I forced myself to breathe.

Sanders was speaking to the judge. "Your Honor, the victim, Mrs. Meredith Hutchins, has provided me with her sworn statement. She is not looking for Miss O'Neill to serve time. She would ask only that Miss O'Neill be required to pay restitution."

Had Sanders told me this outside my holding cell? How had I missed this piece of good news?

The judge's frown forced his eyebrows closer together. "Is Mrs. Hutchins in court today?"

"No, sir. She has returned to New York State, where she is a resident. This is her sworn statement." He handed a paper to the judge, who put on reading glasses and studied the document.

The judge glanced at the prosecutor. "Mrs. Hutchins has pointed out that restitution will be difficult to accomplish if Miss O'Neill is sentenced to prison." He set the paper down and looked at me again.

"I am considering placing you on probation. Will you agree to make restitution to the victim, Meredith Hutchins."

"Yes, sir," I said, nodding. "I will." How would that ever happen?

He turned to the blond prosecutor. "Is the State amenable to this resolution?"

"Yes, your Honor."

It was like a stage performance where the other players had written the lines. They'd set the scenes ahead of time, they'd only been acting, and now the predetermined plot was reaching its conclusion.

Seconds later, I was granted probation, given three years to pay my debt, and led back to the small holding cell.

21

The detention center released me the next morning, giving me back my phone and a bag with the dirty things I'd worn the day I was arrested. Aunt Mary had left street clothes for me the night before, giving me something to wear other than the muddy riding britches, and boots needled with the imprints of Runford's big teeth.

I was grateful to Mary because I'd dreaded putting on the clothes I'd worn the day my da had died, the day my life changed forever.

Beyond the chain-link fence surrounding the jail, a black Cadillac Escalade with dark tinted windows idled in the parking lot.

I paused before walking through the detention center gate and sucked in a deep breath of fresh air. The scent and taste were wonderful. Small white clouds dotted the blue sky overhead, and I felt like busting into a wild sprint fueled by pure joy.

Reality brought me down from the clouds, as I stared at the Cadillac. The window tint was too dark to see inside, but when I passed through the razor-wired chain-fence, the passenger window slid down, revealing Sandy Sanders behind the wheel.

He'd told me he would be there to take me to the farm, but I hadn't expected him to show up in a thug mobile. Still, I didn't really know the man. In fact, I didn't know anything anymore. I should probably forget any assumptions I had about him or my future.

Breathing in the fragrance of leather and mint, I climbed into the passenger seat. It was a huge improvement over the fear and sour vomit smell in the police cruiser that brought me in. Maybe things would get better for me.

"I think you'll like this place, Quinn," Sanders said as he steered the Escalade from the parking lot and made a right onto Wire Road. "You girls usually like horses and there's a bunch of them on this farm. I think they call them Gypsy Vanners."

Where had I heard that name before? The memory eluded me. "I don't know anything about horses," I said. "But I do think they're pretty cool."

"Good. Because you'll be working with them. The idea is to give you new skills, something you can use on a job application, right?"

"Sure."

Turning away from Sanders, and staring through the tinted window, I reveled in the sunlight and space that surrounded us. Sanders took a left off Wire, then minutes later made a right onto Park Avenue, like we were going back to the courthouse.

"Where is this farm?" I asked, confused. "It looks like we're heading downtown."

"You don't know much about Aiken, do you?"

"Just to go shopping on Laurens Street, and where I went to –"

"Swipe the sapphire?"

"Yeah, that."

"Aiken's kind of an amazing town, Quinn. It's got three race tracks, horse farms, several polo fields, and the twenty-one-hundred-acre Hitchcock Woods, all within the city limits."

"I've never seen that stuff. Just the woods." I almost didn't believe him.

"That's because much of it is hidden in the historic district."

Whatever.

But when he turned off Park onto a side street, things changed fast. Quaint wooden bungalows that looked like they'd been there forever were parked right next to homes as grand as Mrs. Dearborn's house. Crossing another paved road, the street we'd been traveling turned into gravel and dirt.

Curious, I glanced at Sanders. "This is a wealthy neighborhood. Why would these people settle for a dirt road?"

"So they can ride their horses and drive their carriages."

"Seriously?" When he nodded, I said, "But we are in the middle of the city. They allow it?"

"It's Aiken," he said, as if that explained everything.

I stopped talking, staring at what I could see of the homes around us. Huge live oaks spread graceful branches above ancient trunks. Evergreen hedges and bushes formed visually impenetrable fences. Only through leaves, or a gate set in a stone or brick wall was I allowed an occasional glimpse of a hidden, stately home. I'd never seen anything like it.

We turned onto a different dirt lane that dead ended about a hundred yards in. A handsome brick wall, with black and gold iron railing crowning the top, blocked the view ahead. The road jogged to the right and approached an ornate gate set in the wall. A large plaque read, "Ballymoor."

Looking through the gate, I couldn't curb my reaction. "Holy shit!"

"I thought you'd like it." Sanders had an odd smile on his face—smug, yet sly, it left me uneasy. But staring through the gate again, I forgot about Sanders.

We rolled through onto white, finely crushed stone that was as smooth as sand. It stretched ahead and formed a circular drive before the grandest home I'd ever seen. More like a hotel. Two stories, brick, slate roof, tall soaring windows, a wing at each end, and four chimneys.

Two ancient live oaks, their limbs massive and heavy, stood like sentinels before the wings. That Ballymoor's owners had preserved instead of destroying these beautiful trees when building their home spoke volumes.

Set apart, on either side of the oval drive, were two handsome brick buildings. I had no idea what they were. They didn't exactly look like houses. One had an entrance door that looked like it belonged to a giant.

"What is this place?"

"Ballymoor, like the sign says." He pointed to the grand brick home. "That's the house. That," he said pointing to the building with the ridiculously tall door, "is the carriage house." He gestured to the building immediately to our right and kept going until we could look back at it. "And that's the horse stable."

Stall doors covered most of the front of the building. The top half of each door was open, and dozens of horse heads stared back at me.

"Holy moly," I said, remembering the horse trailer from that morning in Georgia. The beautiful black and white horse with the long bangs and endless mane and tail. "Gypsy Vanners."

"Yep, that's them."

Was it possible the people I'd seen with that horse were from this farm? I remembered the two men, especially the handsome guy with the intense green eyes. As if summoned by my memory, he emerged from the center door of the barn and stared at the Escalade. Shadowed beneath the same tweed cap, his expression was unreadable.

Sanders fed the Cadillac some gas and followed the oval drive around to the front of the house. Letting his engine idle, he grabbed his phone and tapped in a number.

"Presto, we're here. Are you coming out, or should I just take her—" Indistinct words came through Sanders' phone.

"All right," Sanders said, and disconnected.

From the Cadillac's window, I gazed at the home's entrance. Carved stone steps led to a handsome brick portico with a heavy slate roof. Beneath it, the home's massive wooden door and brass knocker were flanked by tall, narrow side-windows.

The door opened and the man I'd seen at the RV camp, the one with the pompadour and sideburns, stepped onto the stone floor of the portico. He really did look like Elvis Presley.

"Okay, Quinn," Sanders said, "let's get out and meet your new boss."

We did, and the smell of recently mown lawn and the perfume of blooming flowers drifted to me. The Elvis wannabe walked down four stone steps to the driveway.

He must be the barn manager. He couldn't be the owner, could he? His style didn't fit with the careful attention to detail paid to the home. He chewed gum enthusiastically, and he wore a jean jacket with the collar turned up so that his long black hair and sideburns touched the edges of the collar. He looked to be late thirties, maybe early forties.

"Well, Missy, welcome to my kingdom."

Seriously?

"Hi," I said. "You must be Mr. DuPriest."

"Call me Presto," he said with a grin and a wink. "We don't stand on ceremony 'round here."

"Yes, sir."

One time when I'd been at Mary's house, we'd watched an old TV interview with Elvis Presley. He'd grinned and winked at the interviewer. It had worked better for him than it did for Presto, who had just turned to his reflection in the window of Sanders' Cadillac and was finger combing his pompadour.

When he finished primping, he turned back to us. Sliding his phone out, he said, "Let me get Jase up here, and he can show you where you're going to stay."

Jase? Was he the stunning blonde with the green eyes? It made me feel nervous, but in a good way.

I studied Presto as he used the phone. Tall, with dark, Elvis eyes, he would have been good looking if it wasn't for a high bulbous forehead, sadly accentuated by the pompadour. His lips were full and had a well-defined cupid's bow. I'd swear he'd done like Maeve and had his lips injected with filler.

"Hey, Jase," he said. "Miss Quinn's here. Be nice if you'd come up and show her around." He frowned. "What do you think? Show her the barn, her room. She's here to work. Thought you'd appreciate more help."

He shook his head, then winked at Sanders. "That's right, Jase. Hurry up."

Jase didn't seem very excited about my arrival. The previously pleasant tingle of nerves had changed to apprehension.

Presto sent me a big smile. "Jase had a little run-in with the law his self. But he's a good boy, and I'd like to say I have a feeling you're a real nice young lady. I like helping people out, Quinn. I do, and I hope you'll be happy here."

"I know she'll be," Sanders said. "How could she not?" He spread his arms to indicate the beautiful grounds and buildings. His phone buzzed, and he turned away from us to take the call.

In the distance, the blond guy came out of the barn and walked toward us on the sandy drive.

"Something's come up," Sanders said. "Got to hit the road. Quinn, I think you'll be fine here. You need anything, you call me, right?"

"Yes, sir. And, and thank you for everything. He'd left his engine idling the entire time, like he'd planned to leave in a hurry."

Sanders waved off my thanks, got in his car, and drove away, leaving me with two men I knew nothing about. Was there a Mrs. Du-Priest? Children? Other workers?

On the surface, everything looked beautiful. But so had the plan to steal the sapphire.

22

As Jase approached, Presto and I were silent. I tried not to stare as the man got closer. He looked to be in his early twenties. His face was thin, almost ascetic, as if he denied himself. Presto, by comparison, had a fleshy face that suggested enjoyment of life's pleasures.

When Jase finally reached us, he put out a hand with long tapered fingers and dirty, broken nails. When I grasped his hand, he said, "I'm Jase Jones."

"Quinn O'Neill," I said, liking that his hand was warm, dry, and his grip firm. His wavy, long blond hair softened his thin face. Lifting my gaze to his intense, green eyes, I drew back, breaking the connection.

"Let me see now," Presto said, looking at Jase. "Show her the barn and the horses first. Then take her up to her room. Tell her what she needs to know, and," he said, swiveling his gaze to me, "if you have any questions, Miss Quinn, you be sure to ask Jase, all right?"

I nodded. Tension seemed to vibrate between these two men, but then I was nervous and probably imagining it. But something about the down-home way Presto spoke rang false. His Elvis Presley act and perfectly manicured nails rubbed me the wrong way.

"All right, then," he said. He turned, walked up the stone steps, and disappeared through the front door of his opulent home.

"Come on." Jase pivoted away from me and headed for the barn.

I had to trot to catch up with him. He was taller than my five feet seven inches, probably just under six feet. His long legs appeared muscular and fit beneath tight blue jeans.

We were heading for the end of the barn that faced the drive where I'd first come in with Sanders. A large, arched-brick opening provided room for both people and horses to enter the building.

Like Presto's home, the brickwork was a soft rose color. The Ballymoor buildings were new but had been built to look old, and I loved the effect.

We walked through the arch and after my eyes adjusted from the bright sun outside, I realized the interior was filled with shafts of light from the open top doors and windows in each stall. The illumination spilled through the attractive grill work of stalls that lined the aisleway before me.

The ceilings were high, and the barn was airy. The floor in the center aisle was laid with rubber pavers. The stalls were solid paneled wood to about four feet high, with hunter green railing above. Each set of railings rose about eight feet and were crowned with polished brass finials. On the opposite side of the wide center aisle, a wall of paneled wood was broken by several human-sized doors.

The door closest to me was open, and inside I could see counters, cabinets, and all the kitchen appliances you could want.

Jase had not spoken since his abrupt, "Come on." But now he turned to me with an exasperated sigh, and a look that said he expected me to be a total pain.

This annoyed me. "I'm sorry to be such trouble for you, Jase."

His eyes widened slightly. "It's that obvious, yeah?"

I liked his British accent almost as much as I liked the sudden hint of humor in his eyes, but he didn't need to know either of these things.

"Yes," I said. "It is."

"I met you before, didn't I? At that RV camp."

I nodded, surprised he remembered.

"As I recall, you went right into the trailer with our stallion, didn't you?"

Spreading my palms, I said, "Guilty."

If a smile was trying to tease the corners of his mouth, he killed it. "Come and meet Gypsy Moor properly, then." He gestured at the closest stall.

The black and white stallion with the long white bangs stared out at me. He had a sweet face, but hadn't I heard stallions were vicious?

"Can I touch him?" I asked.

"I thought you already did."

The gravitational pull of this horse amazed me, and I went right to him. As before, he pressed his nose into my outstretched palm.

"You've been around horses before, yeah?"

"No. Never."

"But you offered him the flat of your palm instead of fingers to bite."

"Dumb luck."

He shrugged.

Standing next to the horse, I took in the gloss of his coat, and inhaled his horsey scent and the grassy smell of hay in his wall rack.

"How come it smells like oatmeal cookies in here?" I asked.

"That's from his morning feed. Oats and molasses."

"It smells nice," I said, stepping away from the horse and spreading my arms to indicate the entire barn. "Even the poop doesn't smell bad."

"Manure, not poop."

"Whatever." Up the center aisle, at least a dozen horse heads stretched out, their eyes inquisitive, nostrils dilating as if to take in my scent. "Why do you keep their bangs so long?"

Jase rolled his eyes. "Forelocks, not bangs."

"Why do they call them forelocks? Isn't it hard to clean that long hair? And they've got those things on their feet. What do you call those things? How do you clean them?"

Jase raised his arms, palms out. "Stop! Just stop with the questions."

His outburst made me feel about a foot tall, and it probably showed on my face. For some reason, with these horses and this man, my impassive face had deserted me.

"Look, Quinn, I admire your enthusiasm, but you don't know anything. If you think to learn it on day one, you're nuts."

He paused and took a breath. In a softer voice, he said, "The 'things' on their feet are called feathers. You'll soon learn how hard it is to keep them clean. It'll be one of your jobs, yeah?"

I nodded instead of speaking. If he thought I'd hate washing the horses, he was wrong. It sounded delightful. But where had this reaction come from? It wasn't like me.

"This," Jase said, moving to the next stall, "is Irish Mist."

The horse had a dark gray coat speckled with dabs of white and a long white blaze. Looking down, I saw her feathers were white, too.

"She's beautiful," I said.

"He is a gelding." Jase gave another eye roll, then steered me down the aisle to meet the rest of the gang. As we reached Bally Girl, a black mare with white feathers, mane, and forelock, something darkened the barn entrance.

Turning, I saw a wide, female figure. At first, I thought it might be Presto's wife, but as she came closer, I realized she had to be at least fifty. She had a pear-shaped figure with a lot of extra fruit at the bottom. A few of the Tinkers Town women were like that, and I knew if she dieted enough to trim off the extra fruit, she'd end up with a gaunt face, and starved looking shoulders and collarbones.

She also had a full moon face that, due to a large nose and small mouth, wasn't very attractive. Yet she wore an expensive looking knit pantsuit, with a snazzy pair of cowgirl boots, so she wasn't stable help. Yet she couldn't be Presto's wife, so who was she?

23

Jase didn't notice the newcomer at first. When he did, he immediately broke into a grin.

"Hiya. Sylvie, meet the new stable help."

"Didn't know we were hiring," the woman said. Stopping before me, she stuck out her hand. "Sylvie DuPriest."

Was she Presto's mother? Not about to risk sticking my foot in it, I smiled, told her my name, and kept quiet.

Appearing confused, she turned to Jase. "Did we need to hire more help? What with you, Timmy and Carl, I thought we had enough."

Whatever the relation between the two DuPriests, communication wasn't its strong point. Her question left me feeling awkward.

"Quinn's like me and the guys," Jase said, "She had a run in with the law. She's on probation."

Sylvie's puzzled expression splintered, immediately replaced by a warm smile. "That's all right then. I'm glad you're here, Quinn. Presto and I like helping people."

She closed her plump fingers over my hand. "You need anything, you come to me, and I'll fix it. Your life must be hard enough without being thrown into a strange place where you don't know anybody."

Her smile revealed short teeth and a lot of gum. But she had kind, blue eyes that revealed an inner beauty. I liked that her words were straightforward and rang true. Unlike Presto, there were no affectations here.

If by chance she was Presto's wife, I thought she'd gotten the short end of the stick.

"Have you shown her the carriages yet?"

"She just got here. I—"

The barn entrance darkened once more. The new figure was silhouetted by the sunlight behind it.

"Quinn?"

I'd know that voice anywhere. I raced down the aisle and threw myself into Uncle Paddy's open arms. Burying my face against his chest, I burst into tears.

"Ah, darlin'. We all miss him."

But it was the sight of his familiar face that had brought my tears. "I've missed you and Aunt Mary so much."

Trying to distract me, he said, "I know you didn't see me in the courthouse, but I was at your hearing yesterday. You were so brave, and our Sanders did good for you."

He put his hands on my shoulders and pushed me back, so he could look at me.

"You've lost weight, girl. Now stop your crying. Your new employers are staring. Let 'em know that we O'Neills are tough." He pulled a handkerchief from the pocket of his lightweight jacket and handed it to me.

I mopped up the tears and tried to get a grip. "Paddy, I'm so glad you're here. It's been so hard . . ."

Sensing I was breaking again, Paddy squeezed my shoulders. "Now listen to me. I stopped and spoke to Mr. DuPriest at the house. Your Da's funeral is tomorrow, and DuPriest says you can go."

The world seemed to stop. Da's funeral? I couldn't accept there was need for a funeral, let alone attend such a thing. I had a wild desire to stop it.

"No," I said.

"I know it's hard, darlin', but this is where we are."

I shook my head. "I can't." I searched for a way out. "I have no clothes."

"Aunt Mary packed two suitcases for you. They're out in the car. She even found a black dress."

When he saw I was still shaking my head, he gave me a lost look, like he wasn't sure what to do. He tried again.

"Your Aunt Mary will be with you. We'll be on either side of you in the church, with you the whole day." He paused before his next words rushed out. "You don't have to talk to Maeve."

I stared at him. "Thank you." And I'd thought I done such a good job of hiding my hatred for the woman.

"I was sure I'd missed his funeral. It's been almost a week."

"Too much crazy stuff going on, lass. So many arrests in the family. It's been hard to plan anything."

I wasn't the only one with troubles. I nodded and squared my shoulders. "Okay, I'll go. Of course, I will."

That night, I lay on a comfortable double bed in the dormer room I'd been given, above the horses. It was up a steep set of narrow stairs, at the end of the barn, over the arched entrance. It had a large window from which I could see much of the grounds.

I liked being above Gypsy Moor, and I could hear him and Irish Mist rustling in the deep straw below me.

I lay there remembering my afternoon. Jase had shown me my room and adjoining bath, before putting me to work filling fourteen water buckets from the heavy hose I'd dragged about the barn aisle. After that, I'd learned how to clean a stall properly.

Luckily, after a few hours of this, Sylvie had returned to the barn to check on my progress.

Watching me drag and recoil the heavy hose, she'd said, "You'll be surprised how much muscle and fitness you'll develop working here." Then she'd turned to Jase. "The girl needs time to settle in. Let her off for the rest of the day, okay?"

As Jase nodded his consent, I realized how little physical labor I'd done in my life. I was already exhausted and wondered about making it through the next few days.

After gazing at me for a moment, Sylvie had sent me a smile that reached her warm eyes. "I meant what I said, earlier. If you need anything, you come to me."

I counted her as a blessing. She seemed a genuinely sweet woman and having another female around was comforting.

I hadn't met the grooms, Timmy and Carl, who'd been given the afternoon off while Jase and I worked. As sore as my arms and legs were, I envisioned the two of them as tall, big, and bulging with muscles. They had quarters on the ground floor with Jase. Their rooms were behind the doors I'd seen in the paneled wall opposite the stalls.

I was glad to be on a different floor; it gave me a sense of privacy. If I'd been downstairs, I'd have been forced to share a communal bathroom and shower. I'd had enough of that in jail, thank you very much.

Knowing the next day would be tough, I closed the book I'd been unsuccessfully trying to read and turned off the bedside lamp. So many changes. A new life with countless unknowns. And tomorrow, I'd face the worst of my past.

I closed my eyes, hoping for sleep, but thoughts of the impending funeral crowded my head. There would be few O'Carroll's in attendance. Hell, they were all in jail, including Lara. But Maeve would be there, probably wringing her hands. No doubt her grief would be loud and dramatic. And my darling stepbrother, Connor.

I gritted my teeth and made myself count the horses and try to recite their names. It must have worked, for I awakened later. But instead of feeling rested, I was rigid with fear.

I'd been dreaming about . . . Maeve. The dream had dissolved, and the only fragment I could grasp was an image of our Tinkers Town kitchen. She stood before the open knife drawer, staring inside. She raised her gaze to meet mine and a sick smile curved her lips. I couldn't see Connor, but I heard him laughing.

24

Strangers were not welcome at St. Michael's Catholic Church. The accepted place of worship for the Traveller's community, the building stood on the corner of Edgefield and Tinkers Streets.

In the past, I'd seen outsiders make the mistake of entering the church for services. They were invariably treated with cold stares and angry looks of disapproval. Most left and never returned. If they did, they regretted it.

More than once I'd seen Traveller men corner a two-time interloper in the church parking lot before "helping" him into his car and escorting him off the property. Sometimes, fights broke out. I'd never seen an outsider return more than once.

Now, I knew what an outsider felt like. With Tommy indefinitely in jail, my role as an O'Carroll family member had dissolved. Da was dead, and I'd been forced to live among strangers. Even my childhood friend, Kayla Riley, refused to return my calls.

I tried to banish these dark thoughts as Paddy drove Mary and me into the church lot. I was so lucky to have the two of them. They'd picked me up at Ballymoor that morning, stuffing me into the seat between them. Without words, they seemed to know their physical presence was as important to me as their moral support.

Outside Paddy's truck, a crowd of mourners filled the sidewalk and steps before the church as people slowly made their way inside. Nerves on edge, I searched for Maeve and Connor, but didn't see them as we climbed from the truck.

My stepmother had made no effort to contact me in prison or during the short time since I'd been released. I'd made no effort to call her. If I never spoke to her or Connor again, that would be fine with me.

Still securely sandwiched between Paddy and Mary, I reached the top of the church steps, where I gazed at the crowd inside St. Michael's. The church was almost full. Walking toward the front pews, I could feel the staring eyes, and hear low murmurs that sounded more like curiosity than sympathy.

Ahead, easels holding three photographs stood just before the step leading to the altar and tabernacle beyond. Behind them, stained glass windows rose high to the ceiling, lighting the figure of Christ on his cross.

As we drew closer, the sickly-sweet smell of lilies drew my eyes to the mounds of white flowers on the floor before the altar. Votive candles burned and the scent of incense mingling with the smell of the lilies was cloying and made me want to bolt from the church.

We had reached the front pews before I saw the back of Maeve and Connor's heads. I stiffened slightly, then almost bumped into Mary, who'd stopped dead in front of me.

"Sweet mother of God! What is she thinking?" Mary was staring at the three photographs.

I'd avoided looking at them, certain that photos of Da would be my undoing. But now, my gaze flew to the pictures. Yes, there was the portrait photo of Da in the middle. But, before that blade could slice my heart, I saw on the right, a photo of him and Maeve with their arms around each other. On the left, a picture of Da, Maeve, and Connor stared back me.

With his death, Maeve had tossed the role of loving stepmother. Still, I was shocked to realize her brothers, the McCarthy boys, and their families filled up the two front pews on both sides of the aisle.

Lips compressed with anger, Paddy moved quickly to the front pew on the right, away from where Maeve and Connor sat. Glowering at Maeve's family, he cleared his throat loudly enough to turn heads.

"Excuse me. I'm Rory's brother and this is Quinn, his daughter. Could you make some room for us, please?"

At first, no one moved. "What is wrong with you people?" Mary whispered harshly.

Maeve's brother, Jimmy McCarthy, was sitting next to the aisle. He smiled at her, then looked the other way. Hot rage swept through me. I pushed past Paddy and Mary. Weeping, I stumbled and fell against my step-uncle.

Staring into his face, I cried, "Oh, God! My Da, my Da! How could God take him from me?"

By now I was on my knees, wailing and clinging to Jimmy McCarthy's arm, as if I'd slide to the floor without its support. I'd made such a spectacle of myself and the McCarthy family, they began to stand and shuffle along the pew, getting as far away from me as possible.

Maeve had risen from her seat. She stared at me with hatred in her eyes, her lips parting to speak. Then, as if recalling her surroundings, she sat and faced straight ahead.

As soon as room was provided, Mary marched her stout figure into the pew first. Once again, the only two people I trusted made sure I was safely wedged between them.

Somehow, I'd never quite believed Da was dead. It didn't bear thinking about. But a sudden murmur and intake of breath caused me to look back toward the congregation. My father's casket was being rolled down the aisle toward me.

Most of the congregation stood, but my knees buckled when I tried to rise. Sagging back into the pew, I thanked God when I realized the casket was closed. I wanted to remember Da, smiling, whistling a tune. Picture his eyes bright with humor.

The service began. We stood, we knelt, we sang, then the pastor extolled Da's virtues. I still burned with anger at the McCarthy family and my eyes remained hot and dry.

Things had happened too fast. I'd been allowed no part in planning this service and hadn't thought about speaking. But Paddy went to the microphone and spoke so beautifully about Da, that I clutched Mary's hand until she winced in pain. Afterwards, Connor, and finally, Maeve stood to speak.

With her long bony fingers clasped tightly, as if in prayer, Maeve's performance was pure soap queen. Except her eyes had so much black makeup, and her lips were painted so red, she looked like a bit player in a vampire movie, a vampire with an exceptionally short black skirt and lace blouse that revealed too much skin.

"You all know how much I loved Rory O'Neill. This day, I am stricken by grief. Such a terrible blow for me and Connor now that our Rory has been torn from us." She emphasized her words with a pathetic little sob.

I waited for her black mascara and eyeliner to run, but of course, she'd applied waterproof everything.

"A son without a father is a terrible thing," she continued before bursting into tears and sobbing loudly into the microphone.

Her act outrivaled my earlier one with Jimmy, but I didn't believe for one minute she had loved Da. She'd been along for the ride. She loved only herself, money, and her little mini Maeve, Connor.

She gasped for air, clasped a hand to her forehead, then squared her shoulders, and continued like the bravest of martyred saints.

"My Connor is the man of the house now, and he will take Rory's place with honor and distinction. He will be a true asset to Tinkers Town. And I (sob)... shall somehow go on without my Rory because I know this is what he would want."

Turning beseeching eyes to the congregation, she said, "Thank you all for your support and for coming here today for me and Connor."

One of the McCarthy men rushed forward to help the sobbing woman stagger back to her seat. I exchanged a look with Mary, who sent me an eyeroll so pronounced, I thought it might bounce off the ceiling.

Mercifully, the service ended, and we followed Da's casket from the church to the graveyard. When the interment finally ended, I clutched Paddy's wrist.

"I can't go to the house afterwards. I don't want to see her."

"After her performance, why would you? No, of course you needn't go."

As relief flooded me, I was surprised to see Sanders walking toward us. But why wouldn't he be here? The lawyer had worked for half of the congregation and no doubt had represented Da more than once.

With a sympathetic expression of concern, he asked, "How are you holding up, Quinn?"

"I'm all right."

"My heart goes out to you, dear. You've been through so much."

"Thank you," I said.

But he wasn't finished. "Maeve is having everyone into the house afterward."

"I know that. But I'm not going."

Sanders turned to Paddy. "Maeve has asked me to read the will after the crowd disperses. I thought you'd been told that Rory designated me his executor. You and Quinn need to be present. Everyone concerned is available, so it's an excellent time to get on with it, don't you think?"

Paddy appeared surprised by this announcement. "So, you're running things, are you?"

"No," Sanders said, gesturing at the crowd around us. "Maeve made all these arrangements."

At the mention of her name, Paddy made a sound of contempt.

"She is his wife, Paddy," Sanders said patiently.

"More's the pity."

Paddy's low opinion of his sister-in-law was center stage and fully illuminated. Glancing at me, his raised brows asked the question.

"All right," I said. "I guess we'll have to go."

I intended to escape to my room until the reading of the will. I did not want to be around my stepfamily any longer than I was forced to be.

Maeve had told Mary that everything was left to her, so what was the point of me being present when the will was read? Maybe Sanders thought if I heard the words Da had written, I'd more readily accept Maeve as recipient of the family wealth.

Damn, the woman had blinded Da. He'd believed she loved me, but I knew Maeve would never let me near that money, before or after her death. It would go to Connor, and Da must have known this.

The sensation of being on the outside looking in was almost crippling. I couldn't bear seeing Maeve's smug expression, or the triumph in her eyes when I was informed that she got everything, and I got nothing.

Yet some part of me refused to show weakness by ducking out. When the will was read, I planned to give her my best impassive face. It was the only weapon I had.

25

Inside what had once been my home, black wreaths draped every print, painting, and mirror on the walls. When I walked past Maeve's plastic chapel, a new saint stood on the floor, St. Jude, the patron saint of impossible situations. How appropriate.

With anguished eyes, he stared up at the statue of the Madonna holding the baby Jesus. I felt like gagging.

"I'm going to my room," I told Mary. "Can you let me know when it's time to come down?"

"I will," she said. "But in the meantime, since your stepmother is having Salvatore's cater today, I'll bring you some food."

I shook my head. "I don't want any."

"Nonsense, you need to eat. I'll bring you a plate."

I felt like waving her off with, "Whatever," but it was time to grow up and be grateful for the things I still had. So, I hugged and thanked her before rushing upstairs.

Hurrying past Maeve's flower arrangement on the landing, the metallic gold angels rattled like angry skeletons. I couldn't get out of that house fast enough. Zipping up the last set of stairs, I turned toward the sanctuary of my room, and stopped.

My door was gone. In its place stood a panel of unpainted sheetrock, a bucket of joint compound, and plastic sheeting to protect Maeve's black carpet.

My step-mother was already ripping my room apart to make the apartment for Connor and his bride to be. Damn the woman.

I rushed down the hall to Connor's room, threw his door open, and went inside. The wall between his room and mine was gone. My belongings were stuffed in the far corner of what had once been my room.

My moss-green and burgundy carpet was rolled up on the floor, with my leather chair shoved on top. My beautiful Munnings print lay face down on the floor under a pile of clothes and shoes that had been ripped from my closet. She and Connor had left my desk on its side, emptied my drawers, and piled the contents haphazardly on the clothes and shoes.

As my eyes continued scanning the mess, I realized my bed was gone. So much for hiding out in my room until the will was read.

I heard footsteps in the hall, and whirled toward the door, ready to vent my rage if Connor or Maeve appeared. But it was Mary who stood in the doorway, holding a plate of food.

"Joseph, Mary, and Jesus!" She crossed herself. "Has she no shame?"

"Apparently not," I said.

Mary marched into the room and set the plate on my empty bookshelf. "What has she done with your books? You had so many. Doesn't she know how much you love them?"

I raised my brows.

"Ah, you're right." Mary sighed, her fingers reaching for the gold cross on her chest. "That's why she took them. She hates you for educating yourself and rising above her and Connor. I never liked the woman, but now I see her clearly. She's a jealous hag."

I felt my lips curve up. "Yeah, you could say that."

Mary walked to my leather chair, righted it, and retrieved my racehorse print from the floor. She lay the print on the leather chair-seat and wiped her palms on her black dress. Then she picked up my desk chair from where it had been thrown on the floor.

"Don't worry, darlin'. Paddy and I will help you load this stuff into his truck."

"I have no place to put them," I said, picturing my small dormer room at Ballymoor.

She waved a dismissal. "We'll store everything at home. Your Uncle Paddy will see to the books. If she doesn't have them, you make a list, and Paddy will make her replace them. Even she knows better than to get on the wrong side of his temper."

Her last words brought another smile and suddenly, I was hungry. I retrieved the plate, and sitting cross legged on the floor, I wolfed down an entire veal cutlet, and a side of spaghetti.

Mary sat near me in the desk chair, and when I was almost done, she stood. "I have something to give you, Quinn."

"What?" I asked, wondering about the nervous edge in her voice.

She left the room saying she'd be right back and returned with her pocketbook. Snapping it open, she withdrew an envelope.

"I didn't dare give this to you while Rory was alive. I swore to him I'd destroyed it."

Nerves prickled my skin as I watched her withdraw a photograph. I snatched it from her hand and stared at the image.

A lovely blonde with a slender nose, full lips, high cheek bones and my blue eyes stared back at me. My hands began to tremble.

"I know," Mary said. "It's like looking in a mirror."

"And seeing a ghost," I said. "But she's way prettier than I am."

"Don't sell yourself short. You got more than enough from her."

As I held the image of my mother, a knife sliced at my heart. Rage swept in right behind it.

"Why did she leave me? Is she still alive?" I glared at Mary. "Have you ever spoken to her?"

Unable to meet my gaze, she stared at the floor without speaking.

"How could you have kept this from me?"

She sighed, finally raising guilty eyes to meet mine. "I wanted to give this to you a thousand times, but Rory's anger–

A loud bubble of laughter from the so-called mourners below floated up the stairs. A strong smell of Italian meat sauce and garlic came with it, making the veal in my stomach churn unpleasantly.

"Go on," I said. "You were saying Da's anger frightened you."

"It did, Quinn. As God is my witness, his anger was that fearsome. And my Paddy supported him, told me to stay out of it." Her front teeth pressed into her lip, then her words came faster.

"And I was never that close to your mother, Quinn. The only connection I have with her is this photo. I'm sorry."

"But you knew her. What was she like?"

Mary's gaze fixed on a point behind my shoulder. Her thoughts inward, searching the past.

"She had a lovely laugh. When she first came to Tinkers Town, she was bright and happy. She fell so hard for Rory. They were crazy in love. But they married too quick. I've always thought the town's opposition to your mother as an outsider is part of what spurred Rory on. Then when she left him . . . it was horrible. He hardened. I've never seen such bitterness."

"I know everything there is to know about that! But what about her? She must have said something to you! Did Da frighten her? What did she say?"

Mary had shrunk back in her chair. "Quinn, I already told you what I know. Jennifer didn't realize how strong the Travellers' ways were ingrained in Rory. She thought she could change him."

"Make him an honest man? I thought she was supposed to be so smart, with her PhD and everything. Only a fool would think they could change Da!"

"I know you're angry with her, Quinn, but she was a woman in love. There's a reason they say love is blind."

"I guess that makes two of them. A man would have to be blind to fall for Maeve."

In an instant my anger drained away, leaving only emptiness. Still cross legged on the floor, I dropped my head in my hands and wept.

Mary rushed to me, her knees creaking as she knelt by my side. Gently, she took the tear streaked photo from my hand, wiped it on her dress, and slid it into the envelope.

"Don't ruin what's left of her, Quinn." She put an arm around my shoulders a moment, then stood. "I'll let you know when it's time."

I nodded. "And when we're finished, I'll leave this house and never come back."

26

I seated myself at the dining table and folded my hands firmly in my lap. If I didn't, I was afraid I'd grab a lock of hair and twist it until it tore from my scalp.

Maeve and Connor sat across from me, their expressions smug, their eyes filled with anticipation.

On the pink wall behind them, one of Maeve's cheap religious prints was partially hidden beneath a black wreath tied with pink ribbons. Above me, the saccharine scent of spray incense drifted from the air conditioning vent. I couldn't escape this place soon enough.

While Paddy settled himself next to me, Sanders pulled out a chair at the head of the table.

I leaned to my uncle and whispered, "Where's Aunt Mary?"

He whispered back, "Not invited. She's not mentioned in the will."

So why invite me? Oh, right, to provide entertainment for Maeve. I didn't want to star in the "let's-humiliate-Quinn-show" and would have bailed, except I wouldn't give her the satisfaction of showing vulnerability.

Sanders got the room's attention by opening the folder before him. The familiar fragrance of mint aftershave reached me as I caught my first glimpse of Da's will.

Since it lay at a forty-five-degree angle, only the words "Last Will and Testament" were large enough to read.

Sanders cleared his throat before he spoke. "There are two ways I can do this. I can read this will in its entirety and then answer questions the legal terms might raise for you."

He glanced around the room, making eye contact with each of us. As I watched, he set his reading glasses on the bridge of his nose and lifted the document. Maybe it was just the lighting in the room, but the lines at the corners of his eyes appeared deeper.

"Or," he continued, "I can simply tell you the gist of the will first. This would answer your immediate questions of who gets what. You might prefer this option as it will avoid having to listen to what I'm sure you will find a tedious reading of this nine-page document."

"Nine pages?" Maeve asked. "I can't imagine why it needs to be so long."

Sanders picked up a pen and twirled it between his fingers.

Connor frowned at him. "Just give us the fucking score. Right, Mom?"

She scowled at him, then turned to Sanders. "You'll have to excuse Connor, Sandy. He's been so upset by Rory's death. But he's right. Just give us the short version."

She smiled at Sanders, then turned to look at me. Tilting her head so she could look down her nose at me, Maeve's mouth became a sneer. I gave her my impassive face and glanced at Sanders.

Something wasn't right with him. His eyes were blinking rapidly, and his hands dropped the pen he'd been fidgeting with.

"Three months ago, Rory wrote a new will."

"What do you mean a new will?" Maeve's heavy brows shot together, plowing an ugly furrow in her forehead.

Sanders set the papers down. He had to clear his throat again before he could continue.

"Just that, Maeve, a new will." He didn't look at the document again. "In this will, Rory has bequeathed five-hundred thousand dollars, in cash, to his brother Paddy O'Neill."

"What?" Maeve asked, her long nose quivering. "Why didn't you tell me this?"

"You know I couldn't do that. Just try to grasp what I'm saying." His next words rushed out. "This house and the property it sits on, are left to you, Maeve. The rest of his estate, which is considerable, is to be divided equally between you and Quinn."

Connor stood up so fast he knocked his chair over. "What about me?"

His nostrils flared with rage as his furious gaze landed on me, causing the hairs on the back of my neck to rise.

His sharp face and long nose reminded me more of Maeve than ever as he continued. "She gets half of everything? What do I get? This is—"

"No!" Maeve shouted. "Rory promised me. Sandy, you know he promised me."

Sanders spread his palms. "The change is legal. The new document is legal, Maeve, and will stand up if you take it to court. I'm sorry."

I rose from my chair and stared at her. "Maybe Da wasn't as dumb as you thought."

She stood up fast, leaning over the table, pushing her face closer to mine. "Get out of my fucking house!" To Connor, she said, "I have to talk to you. In private."

As they stormed from the room, Paddy burst out laughing until he had to wipe tears from his eyes. "Ah, this is so sweet!"

I didn't feel like laughing, I was too numb. Da had not forgotten me.

He was protecting me from Maeve! My tightly structured defenses shifted as this new reality enveloped me. I felt a stab of guilt for doubting him. But why wouldn't I have doubted him? The scoundrel had fooled everyone.

"I'm happy for you, Quinn," Sanders said.

Paddy slapped his palms together. "Now she can pay off that restitution, right?"

"It will take a while to settle the estate. It's structured in a complicated fashion. Rory bought land in Georgia and South Carolina. Did you know that, Paddy?"

"No. My brother played it close to the vest. We all do. But isn't there enough cash to let Quinn pay off her debt?"

I waited for Sander's answer, thinking how incredible it would be to get out from under the law.

"It doesn't work that way," Sanders said. "Rory also owned stocks, an interest in a car dealership, the list goes on. The estate must be liquidated and divided evenly. If I was to give cash to Quinn before then, Maeve would go ballistic and have me up on charges."

I sighed. "Looks like it's back to Ballymoor for now. How long?" I asked. "How long will I have to wait?"

"I haven't had a chance to look at any of this, Quinn. Rory's death was so sudden, so unexpected. But I'll get the wheels turning and keep you notified every step of the way."

"That's settled, then," Paddy said. "Come on Quinn, let's find your Aunt Mary and give her the news." He laughed again and said, "This is so lovely."

We found Mary in my wrecked bedroom where she was stuffing my clothes and shoes into two large suitcases.

"What happened to this place?" Paddy's hawk-like face drew tight with anger.

"Step-monster had a go at it," Mary said.

He waved a disdainful hand. "Quinn's well out of this place anyway."

"But it's her room."

"Not anymore," I said. "Da left the house to Maeve."

Paddy raised a palm to Mary, who was about to break into a tirade. "But there's good news. Wonderful news. Tell her, Quinn!"

I did, and before I was finished, Mary attempted to dance a jig around the room, but caught her foot on Connor's bedspread, and ended up bent over, rubbing her ankle.

"I'm too old for this nonsense."

I was about to say she was no such thing when I did a double take. An object under the bed was revealed where Mary had tripped and pulled the spread back.

I raced to the spot, dropped to my hands and knees, and reached under. A thrill of recognition shot through my fingers as they touched the texture of velvet. I snatched the box from beneath the bed.

"Connor," I whispered. "That little shit took it!"

"Took what?" Mary asked.

I glanced fearfully at the door and peeked into the hall to make sure we were alone. But Maeve and Connor must still have been locked in Da's office, gnashing their teeth and thinking devious thoughts.

"The box. The box that held the sapphire."

"Sweet Mary, Mother of God." Mary clutched at her gold cross. "Is it in there?"

The box wasn't locked this time, but when I flipped it open, it was empty.

"He'll have put it in his safe," Paddy said.

"Or sold it already."

"No, Quinn," he said. "I doubt he could have done it that fast."

I placed the box back on the floor near the bed and snapped a couple of photos with my phone. Then I slid it back to where I'd found it beneath the bed.

"So, what do we do?" I asked.

"I don't know yet." Paddy turned in a slow circle staring about the room. "But if you want the sapphire back, we need to find it before she changes the locks on this house. And you need to tell Sandy."

He was right on both counts. Yet for some reason, I felt uneasy about revealing what we'd just learned.

27

By the time I returned to Ballymoor, the horses had been fed and because the weather was warmer, they'd been turned out for the night.

After climbing the narrow stairs to my room, I shed my black dress, changed into jeans, and put on a V-neck top that didn't plunge as low as most of my pullovers.

From what I knew about Sylvie, cheap was not her thing. I liked her and cared about her opinion. Besides, I was living in a barn with three males and no Travellers men to protect me. It seemed wise to avoid trouble.

I walked to my window and gazed out. Since my trip to Georgia, the early spring had edged onward. The weather was mild, and at eight o'clock the light still strong. I wanted to see the horses and walk the grounds before I settled in my room for the night.

Easing through the door at the bottom of my staircase, I breathed in the new, but now familiar scent of hay, sweet feed, and horses. I found it comforting.

Light and voices were coming from the kitchen off the barn aisle. When I stepped inside, the voices stopped. Jase, his hair still damp from a shower, sat at one end of the rectangular wood table.

The slicked back hair accentuated the bones of his face, which were refined and well proportioned. No wonder he was so good looking.

Two men I hadn't seen before were digging pizza out of a box labeled Pizza Di Napoli. The aroma of melted cheese and rich tomato sauce was enticing.

One of the new guys stared at me as Jase said, "This is Quinn, our new stable help." The other man was seated with his back to me.

The staring man smiled and said, "I'm Carl. Welcome aboard our little ship." Like Jase, he had a British accent.

When the third man turned to me, his eyes widened slightly, and his lips curved up. He sketched a wave.

"Timmy, here." Glancing at Carl, he said, "She's easy on the eyes, yeah?" To me, he said, "Hear you had a scrape with the coppers just like the rest of us. You aren't a hooker by any lucky chance, are ya?

"No," Jase said. "She's not."

"Didn't mean no harm," Timmy said. "Was just joking with ya, yeah?"

I smiled at him. "If you must know, I'm a thief."

"Oh, well that's fine then," Carl said. "You'll fit right in with me mates here. Grab a chair and some pizza. There's beer and sodas in the fridge."

Far from the brawny physiques I'd pictured, the two new additions were average height and wiry, with the ropy muscles that come from labor as opposed to gym work. Carl had a buzz cut, a closely-trimmed beard, and a topless mermaid tattooed on his neck.

Timmy, on the other hand, had long, limp brown hair and a forest of tattoos on his neck and arms. They looked like prison tattoos. Among my favorites was a fanged snake and a spider's web with a cockroach tangled in it. Later I learned the letters inked on his neck and his knuckles, ACAB, stood for "All Coppers Are Bastards." He wore a wife beater tee shirt and had a missing front tooth.

I decided I'd prefer not to know what he'd been in for, then almost laughed out loud. How was I supposed to move away from crime if they stuck me with ex-cons?

While Timmy continued his rude stare, I went to the refrigerator and grabbed a Diet Coke. Pulling out the chair at the opposite end of the table from Jase, I sat. Leaning forward, I smiled at everyone, grabbed a piece of pizza and took a big bite.

"There, you see?" Carl said. "She fits right in."

"I'd like to fit right in her," Timmy said, under his breath.

This guy frightened me, but instinct told me to hit fast and hit hard, or there'd be no end to it.

With my best poker face, I leaned toward him. "What did you say?"

His gaze dropped to the kitchen tabletop. "Nothin.'"

Typical bully, he was a coward underneath. Thankfully, Jase and Carl appeared as annoyed by his comment as I was.

We finished our drinks and pizza without further incident. When I rose from the table and said I was going to take a walk, Jase stood. "I'll go with you, show you what's what."

Timmy said, "I bet you will."

"Sod off," Jase said, and together, we left the two men behind in the kitchen.

Leaving the barn through the wide horse entrance, we stepped onto the sandy path that led to the DuPriest mansion. The air was soft and warm. Something sweet and heady was blooming nearby, and Jase walked close to me. With a small side step, I widened the gap between us.

The path we walked was cut with hoof prints. I liked the way seeing them made me feel. Like maybe the world here was a better, safer place.

"Where are the horses?" I asked.

He pointed toward the side of the DuPriest home. "There's more land behind the house. See up ahead, how the path goes by the side of the house? The paddocks are out back. Come on, I'll show you."

The house loomed before us. The wing we were about to walk beside was easily as big as Maeve's McMansion.

"Who lives here?" I asked. "I mean, are there children, relatives?"

"That's the thing. No children, no family. Just the two of them, except Presto does have a younger brother I see occasionally."

"Why would they buy such a huge place for two people?"

"They didn't. She built if for him, because it was what he wanted."

"She built it? So," I said, "it's her money."

"Quick on the uptake, yeah?"

"I'm a Traveller. Following the money is what I do."

"So that's your story, is it?"

"Now you know. What's yours?"

His eyes shuttered. "Some other time, Quinn. Come on. I thought you wanted to see the horses."

As he hurried ahead of me, I wondered what had happened to him. But when the Gypsy Vanners in the paddock before us lifted their heads and raced toward us, I forgot everything.

They came so fast and with so much power, I thought they'd come right through the fence. I turned and sprinted sideways to prevent being trampled.

Then I heard Jase snort and turned to look. He almost had tears in his eyes he was laughing so hard. "I'd pay money to see that again."

Ignoring him, I looked back to see the horses had halted at the fence. Two of them were on their hind legs, pawing the air. When they came down, they whirled, and the whole crowd took off and ran in the opposite direction, tossing their heads, leaping and plunging.

"They're laughing at you, Quinn."

I was too busy watching them to care. Black manes on cream bodies, white manes on black coats, and dark grays with dapples like silver coins. Their manes and forelocks were so long the horses appeared to have sprouted wings.

I could feel the earth tremble beneath my feet as they pounded past again. I could sense their movement in the air currents around me. I could smell them. In awe, I stared at a palomino that flew past. The bright dapples on his coat resembled a floating treasure of gold doubloons.

"I've never seen anything this beautiful," I said. "They're not paintings or pictures, they're alive!"

"You Travellers don't get out much, do you?" Jase wasn't laughing now, just watching me with those intense eyes.

"No one has horses in Tinkers Town," I said.

"That's too bad. You're totally smitten with them, aren't you?"

"Why would I be? I don't know anything about them."

"That may be true, but any fool can see you're dying to learn."

I was about to answer, but an angry voice called out. "Now this here is something I don't particularly like."

I whirled to see Presto DuPriest striding toward us. His stacked-up pompadour was reminiscent of Runford's angry hackles. I hoped his bark was worse than his bite.

"Don't be running those horses like that! You'll get 'em hurt." Glaring at me, he continued, "Are you looking for more trouble, Missy?"

"No sir, I'm not." I worked hard to remain expressionless as I took in his high collared white shirt spangled with rhinestones and his bellbottomed white pants and white boots.

"Well then, what exactly are you doing?"

"Presto," Jase said, "She's fallen in love with your Gypsy Vanners, and I think the horses can read her excitement. You know how smart they are."

Jase's flattery was absurdly obvious. But it worked. Presto's glaring expression softened.

"Well, now that's very nice Miss Quinn. They're spiritual, these horses. You know, Elvis always said, 'It's surprising how much you can look forward to the morning when you have a horse waiting on you.'"

Jase turned away enough that Presto couldn't see his face. But I could. He rolled his eyes and his lips silently recited the words with Presto. Apparently, he'd heard Elvis sayings before.

I bit the inside of my cheek, so I wouldn't laugh. "Uh, no. I didn't know Elvis liked horses."

"Loved 'em. Kept them at Graceland just like I keep 'em here."

I wasn't sure how to respond to that and smiled instead. Thankfully, the conversation trailed off, and Jase and I left for the barn.

Climbing the stairs to my room, I pictured the clothes Presto had worn. What was it with this guy and Elvis? When I'd first met him, he'd welcomed me to the "Kingdom." How weird was that?

28

When I saw Jase the next morning, he'd pulled his blond mane back and secured it with a rubber band. Like when it had been wet from the shower, it accentuated the planes of his face and if possible, made him even more handsome.

Unfortunately, he was in lecture mode and watched my every move like a drill sergeant as I loaded breakfast buckets for the horses. I squatted on the floor next to grain bins and shelves that held various cartons and bottles of stuff I'd never heard of, like Succeed and Flex Force.

How much information was I supposed to soak up in one morning, anyway?

"Am I boring you, Quinn?"

"No. Not at all," I replied resisting an eye roll.

"Then, stay with me. You can't ever forget pregnant mares get different feed and supplements than the stallion does, and he needs different products than the geldings and fillies."

About the time my eyes were about to roll up to the back of my head, he left for the kitchen and returned with two water bottles, handing me one. After a couple of sips, he said, "And another thing you should know—"

"Can I ask you a question?" Without waiting, I plowed ahead. "What's this thing Presto has with Elvis Presley?"

He seemed unfazed by the abrupt change of subject. "He is right fond of his man, Elvis, isn't he?"

"More like obsessed." We both grinned, and I realized how much I liked his sense of humor.

But his smile faded as he continued. "But, that's how he made his money and hooked Sylvie, isn't it?"

"It is?"

"Yeah, the wanker was an Elvis impersonator."

"Seriously?"

"Played Las Vegas."

"He sang and stuff?"

Jase nodded. "Don't worry, you'll be sure to hear him sing and play before long."

"So that explains his flashy clothes and country boy act."

Jase gave me a sharp look. "Act is exactly the right word. No flies on you, yeah?"

I shrugged. "I try. But I can't understand why Sylvie fell for him?"

"The woman's been Elvis crazy since she was a nipper. From what she's told me, I figure the day Presto met her, he locked onto her like a heat-seeking missile."

"The heat of money," I said.

"You're exactly right."

We grinned again, and I felt a strong connection pulling me to him. The palomino, Irish Jewel, broke the spell by grabbing his empty feed bucket in his teeth and banging it against the wall. Words couldn't have been as eloquent as the bang of the bucket.

"Come on," Jase said, "He's tired of waiting. You don't want to get on the wrong side of him. He can be difficult."

I gazed at the doubloon-like dapples on the horse's side, at the spirit shining from his eyes. "He's beautiful."

"That may be true, but we haven't even gotten him broke yet and he's three already. He's by a top Vanner in Florida named Jewel of the Crown."

"What do you mean 'by?'" I asked.

Patiently, he said, "When talking about a horse, he is 'by' his papa and 'out of' his momma. See?"

I nodded. I had so much to learn.

When I called Sanders early that afternoon, I couldn't wait to tell him about the sapphire box. My timing was fortunate. Court was in recess for lunch and his secretary put him through immediately.

"Quinn, what's up?"

"We found the velvet box yesterday! The box the sapphire was in. It was in Connor's room!"

"Slow down, Quinn. Are you sure it's the same box?"

"Of course, I'm sure. It had the red MH initials stamped on it. Except there was nothing in it. What do we do now? Talk to the judge? The prosecutor?

There was a moment's silence, then, "Who is the 'we' that found the box?"

"What difference does it make?" When he didn't answer, I paused, trying to collect my thoughts.

More slowly, I said, "I was in Connor's room with my Aunt Mary and Uncle Paddy. It was right after you left the house yesterday, after you read the will. The box was under Connor's bed."

"Okay. This changes things. I'm due back in court now, but I'll take care of this for you, Quinn. Sounds like you got a bum deal."

"But, how are you going to 'take care' of it?"

"Let me talk to Maeve. When she realizes what Connor's done, she may get him to hand over the sapphire. She's smart enough to know turning it over now could keep him out of jail. The boy has no record. I could get him off and that could be an end to this whole mess."

"She won't do that," I said. "She adores Connor. She'd never turn him in. And she'd never help me."

Was Sanders really dumb enough to think Maeve didn't know what had happened?

"Quinn," he said, "I think you have the wrong idea about Maeve. I know there was some jealousy between you two, but Maeve is not a bad person."

I gritted my teeth tight to keep from yelling that he was a fool if he believed that. Instead, I said, "Please, just get me out from under this charge and the debt for a ring I've never even seen."

There was a long pause, then, "Please, trust me Quinn, I'm on your side. I meant it when I said you got a bum deal. I think Connor set you up, and once Maeve realizes this, she'll be willing to get him to work something out. We'll fix this."

"I hope so," I said, knowing it was more likely she'd throw a party for Connor for being clever enough to set me up.

By the end of that week, Jase had stuffed my head with so much information about the importance of calcium-to-phosphorous ratios, hoof paint, hair-coat supplements, leather cleaners, and pasture maintenance, I thought my brain would explode.

I soon realized that Timmy and Carl spent most of their time outside the barn working with leaf blowers, hedge trimmers, weed whackers, and other gardening tools.

Jase, on the other hand, held the more important job of training the horses. Apparently, he'd trained show horses in England and held seniority over the rest of us. Sometimes he drove the tractor, dragging a piece of heavy chain-link fence across the paddocks to break up the manure clumps. Or he'd use its front-end bucket to pile up the waste we forked from the stalls.

Once a week, a local mushroom farm sent a truck to load the stuff up for fertilizer. After this discovery, I picked the mushrooms off the pizzas we shared in the kitchen.

One day, I followed him and the gray gelding, Irish Mist, through the huge door of the carriage house. I was fascinated how easily Jase sorted out a tangle of leather harness, fit it neatly onto the horse, and hooked him up to what he called a training cart.

The cart had only one seat, and when Jase and Irish Mist wheeled out of the barn, I examined the other carts and carriages. There was a two-seat cart called a phaeton, an open carriage that held four passengers, and a large surrey with fringe on top that could hold eight people. This last carriage was pulled by six horses and was very tall. I finally understood why the building's door was so gigantic.

During that week, I heard nothing from Sandy, and had no idea if he'd spoken to Maeve, or how the liquidation of Da's estate was going. Though I was anxious for answers, I was surprised how calming and positive it was to care for animals and work on something besides fleecing people.

The last day of that week, Jase saddled one of the older mares, and helped me climb aboard. He led us around the circular driveway, and I loved it. For those few magical moments, Da's death and the rest of it ceased to exist.

If only it could have stayed that way.

29

By the end of June, I'd learned the basics of horseback riding. I loved everything about it, from the feel of the reins in my hands, to the smell of the horse beneath me and his glossy neck under my hand. That these animals trusted me and carried me where I wanted to go amazed me.

But by the first of July, I was angry that I hadn't heard from Sanders. He knew Connor was the real jewel thief. But I didn't hear a word about it or anything regarding the liquidation of the estate. He hadn't returned my calls and that rang a little bell of alarm.

When I called Sanders' office again and was told he was on vacation until mid-July, I was furious. Since I wasn't supposed to leave the estate without permission and didn't trust the privacy of my cell phone, I asked Paddy to drive over for a powwow.

He came the next day during my lunch break. We ate the food he brought beneath the shade of a live oak, using one of Presto's decorative stone tables and benches to eat our deli sandwiches.

After demolishing the food, we sipped sweet iced tea, and I told Paddy about my last conversation with Sanders.

"I don't blame you for being troubled lass. Something's not right there and I can't quite put my finger on it."

"Is he really dumb enough to think Maeve would be helpful? He never got back to me and now he's on vacation."

Paddy thought for a minute. "He's not stupid, but Maeve has her tricks and might have pulled the wool over his eyes. But even if he fell for her womanly ways, there's something else going on, and it's a puzzle I can't put together."

"Womanly ways?" I asked. "Don't you mean skanky? All the men in Tinkers Town go for her tarty clothes. That's probably what it is with Sanders. What else could it be?"

"I don't know," he said. "But it seems like something I can't see is happening below the surface, and it worries me."

"What do you mean?

"I can't explain it. Don't worry, lass. Maybe it's just a bad feeling."

His words left me doubtful and chilled.

Each day folded into another as I rode in one of the paddocks every evening after work. Because my weight was so much less than the guys, I became Jase's go-to rider for the younger horses.

Somehow, I'd managed to coax Irish Jewel to let me sit on him bareback in his stall. With patience and an ability I barely believed I possessed, I got him walking when I clucked and slowing when I said whoa.

When Jase said the horse had trust issues, I began reading everything I could get my hands on about difficult horses. Sylvie had opened her library to me, loaning me the books of "horse whisperers" like Monty Roberts.

Curious as to what had caused the horse to be so wary, I'd finally pried the reason out of Jase. A year earlier, Timmy had lost his temper with the horse and beaten him repeatedly with a riding crop. Jase had immediately fired Timmy, but for some reason, Presto had stepped in and insisted that Timmy remain on staff.

This, I decided, must be the reason for the tension between Jase and Presto.

One evening, Presto came out with Jase to watch me ride in one of the paddocks. As usual, he chewed gum. Standing next to Jase, he winked at me.

"To tell the truth, missy, it's not just that you weigh less than the boys; I believe you have some natural balance and good instincts with these animals."

"That she does," Jase said. "And she tells me riding your Vanners sends all her worries out the back door."

Jase never lost an opportunity to flatter Presto. I wondered what that said about both their characters. Or had he flattered Presto on my behalf?

Losing Da, watching Maeve operate at the funeral, and spending time in jail had made me as wary of people as Irish Jewel was. It seemed everyone had a hidden agenda.

Presto didn't seem to mind Aiken's fierce southern heat that sent many of the wealthy neighbors around Ballymoor north. Many of them had homes in Maine, New Hampshire, or Millbrook and Saratoga Springs in upstate New York.

Presto came to the barn every morning to ride. He usually wore a sleeveless leather vest. He had them in many colors–black, blues, and reds, and shades in between like lavender. He had boleros in colorful hues, and several western hats.

He usually used thin leather gloves to protect his manicured nails and wore white jeans and cowboy boots when he rode. He had three or four silver-studded western saddles.

Apparently, Sylvie, who often came to watch him ride, gave him whatever he wanted.

One morning after Elvis and Sylvie left the barn, I was jerked back to my other world when Lara O'Carroll showed up in one of the few luxury cars that hadn't been confiscated by the feds. This one was a Lexus.

Stepping outside the barn, I watched her climb out. Her short skirt exposed an enticing view of long thighs and legs. She'd obviously been out of jail long enough the get her hair done as the black roots that had been showing in the detention center were now white blond. Her makeup was back in place, too.

Carl and Timmy who were trimming weeds along a nearby fence line stopped working and stared. I was glad Timmy wasn't within hearing distance as I could imagine the lewd comments he might make about Lara.

"Hey," I called, "when did you get out?"

"Three days ago. How's it going, Quinn?"

I spread my palms to take in Ballymoor. "Could be worse."

At that moment, Jase emerged from the barn. In the sunlight, his natural blond hair was iridescent.

Lara breathed in sharply. "Yeah. Could be a whole lot worse."

I introduced them, Timmy and Carl went back to work, and the three of us stepped beneath the shade of a towering oak.

"You a Traveller too?" Jase asked. But his tone indicated he had no problem with her being one, and one side of his mouth twitched up into the suggestion of a smile.

"I am and I just got out of jail, too. You got a problem with that?"

"Absolutely not," he answered with a grin. "All of us just got out at some point." He gestured with his arm, taking in all four of us Ballymoor staff members. We're a right motley crew."

Jase had broken the ice nicely and the three of us talked a bit about our time in jail. That is, Lara and I did. Jase was more close-mouthed, more careful. He managed to let us know he'd been incarcerated in England but never let on why.

"I should probably get back to work," I said.

But Jase surprised me. "Talk to your mate here a bit longer. I like learning more about you, yeah?"

As I glanced at him, I suddenly remembered one of the things that was troubling me. Turning from him to Lara, I asked, "Did Sandy represent you in court to get you out?"

"Yeah, he's our man."

"So that was three days ago?" When she nodded, I said, "He hasn't returned my calls and his secretary told me he was out of town until mid-July."

Lara frowned. "I don't know why she'd say that. He was here three days ago."

"I don't either. It's weird, and you know what else?" Lara and Jase listened with interest as I explained about finding the velvet box beneath Connor's bed.

"Seems your lawyer's stonewalling you," Jase said.

"If he is, screw him," Lara said. "We should get into Maeve's house, break into that safe and get the stone back. This whole thing sounds like bullshit!"

"If I did that, even if I found the sapphire, I'd be back in jail. I don't want to risk it, Lara."

She made a noise of disgust. "I thought you were tougher than that."

"She's tough enough," Jase said.

Just then, Presto came out of the main house and got into the white Range Rover he usually drove.

"I've seen him before," Lara said with a frown. "He's that guy looks like Elvis."

"Hard to miss him," I said.

"But when I saw him, guess who he was with?"

"Priscilla Presley?"

"This isn't a joke, Quinn. I saw him with Maeve."

30

Confused, I stared at Lara. "You saw Presto with Maeve? That's crazy. They don't even know each other!"

"Appears you're wrong about that," Jase said. Having no idea how Lara's words affected me, he was grinning like it was a joke. Turning to Lara, he said, "Can't have you upsetting the staff like this, love. You'll get Quinn's knickers all in a twist."

"You don't understand. She should be upset," Lara said, glaring at Jase. "You know nothing about Maeve. She's mean and cunning."

When he turned back to me, his grin had faded. "This Maeve is your step-mother, yeah?"

"Step-monster's more like it," I said. "Lara, you're sure it was Presto with her?

She waved a hand toward the white Range Rover that was going past us. "If that's Presto, then that's who I saw."

"When?" I asked.

"Yesterday afternoon, after I got my hair done in Augusta. They were going into a bar on Broad Street."

"I don't suppose you followed them inside?"

"Why would I do that? I just figured she was already on the prowl, and your da barely in the ground. Be just like the bitch."

I shook my head in disbelief. "I don't like her talking to Presto. Is she spying on me or something?"

"Listen, Quinn, whatever she's up to, you should reconsider what I said. You need to get that sapphire back before it disappears. She's probably got it in your da's safe, and I've got a cousin who could get it out."

Again, I told her the idea made me uneasy, and again she gave me a look of disgust. "Well, if you change your mind, you have my number." She sketched a wave at us as she walked away. A moment later, she'd climbed in her Lexus.

"She's a tough one, isn't she?" Jase said, as the car disappeared down the drive.

"She is, but she saved my butt in jail from a gal that was beating me up. Lara knocked the crap out of her," I said, smiling at the memory.

"Well, she's all right then, isn't she?"

I nodded.

Standing in the shade of the oak tree, the noisy buzzing and clicking of summer bugs surrounded us. Presto's elaborate sprinkler system had given the grass beneath our feet a fresh, moist scent. Both Sylvie and Presto were absent, and for once, Jase didn't seem to be in a hurry to get back to work.

"So, what does your step-mother look like, anyway?"

"Why?"

"Maybe I've seen her around."

When I described her tall thin form, heavy dark brows and long sharp nose, he said, "I may have seen her. You got a photo?"

"God, no. But, where would you have seen her?"

"Won't know until I get a picture. Come on, then. Let's see if we can't find out." He motioned me to follow him to the barn.

A moment later, he opened one of the doors off the aisle that led to the grooms' quarters. I was surprised by Jase's set up. It was much nicer than what Timmy and Carl had. I knew those two bunked together, as I'd glimpsed their twin beds through their open door.

Jase had a foyer with a second door that must lead to his room. The foyer had a boot scraper, hooks for coats and a heavy mat for wiping boots and shoes.

We used the mat, and he opened the door to his room. Inside, most of the floor was covered with a good quality rug in muted shades of brown and red. He had a wooden dresser, a desk and chair, and shelves with books. The single bed was neatly made, the whole room tidy.

The walls had several framed photos of him on horseback sailing over big jumps as crowds of spectators looked on. I noticed a wide set of sliding doors that probably hid a closet. Nearby, a large-screen monitor sat on his desk and two powerful looking computer towers stood beneath it.

"Hold on a minute," he said, "while I boot up Mr. X."

"You have names for your computers? And why do you have two, anyway?"

"Truth is, I'm not supposed to have Mr. X. Usually keep him hidden in the closet, but there was something I had to look up last night.

He gave me a sly grin and I suspected I was about to meet Jase the criminal.

"I built him myself and wrote some very useful programs for him."

"Look, Jase, if you're a hacker or something, maybe you don't want to tell me this stuff."

"You say anything, I'll deny it. Even if the coppers took Mr. X in, they'd never find what they wanted. They've tried it before." He smiled as if remembering the thwarted efforts and frustration he'd caused.

When Mr. X was up and humming, he typed in a paragraph-length string of letters that must be his password. Two more screens and sets of passwords later, a third screen opened.

"Does she have a middle name, your step-monster?"

"McCarthy."

"I'm assuming she uses a computer?"

"Yeah, we all do."

He typed in her name and location. The program appeared to zero in on her computer in Tinkers Town. It asked for her password. Jase raised his brows at me.

"I have no idea," I said.

As I stood close behind him and peered over his shoulder, I noticed how clean and thick his blond hair was. I could smell a faint trace of his sweat and his male scent. It made me giddy.

Jase's fingers flew over the keyboard and the computer's screen suddenly flashed with a million letters, symbols and numbers that zipped by faster and faster until they became a blur of light. Then everything stopped. Highlighted in the center of the screen was what must be a password.

His fingers flew once more, and we entered Maeve's private world. He opened her photo file. "That her?"

Maeve, in her signature pink lipstick and black eye makeup, stared back at me. "Yeah, that's her."

He sifted through the photos stopping on a profile shot of her face, and a more distant photo that showed her entire body, including a pair of gold, stiletto-heeled, platform shoes.

"I saw her once," Jase said. "She was here. Before you came."

"You mean here at Ballymoor?"

"'Fraid so, love. She came and met Presto. He showed her around the barn and the carriage house. Even took her into the main house. He told me later that she was interested in buying a horse."

"Buying a horse? That's a big fat lie. She hates animals." My mind spun like a slot machine and settled on one question. "Was Sylvie here that day?"

Jase turned his head and gave me a sharp look. "No, she was gone that day."

"How convenient," I said. "How long were they in the house?"

"Long enough."

"Jaysus," I said, unconsciously adopting Da's expression. "She was cheating on him before Da died."

"We don't know that," Jase said. "But it seems likely. I feel bad for Sylvie. If it's true and she finds out, she'll be gutted. Especially with Maeve being so slender and attractive."

I stepped around, so I could see his face. "You think she's attractive?"

"In a tarty sort of way, yes."

I rolled my eyes, realizing it was a man thing and I'd never understand. Or maybe I didn't want to.

"Don't get me wrong, Quinn. I love our Sylvie. She has a big heart. She's been good to me. So, if those other two are shagging, I'd like to punch in Presto's ugly face."

The image of Maeve and Presto "shagging" almost made me gag. My stepmother was shameless, but she was also evil. The thought of those two being together was not only revolting, it was alarming.

31

That evening when it was time to put the horses out, I left my room and trotted downstairs to the barn.

The fans that spun overhead stirred my hair and cooled my skin. Inside each stall, the automatic fly sprayers periodically squirted mist. I didn't like the smell of insecticide but liked fly bites even less. Together, these machines kept Presto's prize animals cool and comfortable during Aiken's summer heat.

I stopped outside Irish Jewel's stall and let him sniff my hand through the railing. Apparently, he went nuts every time they tried to put a bit in his mouth, like he thought the bit was a snake. Didn't matter if it was a simple chifney bit or a soft rubber snaffle. He wasn't having it.

"Hey, pretty boy," I said to the gold horse, "the big boss was complaining about you again today." Mimicking Presto, I said, "Did ya know Elvis Presley's favorite horse was a palomino?"

Sliding my hand through the railing, I stroked Jewel's face. "Listen, your owner's getting mad that he can't ride you. He wants to parade you around the dirt roads of Aiken. You're going to get us all in trouble if you don't clean up your act."

Slipping inside his stall, I put both hands on his withers. Using my toes and arm muscles to spring and pull myself up, I got a leg over his back and was astride. Gypsy Vanners are small compared to most horses, and it hadn't taken me long to realize I could hop on without a mounting block.

Squeezing my legs and clucking, I got him moving around the stall. His ears flicked back to listen to my voice, and he seemed happy to follow my suggestions. Stretching my left leg back and tugging his mane up near his ears toward the left, he turned left for me and moved in a tight circle.

"You are so good with him."

I hadn't heard Jase approach over the whirr of the fans, but I wasn't startled. I was too used to being around him. I threw him a grateful smile before mentioning an idea I'd had while reading one of Sylvie's books.

"You've tried a hackamore, right?" Using the bridle that's designed without a bit seemed such a no-brainer, I was sure they'd tried it. But I could see realization dawning in his eyes.

"Oh, sod me. You'll be having my job next, Quinn. That's brilliant. I'll pick one up in the morning."

Farther down the aisle, Carl and Timmy stepped from their room and picked up some lead shanks. Minutes later the four of us began walking horses from the barn into the warm night outside. When all were done but two, Jase said he and I would handle them.

"Watch that his hands don't handle you, Quinn," Timmy said with a leer.

With a frown Jase said, "Sod off, Timmy. Get your mind outta your bum hole for once."

I'd gotten used to the guys' rough speech. We were all ex-cons, so what did I expect? I'd even stopped worrying about Timmy. But I was glad that Jase didn't talk to me that way.

"So," I said, as we led the last two Vanners to a paddock gate, "you know why I'm at Ballymoor. How'd you wind up here?"

"You know I got in trouble in England, right?"

"For hacking?" I asked.

"Something like that."

We led the horses through the gate and released them. For a moment we didn't talk, just watched the two horses tear off into the moonlight. When the sound of their hooves receded in the night, I turned to Jase.

"I thought you said they never got inside Mr. X."

"Just so," he said. "I didn't have Mr. X when I was across the pond. I had Mr. Z."

"Of course, you did." I wasn't sure if he was teasing or not.

"Look, Quinn," he said, suddenly serious. "I like you, and some things happened in the past you won't like. But I'd rather you hear it from me than someone else."

Unconsciously, I drew back. I didn't want the responsibility that came with knowing his secrets. I liked him, and maybe too much.

But he took a quick breath, and his words rushed out. "My dad, he beat me. He beat Mom, too. One night he started in on my little sister. He could have killed her. I couldn't let him do that, could I? I didn't mean to kill him. It just happened."

I stared at him in the moonlight, realizing my jaw had dropped. I didn't know what to say. He had such a beseeching look on his face. I wished he hadn't told me.

"How badly did he hurt your little sister?" I asked.

"She was in the hospital for a month."

"Jase, I don't blame you for what you did." Where had that come from? But I didn't blame him, if what he said was true. "What happened?"

"They ruled it justifiable, no charges were brought. I went to jail because the internet crime crew found my program on Mr. Z that copied keystrokes. I was hacking the coppers for some mates of mine, and I got caught. Listen, Quinn, I've done my time, and I've learned my lesson."

"So, hopefully, you don't hack into police departments anymore. You don't, do you?"

"Not yet," he said with the sly grin of a con artist.

Hopefully that was mostly in his past. But then who was I to label someone else a con artist?

"So," I said, "You stole information, and I stole jewelry. I don't want to know what Timmy and Carl did, okay?"

He made a zipper motion over his lips.

"You still haven't told me how you ended up here."

"That part's easy. After the thing with my dad, hacking, and prison time, the show horse people wouldn't touch me. The only work I got was cleaning stalls. But there was one toff who stood by me. He knew Sylvie through his American wife. They got me the job and here I am."

He paused a moment, watching a cloud scuttle across the face of the moon. "Listen, Quinn, I don't know what's going on with this Maeve person or your lawyer. He doesn't seem too speedy to me." In the soft light his eyes suddenly grew more intense.

"You could use someone to stand by you, yeah? I know a bit about cracking safes. If getting that sapphire back could set you straight with the law, I could help you."

His words surprised me. "Why would you take that risk?"

"I like you, Quinn."

I couldn't think of a response. His words had given me a tiny thrill and I was glad it was dark so he couldn't see the hot blush I felt on my cheeks.

32

The next day, after morning stable chores, I called Lara from my room. "Yesterday, you said there was something I needed to do. Remember?"

"Sure."

I knew Lara was far too clever to mention "stealing back a sapphire" on the open line of a cell phone, so I didn't worry she'd mention what the "something" was.

"Jase and I want to talk to you about it. Can you come over again?"

"Well, yeah. As cute as he is, I'll drive back, and I'll drive fast. So, he's coming to your rescue? He must like you."

"It's not like that," I said. "He has some talents we could find useful in getting it done."

"Whatever you say, Quinn. Noonish tomorrow?"

I agreed and hung up. I heard Jase in the barn below and then his voice calling up my staircase.

"Want to come with me to pick up that hackamore?"

"Yeah, if I'm allowed to leave the farm."

"It's stable business," he said, "and I'm sure I'll need your help."

"Of course you will."

Rolling off the property in the farm truck with Jase was such a treat. The sudden sense of freedom was intoxicating. He drove the dirt roads through what the locals called the historic district, passing the lovely nineteenth century homes I'd seen on my way in. We drove by horse stables and polo fields, before rolling along Mead and out onto Whiskey Road.

Because people rode horses across Whiskey to access the Hitchcock Woods, the streetlight posts had buttons at rider height, making it easy to call for a green light. I thought that was pretty neat and also liked that the street signs were decorated with horse heads. No wonder Aiken was nicknamed Horse Heaven.

Moments later we pulled into the lot outside Aiken Saddlery on Pinelog Road. Inside, the strong scent of leather was rich and heady as we studied a selection of hackamores. The bridles used a section of finely braided rope or rolled leather that looped under the horse's jaw and over his nose to control and guide. Some of the hackamores had extremely long metal extensions called shanks that extended down from the noseband. The longer the shank, the stronger the pressure on the animal's nose. Leather reins attached to rings on the end of the shanks.

We selected a short-shanked Herm Sprenger model. It was expensive, but it was Sylvie's money and she always wanted the best for Presto and his horses. I wondered if she'd be happy with our purchase if she knew what we suspected about him and Maeve.

"Since I've temporarily rescued you from the farm, how about I take you to lunch at the Brewery?"

I could feel my mouth break into a smile. "Sure."

The restaurant, a popular spot in Aiken, brewed its own beer and served up excellent burgers and fries. We sat beneath umbrellas on the wide sidewalk out front and watched the world go by on Laurens Street.

I was amused by the surreptitious looks Jase received from women at neighboring tables. Who could blame them?

But then, we returned to Ballymoor. It wasn't like I could leave the farm whenever I wanted. As lovely as it was and as much as I adored the horses, when the farm gate shut behind me, I felt locked in again.

At noon the next day, Lara, Jase, and I sat in the shade at the stone table, eating the steak and cheese sandwiches she'd brought in a paper sack.

"So, here's the deal," I said to Lara. "Jason knows how to crack a safe, especially one with a digital lock like Da's. He's willing to help us get the sapphire back."

"So," she said, "my help wasn't good enough? You know damn well I would have called in one of the O'Carroll boys."

That was exactly what I'd been afraid of. "Don't take this the wrong way, but some of your cousins tend to be a bit violent. If this thing goes sideways, I don't want to have assault lumped on top of robbery."

Lips tight, she said, "Whatever, Quinn. Suit yourself."

"Look," Jase said. "No one in Tinkers Town, save you two and Quinn's uncle, know what I look like or who I am."

"I thought you said you'd met Maeve," Lara shot back.

"Saw her. At a distance. Never met her, and she didn't see me." He raised his brows at Lara. She shrugged.

"So," he said, "I have a carpenter's uniform I used to wear for computer jobs in England. Since Maeve's getting that room redone for Quinn's brother–"

"Half-brother," I said quickly.

Jase rolled his eyes and continued. "I could enter the house in the workman's uniform and if anyone questioned me, I could talk my way out. You know, the old 'it's my first day on the job' excuse."

"That could work," Lara said. "I know the girls that do Maeve's hair and nails. Either of them could lift her key, slip it to me, and I'd have it copied and returned before she knew it was missing."

"You're a talented lady," Jase said.

"You have no idea," she said with a flirtatious smile I wasn't too crazy about.

"So," I said, "we need to find out when Maeve and Connor will be absent during the day."

"That's easy," Lara said. "Connor is out of town working with his McCarthy uncles painting houses in Alabama. As for Maeve, she gossips like a sieve with her hair and nail girls. They'll know her schedule."

I swatted at a gnat that was attempting to land in my eye. Jase grabbed the bug out of the air and put it out of my misery by rubbing it against his thigh.

"He's fast," Lara said.

Giving it right back to her, he said, "You have no idea."

I was surprised to see Lara blush. "So," I said, trying not to glare at her, "you'll let us know when you get the new house key copied, and when the house should be empty, right?"

She nodded.

For someone who had been my sworn enemy, she was really helping me out. Or was she? The way her eyes were all over Jase annoyed me more than I liked to admit.

For God's sake, Quinn, focus on getting out from under the law. Forget the rest.

33

Two days later, Lara got Maeve's new housekey copied and dropped it off. Then we waited.

While Lara was working on Maeve's schedule, I finally received a call from Sanders. I was walking from one of the paddocks on my way to the barn when I answered the chime from my phone.

"Quinn, sorry I've taken so long to get back to you," he said. "These federal cases are a bear, and the workload has been immense. The Travellers really screwed themselves this time."

Someone was lying, and my voice reflected my doubt and anger. "Your secretary said you were on vacation, not working on the racketeering and fraud charges."

"She was mistaken, Quinn. I was at the Columbia courthouse ironing out some of the details with the prosecutor. I've been trying to find some sort of deal for Tommy and Desmond O'Carroll. For some of the McCarthy boys, too. That's important to you, right?"

"Of course, it is," I said, knocking off a locust that had landed on my shoulder.

"So, you get that I was out of town and not on vacation, right?"

"If you say so." I didn't like that I'd gotten two different stories, but short of calling him a liar, what could I say? For now, I let it drop, and asked, "So how's that deal going for Tommy and his da?"

"Slowly, very slowly."

It seemed like everything Sanders did was way slower than necessary. But then I didn't have a law degree and knew little about that stuff.

In the grass behind me, my locust buddy began a loud buzzing. Maybe he was angry, too.

"So," I said, working to keep the irritation from my voice, "what about the fact that Connor stole the sapphire? What's up with that?"

"I spoke to Maeve and the conversation went well. I think we can work something out."

"But *what* are you working out, and *when* will it happen? And for that matter, what's up with my inheritance? Are you still liquidating, or what?"

"I know you're impatient, Quinn. And you have every right to be. It shouldn't take much longer. I'm going as fast as possible; you can trust me on that. Selling property and assets is a tricky business. You don't want me to rush to the point where you lose money, do you?"

I sighed. "I guess not."

"Good girl. Listen, I'm due in court. I'll be in touch." He disconnected abruptly, never explaining what he would work out with Maeve or when.

And how much was he billing Da's estate for his time? I felt like throwing my cell phone across the lawn and smashing it against the barn wall. Behind me, the locust's buzzing reached a crescendo.

The next day, Lara called, her voice tight with excitement. "Tell Jase it's happening tomorrow. Maeve's getting her hair cut and highlighted. She should be at the beauty shop for at least two hours. Her appointment's at one."

"Good," I said, watching Jase lead Irish Mist into a wash-stall. It was my turn to shampoo the horse, then scrub and comb out his white feathers, his mane and his tail. Cleaning and grooming a Vanner took almost as much time as Maeve would need for her highlighting job.

"Listen," Lara continued, "Connor's still in Alabama. I checked."

Her news lit a fuse of unease in my blood as I hurried toward Jase. Holding my phone up, to get his attention, I mouthed the word "tomorrow," and he nodded.

On my cell, Lara was still talking. "I still think I should sit watch with Jase outside the house instead of you."

"I know the house better than you do, Lara. He might need me."

"You think you still know the house after all the changes Maeve is making?"

She had a point, but I said, "I'm going with Jase. He wants me there." Was I really squabbling with her over Jase? Yeah, I was.

"Suit yourself, Quinn. But if you're going to Tinkers Town, you'll need a brown wig and dark glasses. That blond hair is like a Quinn billboard."

I spent the rest of the day keeping myself busy with chores, trying not to worry about the next day's agenda. Unfortunately, my mind would dart in that direction and I'd find myself holding a hose over a water bucket that was overflowing into what moments before had been a clean, dry stall.

Fear of Maeve, Connor, and the law had overtaken me in a way I wouldn't have believed possible a year earlier. Fear was a luxury I couldn't afford. If I was up against the likes of Maeve, I had to be as tough as nails in a coffin.

So much for good intentions. I had a rough night, dreaming about the narrow cell I'd shared with Tania, even smelling the stench from its filthy toilet. By morning, I was a wreck. I gave up on sleep early and took a hot shower, hoping to wash away the nightmare.

34

Early the next morning, Paddy called so we could nail down the plans for him and Mary to help us.

"Quinn, I'm thinking if I get my truck to the feed store's parking lot by eleven this morning, that'll be soon enough."

"It will," I said. "Jase and I won't get there before then. And you'll switch the tags before you leave?"

"You know I will, lass. And the sign for 'Roberts & Sons Construction' arrived yesterday."

"Great!" I said.

Paddy had paid for a rush job for the magnetic sign to be made matching the carpenter's uniform Jase had brought with him from England. Paddy didn't mind paying for it. The sign would be useful to him for a future scam on an unwary client.

Since most of the Travellers in Tinkers Town drove almost identical Dodge trucks, Paddy's wouldn't raise a red flag when Jase parked it outside Maeve's house.

"Will Mary follow you so she can drive you home?"

"Yes, lass."

Lara stopped by the barn about the time Paddy would be leaving his truck at the feed store.

When push came to shove, Lara was a true ally and believed the job was more important than who got to do what with Jase. Through the window of her Lexus, she handed me a shopping bag from Ross Dress for Less. This would lead anyone who might be watching to believe she'd brought me something I needed from the discount store.

Inside the bag was a thick, brown wig–the kind a Traveller woman might use. I'd wear it with my dark glasses as I sat watch for Jase after he entered Maeve's house.

"Wish me luck," I said to Lara before she left.

She gave me a perky salute. "May the road rise up to meet you." Then she was gone.

A little after noon, Jase and I left under the ruse of buying supplies at the feed store. As we drove into the store lot, I spotted Paddy's truck. After we parked, Jase smoothed the magnetic company sign onto the pickup's side. We got in, I cranked the engine and drove to Tinkers Town while Jase worked to pull his carpenter's uniform over the shorts and sleeveless tee he was wearing. When he finished squirming into his uniform, he stared at me a moment.

"You look wonky in that wig."

"Well, you look geeky in that uniform."

We exchanged a grin, and I kept on driving.

When I reached Tinkers Town, I drove in at a casual rate of speed—not too fast and not too slow—and stopped before Maeve's house. I hadn't been there since Da's funeral and had to catch my breath when a wave of anguish hit me.

Suddenly, I could hear the pride in his voice when he'd brag about me, saying things like, "But our Quinn is a silver-tongued devil and a clever thief." Maybe not the typical words of a proud father, but he'd loved me. He had truly loved me.

I took a deep breath, trying to control how badly the immense cost of losing him had just blindsided me. It could weaken me in an instant, and I couldn't afford to let that happen.

"Quinn, you look like someone nicked your last mate. You all right?"

"Sorry, I was thinking."

"Well don't, unless you're thinking in the present." He nodded toward Maeve's house. "This it?"

"Yep."

"Bit over the top, isn't it? Across the pond they'd call it chavtastic."

I had no idea what that meant, but it sounded derogatory and that worked fine for me.

We sat quietly for a few minutes with the tinted windows rolled down an inch, so we could listen to the sounds around the house. Someone was mowing a lawn a few houses down and, in the distance, I heard a car door slam.

Jase glanced up and down the street. "This whole place is a bit dodgy, yeah? What's with every house but your stepmother's having the blinds drawn?"

"We value our privacy, and more than that, lots of folks here pretend that their new house still isn't finished. Saves on property tax."

"Quinn, that's wonky. Where are they supposed to be living?"

"Look around," I said. See how most of the homes have a house trailer somewhere on the property? Some people live in those things for a couple of years after their house is finished."

"Your stepmother's blinds are open. So, she's a rebellious cow, yeah?"

"Pretty much. She's always done exactly what she wants. No living in a trailer for her."

"You people are weird."

"Tell me about it."

The smile on his mouth faded, and his eyes narrowed. "Let's get this done."

After a last scan of the street, he opened his door. Relaxed, yet still appearing businesslike, he strolled to the back of the truck, grabbed his tool box, and walked along the side of Maeve's house.

We'd made two copies of Lara's stolen key, so we both had a key to the house. I'd told Jase to use the kitchen door as it was partially hidden from the neighbors by our old trailer and a screen of shrubs and trees.

Moments later, Jase rang my cell. "I'm in. Everything clear out front?"

"Yep. If you're in the kitchen, go to the hall beyond and hang a left into the room with the dark green and red carpeting."

"Uh, you mean the room with the pink and black tile?"

Maeve must have already thrown Da's stuff out. Damn the woman.

"Wait," I said. "Is there a large framed photo of Maeve with a good looking, dark-haired man over the fireplace?"

"Yeah."

That's the room. The safe's behind the photo."

"Got it," he said a moment later. "We still clear out front?"

"Yes. But hurry."

"Call you back in a bit," he said, and disconnected.

I knew he'd brought his illegal gizmo that ran through a million digital combinations until it found the right one. I just hoped it was fast. My nerves were getting raw.

There was never much traffic in Tinkers Town. The streets didn't go through and outsiders were afraid to enter, so when I saw a car coming toward me, my heart rate jumped a notch.

When I saw it was only one of the Murphys, I let go a breath I hadn't realized I was holding. With my dark wig and clothes, I was almost invisible inside the truck's tinted windows. The car passed by and kept on going.

Hurriedly, I glanced at the side of the house, praying I'd see Jase coming toward me. No such luck.

Moments later, a black SUV rolled down the street and appeared to be slowing as it neared Paddy's truck. My pulse raced, and my breath stopped as I recognized it. The SUV belonged to Maeve's brother, Jimmy McCarthy.

The brother who was supposed to be in Alabama painting houses with Connor.

Adrenalin spurted into my veins as McCarthy rolled his black SUV into Maeve's drive. I grabbed my phone to call Jase, my hands shivering like November leaves.

Behind the tinted glass of the SUV I could see the shapes of four men. A rear door opened, and Connor got out with the swagger of a returning conqueror. He moved toward the back of the vehicle, no doubt to grab his gear.

"Yeah?" Jase said in my ear.

"Jaysus, Connor's here! He'll be inside in minutes. Get out!"

"Safe's not open yet."

"I don't care, just get out. He's got three men with him!"

"What door will he come in, Quinn?"

"I–I don't know. He's already got his duffel bag. Get out of there!" My words sputtered with fear.

Calmly, Jase asked me again. "What door, Quinn?"

I told myself to breathe. "He'll want to take his stuff up to his room. He'll use the front door."

"That's all the time I'll need." The line went dead.

"No!" I said, to the empty phone. I'd been pressing the thing so tightly to the side of my head, I was afraid I'd permanently crushed my ear. Gingerly, I rubbed it, while Connor gave a wave to the black SUV and headed for the front door.

He set his bag down, withdrew a key, and entered the house. Without a care in the world, he left the front door wide open. I could see him set his bag down at the base of the stairs and head down the hall toward the kitchen.

Shit! I had to do something.

McCarthy's SUV backed from the drive, J-turned and disappeared down a side street. I threw my door open and ran for the house.

35

I tore up the entry steps and into the house, where I was enveloped by a cloud of Maeve's spray-can incense. I halted just inside the front hall. My heart was pounding so loudly, I was surprised I could hear the ice rattling into a glass from the machine in the kitchen. Connor must be getting a cold drink after his journey.

My breath caught as I heard his footsteps leaving the kitchen. Was he coming my way? I ducked sideways into Maeve's sanctuary, remaining motionless as my ears strained to listen.

Go upstairs Connor, just go upstairs.

But he didn't, because the next thing I heard was his voice yelling from the back of the house.

"Who the fuck are you? What are you doing in here?"

"Oh, hullo. I'm the fellow hired to work on Mrs. O'Neill's computer, yeah?"

"You're full of it dude. She hire you to open her safe, too?"

This was going wrong real fast. I grabbed the resin statue of St. Jude and raced down the hall on tiptoes, somehow managing to be quiet. I entered Da's office behind Connor. He had grabbed a brass poker from the fireplace.

The metal was raised high as he advanced on Jase, who backed away. As he retreated, he slid a small object into his pocket. Connor swung the poker. Jase ducked, but caught a glancing blow high on the side of his arm. He grunted in pain, staggering backwards.

Connor was raising his arm for another blow when I cracked him on the back of his head with the patron saint of impossible situations. I'd never appreciated a saint more. Connor stumbled forward, sinking to the floor on his hands and knees.

Apparently too dazed to function, he remained that way long enough for Jase and me to bust out of the room. We raced down the hall, out the front door, and scrambled into the truck. I gunned the engine and got the hell out of Tinkers Town while Jase sat next to me, one hand pressing on his injured forearm.

We were both panting and didn't speak until we were out of North Augusta.

"Please," I finally said, "tell me you got the sapphire."

"I did."

Pumped up, successful partners-in-crime, we exchanged maniacal grins. Spotting a strip mall ahead, I pulled in and circled behind to the service entrances before pulling up by a garbage container. Seeing no one around, I scrambled from the truck, grabbed the screwdriver and Paddy's old tags from the box behind the cab. I had them switched in a jiffy.

I drove back around to the front and headed for the far end of the strip mall before I stopped the truck again.

"Okay," I said, "let's see it."

"See what?"

"You want your shoulder smacked again?"

Jase put his hands up in surrender. "Uncle, or whatever you Yanks say." He slid his fingers into a front pocket of his jeans and withdrew a small ring box.

I snatched it from him and flipped open the lid. A huge, sparkling, deep-blue sapphire nestled in white silk.

"Wow," I said. "It looks like it's on fire!"

"You never saw it before, did you?"

"No." I touched the stone, then pulled it from the box and slid the ring onto my finger. "Holy moly!"

"At least you can see why you went to jail."

"Somehow, that doesn't ease the pain," I said.

"No, I don't suppose it would, would it?"

The thought of prison quickly dampened my euphoria. "We should get back to Ballymoor." I cranked the truck's engine and rolled from the shopping mall.

Staring at the ring, Jase said, "What are you going to do with it, Quinn?"

"Turn it in. I've had enough of this stuff. I don't care how much it's worth on the black market, I'm calling my lawyer as soon as I get back. He'll know what to do."

When I'd parked Paddy's truck at the feed store, we changed to the farm truck. After that, we bought and loaded bags of grain. When that was done, Jase drove us back to Ballymoor, where Presto appeared to be waiting for us in the barn entrance with a man I'd never seen before.

As we slowed before stopping next to them, I realized the newcomer looked a bit like Presto. Same nice eyes and a similar cupid's bow on his mouth. But his lips were fuller than Presto's and he didn't have the same bulbous, high forehead.

"Is this the younger brother you told me about?" I asked Jase.

"Yeah, that's him, Delbert."

When we stopped by the two men, Presto's jaws were working on a wad of gum. He stared into the truck window as Jase rolled it down. "Where have you two been for so long?"

Jase smiled and patted his stomach. "Since we were in town, we stopped for some burgers and chips. That's okay, yeah?"

"Well, a man's got to eat, I guess," Presto said. "Just get that feed up before it sits too long in this hot sun."

"We're on it," Jase said.

Presto's brother never said a word. He and Presto moved to the side so Jase could roll the truck into the barn and up to the feed room door. When the DuPriest brothers weren't looking, I slid the ring box deep in my jeans pocket, then I helped Jase carry the bags of grain inside. After ripping them open, we dumped them into the rubber storage bins.

By his ability to move it, I knew Jase's arm wasn't broken. I was surprised how much knowing this comforted me. The sweet smell of molasses from the new feed hung in the air, and when I stepped back into the barn aisle, a dozen horse heads were thrust over stall doors. With dilated nostrils, a few snorts and shuffling hooves, the horses' "feed me" message was clear.

"Chill, guys. It's too early." They ignored my words and continued to stare at the feed room door with bright-eyed interest.

As soon as Presto and his brother finished watching and left, Jase and I hit the kitchen refrigerator for food. Stealing stuff builds up an appetite. I grabbed a yogurt and Jase put a cold slice of the previous night's pizza in the microwave. While waiting for it to heat, he wrapped ice in a towel and held it to his arm. It had swollen into a dark red. A nasty bruise was forming.

After scraping the last of the yogurt from its carton, I called Sanders and reached his secretary.

"I need to talk to Mr. Sanders. It's urgent."

"He's just leaving for court. Hold on." I heard a quick muffled conversation and then Sanders.

"Quinn, are you all right?"

"Better than all right. I've got the sapphire!"

"What?"

"I went to Tinkers Town this morning and found the sapphire."

"What did you do? Break into Maeve's safe?" He sounded angry and tense.

"Well, you never got around to getting it back after I told you Connor had it."

"Quinn, you just broke the law. If Maeve or Connor report you, you'll be back in jail."

"Nobody saw me. I'm not an idiot." It occurred to me that was debatable, but it was past time for action. I wanted my life back and it seemed like it would be years before Sanders got the estate liquidated and I got the cash to pay restitution.

On the line, Sanders was silent. Finally, I heard. "It's in your possession now?"

"Yes."

"I have to go to court, but I'll stop by afterwards and get the stone. We need to be able to say you turned it over to me. I just hope I can keep Connor out of trouble."

"Screw Conner! Why does everybody care about him?"

"It's just I promised Maeve that-" He cut his sentence short. I could hear him breathing.

"Promised her what?"

"I'm trying to do the best I can for your family, Quinn. You can trust me on that." His voice softened. "You've been through hell, and I had hoped to clear this business of the sapphire up without anyone else facing charges, and most importantly, without you ever seeing more jail time. Let me talk to some people. I might still be able to smooth this out."

"I hope so." I felt miserable and was suddenly reluctant to give him the ring. Where was the jubilation I'd expected to hear in his voice when he learned I had the sapphire? Apparently, I'd only made things worse.

"Quinn, I've got to go." He hung up, and I stared at the silent phone feeling both sad and frustrated.

36

Sanders parked outside the barn just after five that evening but left the motor running. The day had been hot, and as I greeted him at the barn entrance, his white cotton shirt was damp and as wrinkled as the lines surrounding his eyes.

For the first time, I got no waft of mint aftershave. Instead, I smelled the sweat on him. Mounting a defense against the Feds for his clients must be grinding him down. Not to mention keeping him from settling Da's estate.

When the voices of the guys in the kitchen reached us, Sanders took a step back from the barn door. "How about we sit in the Escalade for privacy?"

I nodded, followed him to the SUV, and climbed into the passenger seat. The AC was on, and the cold air felt good. I dug the ring box out of my jeans' pocket and flipped it open.

Sanders whistled. "What a rock!" He reached his hand across the seat and I experienced a renewed hesitance to relinquish the sapphire.

"Give it to me, Quinn. If I don't turn it in for you, this will only get worse."

Releasing the gem, I said, "Who are you going to turn it over to? Maybe I should come with you when you do."

"That's not how it's done," he said, zipping the ring box into his briefcase. "We have to be very careful now, because the Travellers' reputation just advanced beyond the level of white-collar crime."

"What do you mean?"

The smell of his sweat was stronger inside the Escalade. Nervous fingers plucked at the fabric of his rumpled trousers, and for a moment he seemed far away.

"Last week two men from Tinkers Town drove to Memphis and murdered a woman. Her husband had a large insurance policy on her. He hired them to assassinate her."

His words shocked me. "But we don't do that!" It was one thing to steal, but to murder?

"The killing was especially violent. The men bludgeoned and knifed her to death."

"Jaysus. Who was it?"

"This is where it gets worse. It was two of your step-cousins. Two of the McCarthy boys. Maeve's nephews."

I stared at him, trying to absorb what he was saying. My voice sounded weak to me, "So, now, in the eyes of the law, I'm tied to two murderers?"

He nodded. "Like I said, we have to be very careful."

This development would make the defense of Tommy and the others arrested on federal charges that much harder. No wonder Sanders looked like hell.

I touched his arm lightly. "This is a really rough time for you, isn't it?"

"You're a nice kid," he said. "One of the few I've met who thinks about someone other than themselves."

While I tried to think of a response, he continued.

"Look, Quinn. I'm going to stay on top of this. And to do that, I'd better get back to work."

I nodded and after climbing from the Escalade, I watched its taillights fade in the distance.

After chores were finished the next morning, Jase attempted to slip the new hackamore onto Irish Jewel's head. The horse repeatedly threw his head up to avoid the contraption, but Jase gently insisted that Jewel accept the bridle.

Stepping in close, I stroked the horse's neck, which seemed to calm him. "It's just a halter with reins," I said softly. "No iron in your mouth, I promise."

I giggled when Jase finally got the hackamore on. Jewel was comical as he worked his lips and tongue in search of an offending bit.

When he realized there wasn't one, he nodded his head up in down as if in approval.

"You're silly," I said, stroking him again.

Jase laced his hands together to make a knee cup. "Up you go, Quinn."

I placed my hands on Jewel's withers and my knee in Jase's hands. He tossed me onto Jewel's back like I weighed no more than a ping pong ball, then led us from the barn to a nearby paddock, where he turned us loose.

A gentle squeeze with my legs and heels got Jewel moving forward. The new bridle would apply pressure to the noseband, instead of a bit inside his mouth.

I pulled on my left rein. Jewel turned left. Jason gave me a thumbs up and before long, Jewel was walking in figure eights, halting, and backing up.

"Quick study, this one, yeah?"

I halted the horse and stroked his wither. "He's wonderful!"

"We'll do this for a few days and then put the saddle on him. You'll have him in hand in no time." Jase gave me a sidelong glance, "Presto will be pleased."

In unison, we said, "And when Presto's happy, everybody's happy."

We exchanged a foolish grin that was probably as much about the previous day's sapphire caper as it was about our Elvis-impersonator boss. I was beginning to feel like Jase had been my friend for a long time.

The day rolled on, and the next morning, I rode Jewel into one of the bigger fields behind the house. After a few minutes of walking, I urged him into a canter. It was like sitting on a rocking horse and I could feel my mouth curving in delight.

A noise caused my head to swivel toward the house. Sylvie and Presto were coming out from beneath the rear portico. Presto had on one of his leather vests that showed off his biceps. His eyes were in shadow beneath a western hat.

They joined Jase on the fence line where he'd been watching me and Jewel. The three of them were silent while I worked the horse, and when I was done, they applauded.

Beaming, Sylvie motioned me to the fence. "I have something for you, Quinn," she said. Her hands held what appeared to be a gift, since it was wrapped in silver paper and tied with a gold ribbon.

"Get off that horse and let me give this to you."

Jase held Jewel while I slid off the horse's back and walked to Sylvie.

I wished I could experience the contentment she wore on her face. She obviously didn't worry about much. Her pear shape or the large amount of her gum that showed when she smiled didn't concern her. I liked that about her and that she was in love with Presto and had the money to keep them both happy. She was a lucky lady.

She handed me the gift through the fence. "Open it, Quinn."

I did, untying the ribbon and tearing off the silver paper covering a twelve-inch-square box. I lifted the lid. Wrapped in gold paper was a finely made china statue of a blond-haired girl riding bareback on a golden horse. The dapples the artist had glazed onto the horse's coat were almost iridescent.

"Wow," I said. "This is beautiful. It's Irish Jewel!"

"And you, Quinn." Sylvie's eyes gleamed as she spoke.

"Where did you find it?"

Before she could answer, Presto said, "Now that there was made to order in Austria, missy. That's where it came from, right Sylvie?"

She nodded happily at Presto.

I was so touched by her gesture. "Sylvie, I can't tell you how much–"

But Presto grabbed the stage again. "Like Elvis always said, 'I figure all any kid needs is hope and the feeling they belong. If I can do or say anything that gives some kid that feeling, I believe I have contributed something to the world.'"[2]

Sylvie watched him adoringly as he recited his quote. I refrained from pointing out that the gift was from Sylvie and not Presto, while Jase covered his mouth to turn what would have been a laugh into a cough.

We both knew better than to negate a Presto performance. When I was sure he was finished, I slipped carefully through the fence with the box and gave Sylvie a one-armed hug. I thanked her, this time without interruption.

After the DuPriests returned to the house, I rode Jewel to the barn. Jason followed with the statue, safely tucked in its box. Sylvie's gift meant a lot to me. I would cherish it for a long time.

As if to taunt my happiness, a nasty memory burst into my conscience. Emma Buntings shocked expression, her voice crying out that she had planned to give me a silver spoon. I had repaid that kindness by stealing her family heirlooms.

Guilt tore at me, followed by a flood of relief that I hadn't betrayed the DuPriests. I didn't want to feel that kind of guilt again. Not ever.

That night, I lay awake thinking, my mind racing through a review of the past. Maeve's false affection toward Da. His love that was lost to me forever. Paddy and Mary, the only people I really trusted. Stealing the sapphire. My time in jail and a lawyer who seemed unable to settle Da's estate.

With a start, I realized I didn't think about Tommy anymore. I finally admitted that regardless of what happened, I would never marry him. I couldn't stand the idea of him as a lover. But there was more than that. He was not my friend. I barely knew him.

This realization brought me to the present. To Jase. Thinking about him and the horses eased my mind, and I fell asleep.

---

2.   https://www.inspiringquotes.us/quotes/7TGo_UwWbCDpl

37

The next morning, I returned from dumping the last load of dirty straw to find Presto on one knee, glaring at the spigot in the barn aisle. Water streamed from the spigot and pooled onto the aisle's rubber pavers.

When he saw me, Presto rose to his feet. "Get me that big wrench out of the tack room, would you?"

I nodded and trotted off to retrieve it. I found a hefty chrome wrench in the tool box inside the tack room supply cabinet, took it to Presto, and handed it over. He grabbed it and stared at the spigot, frowning in concentration.

"Well, let me see now. What I have to do here, I believe, is to open this whole thing up so I can get at that washer in there."

I muttered sounds of agreement, left him to his work, and got busy loading fresh hay into the horse's hay nets. We both finished about the same time, and seeing I was done, he handed me the wrench to put back.

By now my hands were dirty and I'd broken a fingernail. Presto, of course, had been wearing his thin leather gloves to keep his manicured hands pretty. He was lucky to be so spoiled by Sylvie.

After replacing the tool, I went to the kitchen and found Timmy and Carl at the table eating deli sandwiches Jase had brought in earlier. After rinsing my hands, I grabbed a ham and cheese sub, and washed it down with a diet soda.

I'd been around the guys long enough that I was almost able to ignore the ugly fanged snake and other sinister tattoos on Timmy's arms. By comparison the topless mermaid on Carl's neck was like a Hallmark card, except when he swallowed, and the mermaid's breasts jiggled. I could have done without that.

When we finished eating, Timmy went to his room, leaving me with Carl, who I'd always preferred. He was the nicer of the two.

"Was that," he asked, "our lord and master I saw fixing the water line?"

"Yep."

"And he knew what the bloody hell he was doing?"

"Seemed to," I said, picking at my broken nail. "But whatever he was doing he kept his hands nice and clean with those leather gloves of his."

Carl looked away from me, his thoughts appearing to have suddenly gone inward. Then with a grin, he said, "He's a prima donna, that one, yeah?"

"Pretty much."

Saying he had one more paddock to mow, Carl pushed away from the table and left.

I stepped outside the barn for a moment and stretched my arms over my head. In the distance, the trees had lost their lush look, the leaves drier, tighter. Mid-August had arrived, and with it, the season was changing. Even the music made by insects had returned to a different composition, one I hadn't heard for a year.

The fear and sorrow of the past months must have heightened my awareness of the world around me. As slow as the summer had been, time was rushing by, and a knot of resentment tightened my stomach. I had no power to rule the seasons of my life. That authority was in the hands of other people.

Trying to shrug it off, I went to my room and spent my break time reading a Dick Francis novel Sylvie had lent me. Because I'd had so little sleep the night before, I put the book down and drifted off.

The sudden, shriek of a siren awakened me. Half asleep, I rolled off my bed, stumbled to the window, and stared outside. An ambulance was pulling up to Ballymoor's front entrance. Presto was gesturing wildly to the ambulance driver from where he stood at the top of the steps.

Sylvie?

I careened down the stairs and ran from the barn, sprinting up the drive. I raced past an Aiken County Sheriff's car that was also parked in front of the house, the flash of its blue and red lights all but drowned by the bright afternoon sun.

Two EMTs rushed up the steps and into the house after Presto. Without thinking, I followed. Brief impressions of large rooms filled with lovely and expensive items brushed past me as I ran after them and into a room where I froze, momentarily unable to move.

Sylvie lay on a pale-blue flowered carpet, a huge pool of blood around her head. Her eyes stared at the ceiling. They seemed lifeless.

One of the EMTs was kneeling next to her. Was she still alive? God, I wanted her to be alive.

There was an unfamiliar scent in the air, like copper pennies. Though I didn't recognize the smell, it brought a visceral reaction that made me shudder.

The EMT shook his head, stood up, and backed away from Sylvie. A sheriff's deputy who'd been standing before wooden shelves of books stared at me. His face was expressionless and hard. "I want everybody out of this room, now.

Another deputy appeared and ushered a silent, ashen-faced Presto from the room. The deputy made sure I was right behind. I couldn't help but glance back at Sylvie, at the pool of blood her head seemed to float in. A book lay on the floor next to her.

In a daze, I realized I was in her library. All around me were books. Like the ones I'd been reading all summer, like the ones she'd given me.

With a gasp, I stifled a sob. Hot on its heels was a flame of anger. Had someone done this to her? Could such horrible damage be caused by a fall to a carpet on the library floor? I didn't think so.

Late that night, Jase, Timmy, Carl and I sat in our kitchen. Earlier, we'd been separated, then interviewed by a detective asking to know what we'd seen or heard. Probably the officer hadn't been happy to discover the four of us knew so little.

Normally we'd be in bed by now, but we were too disturbed by Sylvie's death to think about sleep.

We'd been in the barn all evening, watching the house through the stable door for a sign that something new was happening, that there might be information. But after the crime scene technicians and medical examiner left, there'd been no further police activity.

The only person we'd recognized was Presto's brother, Delbert. The few additional cars that rolled slowly up the drive appeared to be visitors for Presto and were people no one remembered seeing before.

Around me, the scent of coffee filled the kitchen from the latest pot Jase had made. I watched him refill our cups. Did he think a new injection of caffeine would help us solve the mystery of Sylvie's death?

For maybe the fourth time I asked, "Do you think she was murdered?"

Irritated, Carl said, "We don't know, Quinn."

"Besides, like I keep telling you," Timmy said, "everyone loved her. She never got on anyone's nerves like Presto does."

Jase glanced at me, "So when you were in that room, there was nothing on the floor besides the book. Nothing like a weapon?"

"You already asked me that. No. I didn't see anything else."

"Then we don't know anything, do we?"

"No," I said. "We don't." I took a sip from my second cup of coffee, my stomach burning in protest at the acidic liquid.

"Our Presto must be in a sorry state," Carl said.

Timmy's lip formed a sardonic curl. "I don't feel bad for him. He'll be getting all the money, won't he?"

This was something I'd thought about but not voiced because Presto had to be hurting. Sylvie had loved and taken care of him. As far as I could tell, he'd had unlimited access to her money, and this endless conjecturing was leading us nowhere.

In the closeness of the kitchen, the smell of male sweat and stale bodies was strong. Apparently, none of us had showered that evening, yet worrying about hygiene on the heels of Sylvie's death seemed absurd.

Finally, Jase rose from the table, his green eyes sweeping over me. "Want to take a walk, Quinn?"

I shrugged, and for once Timmy and Carl made no comment about us going out together.

It was dark outside, and the air was thick with the humming of insects. A cloud shifted across a quarter moon, leaving Jase's face in a deeper shadow.

"Quinn, nobody's saying it, but this doesn't look good for any of us."

"How do you mean?"

"Think about it. We're all ex-cons. There's a lot of money around this place, and Sylvie's dead, probably murdered. The coppers are going to look at us, Quinn. They're going to look at us hard."

His words brought dismay that wrapped my gut in a coil of nerves. "But none of us have a motive, right?"

"Not that anyone knows about. At least not yet."

"I don't want to talk about this anymore, Jase. It's making me sick."

I turned away from him, walked swiftly into the barn, and ran upstairs to my room. Once inside, I locked the door and remembered something Jase didn't know. Two of the McCarthy boys had just assassinated a woman for money, and even if they weren't blood relatives, I was still a part of their family.

Shaking my head, I sat on my bed alone as the fear of the unknown wormed its way ever deeper inside me.

38

SOMETIME AFTER TWO a.m., I fell asleep. Awake again at 5:30, I crawled from my bed. A hot shower and brisk tooth brushing later, I almost felt human.

Pausing at the barn door downstairs, I stared at the main house, vainly searching for answers. The only unfamiliar car parked up there belonged to Delbert. He must have stayed the night. It was nice of the guy to hang with his bereaved brother, and I was glad for Presto.

To the east, the long leaf pines stretched their needles to touch the first hint of sunrise. The air was humid, and I knew it would be another hot one.

In the barn kitchen, I started the coffee pot, dumped yogurt and granola into a bowl and forced down my breakfast. Since it was still hot, and we brought the horses inside each day, I ventured out to get them.

Taking a shortcut across the grass, the drops of dew that glistened in the dawning light quickly soaked the hems of my jeans. It was earlier than we usually brought them in, but I had to do something to quiet the noises in my head.

I got as far as the field gate when my cell phone rang. Who would call at 6:30 a.m.? When my gaze darted to the phone's screen, Sanders name stared back at me.

"Sandy?" I asked.

"Quinn, I just heard about Sylvie."

"I saw her, Sandy. It was horrible." I could hear the quaver in my voice. "She was lying there . . . with all this blood."

"Look, kid. Get a grip, okay?"

"I'm trying to." I breathed, attempting to steady myself before continuing. "Do you know what caused her death?"

"My contact in the sheriff's office says it's murder."

"*Murder?*" In my heart, I'd known it, but still, my stomach dropped, and my pulse ticked up until it pounded in my ears.

Sanders continued. "A friend in the solicitor's office just called me. She says they have the murder weapon, and don't ask because I don't know what it is. But whatever it is, they're checking for fingerprints."

"How long will it take?"

"I don't know. Could be tomorrow, could be a week."

"Sandy, I'm scared."

"Look, Quinn, hang tight. I'm going to find out everything I can about this. Will you be there all day?"

"Of course. Where else would I be?"

"Good, stay put and I'll come visit you later. We'll talk."

"Okay," I said, but I spoke to dead air. He was already gone.

I spent the rest of the morning going through my chores like an automaton, barely able to eat a bite of my sandwich Jase had brought in for lunch. Since my outburst the night before, he hadn't mentioned Sylvie's death, and now I was too panicked to tell him what I'd heard from Sanders.

As I struggled with my last mouthful of sandwich, Jase stared at me.

"You all right, Quinn? You look knackered."

"I'm fine," I said, my voice short to the point of nasty.

He raised his hands defensively. "Whatever you say."

When I didn't respond, he turned and left me in the kitchen.

During my afternoon break, I tried to nap but gave it up when my mind whirled like a blizzard, building cold banks of fear that smothered me. When I heard tires on the gravel drive, I ran downstairs to see Sanders pulling up outside.

Like before, he left his motor running with the air conditioning blasting. He motioned me inside his Escalade where we'd have privacy. The cold leather on the car seat creaked as I slid onto it. I was used to the summer heat and found the car uncomfortably chilly, especially with the Cadillac's fans blowing an arctic wind across my skin. Even his mint aftershave smelled icy.

I could feel my brows raise into question marks as I stared at him.

Like he'd done right before he'd told me Da was dead, he took a nervous breath before exhaling.

"Quinn, I have news, and it's not good."

His words caused my arms to wrap around my middle, as if to protect myself from whatever came next.

He did another breath thing and spoke. "Are you aware that Sylvie had taken out a million-dollar life insurance policy with you as the beneficiary?"

"What? That's crazy! Why would she do that?"

"That's not the question, Quinn. What matters is, did you *know* she'd done this?"

"No. That's ridiculous. Why would I think she'd do something like that?"

"Presto mentioned she gave you a gift, a statue and–"

"It was nice but would hardly make me think she'd do something like leave me in her will. I don't believe it!"

"Presto seems to think your personal history resonated with her. She may have been extremely wealthy, but apparently there were some problems in her childhood. Evidently, you reminded her of herself and, of course, she liked you."

Tears welled up in my eyes. Sanders was ready with his handkerchief and handed it over. I pressed it against each eye.

"Understand, Quinn, that since it's a million-dollar policy, that's motive for murder."

"What are you saying? I didn't kill her!

"I know that," he said soothingly. "But you're a Traveller and the law knows about the Travellers' penchant for life insurance policies."

Two Traveller men had just committed murder for hire in Memphis. Murder for profit by insurance. Like shards of ice, the knowledge shredded what little composure I had left, leaving me speechless from a new wave of fear.

"Like I said, Quinn, try to get a grip and listen to me. Did you touch anything when you were inside that house yesterday?"

"No, I don't think so."

"Had you been in the house before yesterday?"

"No!" Mentally, I replayed my entry into the house the day before and could not remember touching anything. "All the doors were open. There was no need to grab a door handle or anything else."

"Good. Then you should be fine."

By now it was so cold in the car, my teeth were almost chattering. But I suspected my physical reaction was more from fear than the cold. Then a scrap of thought formed.

"My prints will be on some of Sylvie's books. But a book couldn't have been the murder weapon, could it?"

"Not with the damage her head sustained." He put his hand on my shoulder and gave it a light, reassuring squeeze. "Look, kid, I gotta roll, but I'll call you as soon as I hear anything."

"Thanks," I said, and climbed from the SUV. Standing in the heat of the August sun, I still shivered as he drove away.

39

On the second day after Sylvie's death, the August air hung heavy and unmoving as I waited for Sanders' call. It never came.

I spent the day in a trance of apprehension. When I couldn't reach Sanders, I called Lara to see if she'd learned anything through the Travellers' grapevine. I'd been told the sheriff, with jurisdiction over Tinkers Town, took bribes from our people. If so, he could have information. But if he did, he hadn't told Lara.

Working kept me sane. I cleaned tack, scrubbed manes, tails and the feathered ankles of Presto's horses. I applied hoof polish that wasn't needed and brushed the horses until they were show ready. Except there was no show in August.

I worked on our kitchen, using spray bleach, cleaner, scrub brushes and sponges until every appliance shone, even the inside of the refrigerator.

I was on my knees finishing up the crisper at the bottom of the refrigerator, when Timmy came in. He stood close behind me, smothering me with his smell of gasoline, oil and grass cuttings.

Turning to glance up at him, I saw him frown as he stared inside the refrigerator.

"O'Neill, where's my sub sandwich?"

"You mean the science project you left in there?"

"Wasn't your place to throw it out, was it?"

I glared at him. "The lettuce was slime, and the meat smelled like dead fish. But if you want it, you can dig it out of the trash can."

"Listen, bitch–"

"Hey, you two. Stop it!" Jase had entered the kitchen. His hands were raised, the gesture placating.

"I paid good money for that sandwich," Timmy said, "and the bitch went and tossed it." He backed away from the refrigerator and kicked one of the kitchen chairs, knocking it over.

Jase stepped between us. "We're all gutted by Sylvie's death and nervous as cats with the coppers around, but we need to stick together, yeah?"

Timmy sighed, leaned over to pick up the chair and sagged into it. "This thing is such a cockup. All they need is a tad of luck and they'll find a way to pin this murder on me."

I started laughing. "You? What a joke!"

My laugh wasn't a happy one. In fact, it was uncontrollable, and my hands began shaking.

"Try this one for size, Timmy. Sylvie had a million-dollar life insurance policy, and I'm the beneficiary." My laugh grew louder, rising to near hysteria. "Still think they'll pin it on *you*?"

The way Timmy's mouth formed an O of astonishment, finished me. I dissolved into convulsions of laughter and collapsed into the chair next to his.

Sputtering with amusement, Timmy turned to Jase. "You got to admit, the joke's on her."

Jase's face hardened. "This isn't funny." He grabbed my shoulder and shook me hard. "Stop it, Quinn." His face had blanched, and the vein on his temple pulsed visibly. I'd frightened him.

I stopped laughing and got control of myself.

Jase let go of my shoulder. "When did you find this out?"

"Yesterday."

"And you didn't tell me?"

"Jase, I was stunned. I couldn't talk about it."

He nodded, pulled out a third chair and sat.

With a sigh, I attempted to speak calmly. "Travellers are known for using life insurance scams to make money. And two of my step-cousins just did a contract killing for a guy who wanted to collect on his wife's life insurance."

Timmy whistled. "Blimey, you might as well go to jail now."

Jase remained silent. Then, he stood, saying he'd be right back. He returned with a bottle of whiskey, put ice in three glasses, then passed the booze around.

I started to say I didn't drink but remembered how the whiskey Connor had given me at the Buntings house had steadied me. I took a big sip. It burned all the way down but didn't cause me to choke or sputter.

"Good girl," Jase said. "Now tell me. How good is this Sanders bloke?"

"My people like him, and he got me out of jail."

"But has he worked a murder trial?"

The word murder weighed like a slab of concrete. "No. I doubt it. He defends nonviolent crime. We don't commit violent—"

"But now, you do," Jase said, "and you need a sharp lawyer with an ace record for trying murder cases."

I dropped my head in my hands. A lawyer of that quality would use up much of my inheritance. That is, if I ever received it.

"Quinn," Jase said, "I need to talk to you alone."

We left Timmy in the kitchen, walked along the barn aisle, and stopped before the stall of the gray horse, Irish Mist. He pushed his head over the door, and I didn't resist the urge to run a hand down his long white blaze. He rewarded me with a feeling of comfort, and smiling, I turned to Jase.

His gaze on me was intense, startling. The veil that usually covered the depth of his eyes was missing. I felt like I could see his soul. But this was no time for romance. Would there ever be a right time?

Jase broke the spell, his eyes sliding away from me as he spoke. "Did Sanders mention other insurance policies?"

His words brought me back with a mental head slap. Why hadn't I thought to ask that question? Maybe I wasn't the only one who benefited from insurance when Sylvie died.

"No," I said. "He didn't."

"Then I have some work to do on the internet. It would throw a spanner in the works if Presto bought a policy on Sylvie. And someone else may have done it, too."

"Like who?"

"That," he said, "is what I aim to find out."

"Thank you, Jase." I reached out to touch his shoulder and he pulled me against him and held me a moment. It was a powerful feeling and something I hadn't realized how much I wanted. This scared me a little.

He released me and stepped away. "I'm going to get on my computer. You go find something else to scrub."

I nodded. For a moment we grinned like kids.

The third morning after Sylvie's death, Sanders' Escalade rolled into Ballymoor at seven a.m.

That he would come so early and without warning told me something was up. I set my empty wheelbarrow down and approached the SUV. Observing my dirty clothes, he got out of the car, not asking me to sit inside.

When I got close, I knew he was nervous. He was chewing his bottom lip and there was no smell of mint, like maybe he'd forgotten his aftershave.

"What is it?" I asked.

"I got a call this morning. Quinn, the fingerprints on the murder weapon are yours. And, unfortunately, yours are the only ones on it."

Somehow, I'd known this would happen and though I knew the answer, I asked anyway. "What's the weapon?"

"A wrench was used to kill Sylvie."

I closed my eyes and let my breath out. Opening them again, I said, "If it's the chrome wrench from the barn, Presto told me to get it and hand it to him the day she was killed."

"Did he handle it?"

An image of Presto in the library with the wrench surfaced, and I shuddered.

"Oh, yeah, he did. But he was wearing gloves."

"This could be cause for reasonable doubt. We could argue he set you up."

"Oh, I was framed all right!"

"Can anyone corroborate his involvement with this wrench that morning?"

I thought back, feeling a little thrill when I remembered. "Carl! I talked to Carl about it afterwards. He saw Presto using the wrench to fix the barn spigot. It was leaking that morning."

Sanders seemed to file this away before changing the subject. "Look, Quinn the deputies should be here soon."

Stupidly, I asked, "Why?"

His teeth gripped his bottom lip again. "To arrest you for the murder of Sylvie DuPriest."

40

Moments after Sanders delivered the news that left me stunned and broken, two sheriff's deputies arrived at Ballymoor. I'd been so afraid this would happen yet was shocked when it did.

When they came for me, every detail seemed oddly vivid. The close-cropped hair on their heads, their uniforms, their guns, it was all so familiar but different.

Tyler, the deputy with the bullet-shaped head who'd taken me in after the sapphire theft, was one of the two officers. The grimness on his face was new as was the extra caution they both used when they approached me. They thought I'd committed murder. I could smell it.

I seemed split in two, both myself and a mere bystander who watched and listened as they arrested me for Sylvie's murder. As the new deputy fastened my cuffs, Tyler read me my Miranda Rights. Sanders, who'd stayed with me, said reassuring words as they put me into the back of the car, locking me in their steel cage. As we rolled away from Ballymoor, I had no recollection of what Sanders had said to me.

I huddled in a tight ball behind Tyler, who'd taken the passenger seat. His cold cop eyes stared at me in the rear-view mirror, and I looked away, feeling almost catatonic. I'd been set up for a murder rap and was certain there was no way out.

But Jase will check for another insurance policy, Carl will corroborate about Presto and the wrench. And didn't Lara see Maeve with Presto?

These thoughts were not reassuring. Not when I felt so sure of forces lined up against me that I couldn't see and that Jase would never find, that Sanders or an "ace" lawyer would never beat.

I should have run the second Sanders told me about the wrench. I should have just gone.

I was so lost in these thoughts I might as well have been blind. I saw nothing until after the new deputy yelled, the brakes screamed, and the wire mesh separating the front from the back seats pushed into my face.

Something huge loomed outside the driver's window across from where I sat. Metal smashed steel, grinding and shrieking. I stared at the horizon trying to understand why it was turning vertical. Was the spray of blood a deputy's or mine? The driver's door jutted halfway across the front seat. I was crammed in a narrow space between the car's two rear doors. The twisted steel grill and front end of a truck seemed to have come inside the car.

This is a wreck, I told myself. But you're thinking, so you're alive. Blinking, I tried to sort it out. The car was on its side, but I was on top, still on the car's passenger side. We'd been hit from the left, so we must have rolled all the way over.

You need to get out, Quinn. See if you can get out.

A man was wrenching at my door with a metal tool. Muscles bulging, he struggled with a crowbar. He ripped my door open.

He was big, with a beard and long mustache. Prison tats all over his neck and arms. The driver of the truck that hit us? When he pulled me from the car, I smelled gasoline.

"The deputies!" I cried. My gaze darted back to the deputies inside. The impossible way the driver's neck was turned, his head bloodied, he had to be dead. The one on my side, though bloody, was starting to move. It was Tyler.

The hard eyes of the tattoo guy narrowed. "Fuck 'em."

"No! The car could blow. You have to get him out!" I begged, pointing at Tyler. "He's alive."

"Ah, fuck it." The guy pried open Tyler's door with his crowbar. He had no time to be careful of the deputy's injuries but got him out and dragged him to a safe distance.

I followed, staring at where he lay on the pavement, his eyes locked onto mine. He was too weak to make a sound, but I read his lips as he tried to say, "Thank you."

Shaky, and hurting, I backed away. People were rushing toward us. I was bleeding where the wrecked door had ripped my jeans and cut into my thigh. My face dripped blood from where it hit the wire mesh, but after a glance at the crushed figure in the car, and the resulting wave of nausea, I figured I was lucky.

"Just my goddamned luck to hit cops," the truck driver said. He appeared to be unhurt. He glanced at my hands.

"You're cuffed. What they get you for, DUI?"

"Murder."

He grimaced, then half walked, half dragged me to the rear of his utility truck that somehow, had remained undamaged. Opening a side panel, he threw the crowbar inside, pulled out a pair of bolt cutters. He cut and separated the link between my cuffs.

"Here," he said. "You'll need this."

He pulled some cash from a pocket and thrust it at me. I was wearing a pullover with kangaroo pockets. When I didn't react, he shoved the cash into one of my pockets.

"Put your hands in there so no one sees those cuffs. Can you walk?"

"Yeah."

"Then get the hell out of here."

"What's your name," I asked.

"None of your fucking business."

We were done. One deputy was dead, and Tyler was on his knees crawling away from the gas that leaked onto the pavement. The few people who'd come to the scene of the wreck were evolving into a crowd.

A sudden whup sound was followed by a horrendous explosion. Fames roiled skyward, people screamed, and the heat that rolled toward me was intense. The last thing I saw before I turned and ran was two people helping Tyler get even farther away from the incinerating vehicle.

As fast as I could, I put six blocks between me and the wreck, wondering if I'd be running for the rest of my life.

A while later, I walked into a gas station convenience store, into the bathroom, and rinsed the blood from my face. I was grateful the sheriff's steel mesh had only left shallow scrapes that wouldn't need stitches. Where the metal had ripped my jeans, there wasn't much blood, but I could tell there'd be a lot of swelling and bruising. Still, I was damn lucky.

It made more sense to get what I needed right then. Once the cops started searching for me, I'd have to disappear.

I counted the money, relieved to see the truck driver had given me almost fifty dollars. Outside the bathroom, I grabbed one of those little shopping baskets. I snatched up bandages that came with antiseptic ointment already on them, cheese and peanut butter crackers, two bananas, a premade sandwich, and a bottle of water. I picked out a cheap burner phone. Though it had few features, it had lots of minutes.

As I walked my stuff to the cash register, I prayed. If the dark-skinned woman behind the counter saw my cuffs and called the cops, it would be game over. I set the basket down, hoping she wouldn't notice the metal around my wrist. When she turned to talk to the clerk next to her, I slapped my money on the counter and slid both hands into my pockets.

Eventually, she turned to look at me. "You can take that stuff out yourself, you know."

"Uh, I had a bad fall and I'm having trouble moving."

"Oh, baby girl, you banged up that pretty face, too. I'll take those out for you."

She did and after she totaled my supplies, she counted the money, made change, and left the cash on the counter.

"Sorry to be a pain, but could you put the money in the bag with the other stuff?"

"Sure, hon."

When she finished, I whipped out a cuffed hand and grabbed the bag and started to leave.

"Hey," she said, "what's that on your hand? Is that a handcuff?"

"Uh, yeah. My boyfriend likes kinky sex."

Turning, I sped from the store. I circled around to the back and worked my way through parking lots and down alleys as fast as I could until I found the Aiken Public Library. Once inside, I did my best to make like a ghost in the stacks.

In a deserted corner, I used my new burner.

"Lara," I whispered, when she answered. "I need your help." Quickly, I explained my predicament.

"I'll come for you. But you can't come to Tinkers Town. They'll be all over this place looking for you."

"I know that." I thought a moment and took the plunge. "Call Jase. He can probably help. Will you do that?"

"You trust him? He's not one of us."

"In a way, he is. And yeah, I trust him."

"Okay," Lara said. "Give me half an hour."

We ended the call, and I was surprised to realize that I did trust Jase. I just hoped I wasn't wrong.

41

I left the stacks a few minutes later and stood in the foyer of the Aiken Public Library. When I wasn't glancing anxiously through the glass, hoping to see Lara's car outside, I pretended to study the colorful flyers that were pinned to a large corkboard.

Nervous as a cat with a firecracker tied to its tail, I flinched whenever a car rolled in, or a stranger walked up the steps to the library. Who's to say they weren't unmarked police cars or plain clothes cops?

Though the sweat from running was drying, I could smell the stress rolling off my skin and dirty clothes. People coming and going looked so normal, while my world had spun beyond the universe. Amazing no one seemed to notice me when I was certain a blinking, neon sign shouting, "Criminal!" hung over my head.

I kept my cut, bruised face turned away as best I could. With my cuffed wrists deep in the kangaroo pockets of my pullover and my bag of supplies looped over one forearm, I tried to look inconspicuous.

Good luck with that, Quinn.

When the Lexus finally pulled up near the base of the steps, I steeled myself not to dash down the steep staircase and leap into Lara's car. Closing the distance between us, I was glad to be reminded how beautifully dark and tinted her windows were. Once I was safely ensconced in the passenger's seat, and no whistles or sirens exploded, I breathed a sigh of relief.

I'd never been so glad to see the heavy makeup and super bleached blond hair of this girl I'd once hated. She'd stood by me since the day she'd knocked down Betty Lou Branson in the detention center. She was silent as she focused on driving away from the library quickly and without attracting attention.

"Hey," a voice said behind me, causing me to almost jump out the window. "You got beat up pretty good, yeah?"

It was Jase. I hadn't seen him when I'd dived into the car. The familiar sight of his blond hair and intelligent green eyes was wonderfully comforting.

"You came. I wasn't sure you would."

"You know better than that. Our kind stick together, yeah?"

I nodded, afraid if I tried to say more, I'd start crying.

By now, Lara was on a quiet street in the historic district, not far from Ballymoor.

"The wreck," she said, "and your escape were all over our police scanner. When I was like, a half mile out of Tinkers Town, squad cars were flying toward it. I was lucky I left when I did."

"No one followed you?" I asked.

"No," she said, turning her dark eyes my way. "So, where to?"

"Listen," Jase said. "I've got a panel I put in the back of my closet. There's a little space behind it where you can hide."

"Good," Lara said. "But she can't stay there forever. Have you got a plan?"

"Yeah." He leaned forward and put his hands on the back of my seat. "Quinn, you remember how I told you I used to be big in the British show world, and how that guy over there introduced me to Sylvie?"

"Sure." That was about the only word I could muster. The arrest, the wreck, and running were catching up with me fast. I didn't want to think, just wanted to turn it all off. It was all I could do not to tune them out.

"See, Mark's rich," Jase continued. "Has a home here and one in Saratoga Springs. When I first came over, he had me house sit for him here while he was up north. I still have the key, and guess where he is now?"

"Saratoga, right?" Lara asked.

"Exactly."

"Sure you're not a Traveller?" she asked.

"I could be, yeah?"

"Jase," she said, "why can't we go to this guy Mark's house now?"

"Is there a brain in your head? We gotta wait until dark, don't we?"

I left them to hatch their plot and drifted into an almost semi-conscious state until we pulled into Ballymoor.

When I heard the gravel drive beneath the car's wheels, my eyes snapped open, and fear washed over me. Where was everyone? What was to keep them from seeing me?

"Jaysus," I said, panic sharpening my voice, "Lara, your being here is a dead giveaway!"

My eyes scanned the area outside her car, and I was relieved to see Timmy and Carl were a distance away from us. Even better, they were using noisy gas-powered equipment to trim hedges and a fence line.

"Don't worry so much, Quinn. Lara's going to drive you into the barn, and those two wankers still think you're in jail. So, no one will see you, right?"

Jase's words weren't that reassuring. "What about Presto?"

"He's out with Delbert. They went to see Presto's lawyer about Sylvie's estate. He said he'd be a while. So, it's fine, yeah?"

Lara was about to ease her Lexus into the barn, when a sheriff's car rolled through Ballymoor's entrance gate and headed toward us.

Lara sped into the barn, stopping outside the door to Jase's room. Jase and I sprang from the car, dashed through his little foyer, and into his room. He whipped open the door to his closet, pulled his hanging clothes aside and grabbed a clothes hook nailed into the back wall. A couple of shirts hung from the hook, and when he pulled on it, the rear wall slid open enough for me to slip through.

Jase shut me in, leaving me in total darkness. I heard him scrambling to close doors and get out of his room before the deputy arrived. I sank against the back wall, sliding down into a sitting position, afraid if I so much as breathed, I'd be discovered.

It was totally silent for a while, then I heard what sounded like the door to Jase's room opening, and voices. I recognized Timmy's voice, sounding tough.

"We told you. She ain't here, is she? What gave you the bloody right to mess up my room like that?"

I could almost see the ugly tattoos on his skin expanding and contracting with the anger in his words.

"Take it easy, Timmy, they've got a warrant." Jase's voice.

"You people have rap sheets a mile long," a strange male voice said. "You might want to think twice before you obstruct this investigation."

This last voice, which had to be one of the deputies, grew louder. They were entering Jase's room. In moments, only the thin panel would stand between me and prison. My heart pounded so loud in my ears, I was sure the racket would give me away.

Hearing the closet door open, and the sound of the hangers sliding on the rod, I shrank against the back wall of my tiny hideout. I almost cried out when a couple of thumps sounded on the panel, but the wood held. After I heard them move the bed to make sure I wasn't hiding underneath, the voices and footsteps receded.

I wanted to shriek with relief, but instead, I barely dared to breathe. Eventually, I began to relax, and a while later, when Jase brought me a sandwich and a bottle of water, I was surprised to find I was hungry. Timmy and Carl, he said, had already been in for lunch and were back out in the side field.

After I finished eating, Jase stood in the entrance to the barn to make sure no one was approaching. I darted across the aisle, peed in the nearest empty stall, then fled back to my hide out.

"We leave tonight," Jase said through the closed, thin panel. "We can't drive in, because the neighbors might notice a car. We'll go on horseback. No engine noise, no lights, yeah?"

"Okay," I whispered.

At midnight the stable and grounds were dark as Jase and I carried two lead shanks, one saddle and one bridle to the front paddock. Overhead the stars were out, and a waxing moon was close to full.

Moments later, we had the older foundation mare, Bally Girl, saddled and bridled for me. After clipping a shank to each side ring on Irish Jewel's halter to use as reins, Jase sprang aboard the horse bareback.

"Why not tack him up?" I whispered.

"You're not thinking, are you? What if I got caught leading him back with a saddle and bridle but no rider? Anyone would know you were involved. When I come back, I'll be on Bally Girl leading the youngster. Be easy to say he got loose and ran off, yeah?"

Of course, he was right.

Pointing at the path that went along the side of the main house, Jase spoke in a whisper. "There's a gate in the fence line in the rear field. It's closer to Hitchcock Woods than the main entrance."

I nodded, and silently, we rode the path that passed by the side of the main house on its way to the back field. The blue light of a television glowed from one of the windows, and as we passed by, I glanced inside. The room appeared to be a den, furnished with a couch and deep armchairs upholstered in dark leather.

Presto and Delbert sat on the couch drinking glasses of amber liquid. Presto was smiling, and once again, I was glad for him that his brother was there to support him.

After passing through the gate of the back pasture, we rode without speaking along the deserted dirt roads of the historic district. When we reached the Whiskey Road crossing that led into Hitchcock Woods, a breeze came up, bringing goosebumps to my arms.

Jase didn't press the switch to bring up the walk sign. Instead, we waited back in the shadows until there was no sound of an approaching vehicle, only the rustling as the wind stirred the magnolia trees beside us.

We crossed the road quickly and headed for the park. In an instant, we were swallowed by the vast pine forest.

42

I hadn't been in those woods since the day I'd tried to steal the sapphire. The things that had happened since reeled through my head like a bad movie.

"What is it?" Jase whispered.

"Nothing."

"It's not nothing, is it? You just whimpered like a lost puppy."

"It's nothing. Forget it."

In the dim light of the moon, he shrugged and grew silent.

Overhead, what sounded like the hoot of a great horned owl echoed through the forest. I found it comforting. If the owl felt safe enough to act normally, maybe I'd be safe in his woods too.

Before us, the horse path was wide enough for the moonlight to filter through the pines and light our way. But on either side, the tall oaks and pines crowded together, the undergrowth thickened, and the breeze stirred dark, tangled shadows, causing the hair to rise on the back of my neck.

A sudden loud blowing sound and flashes of white made me stifle a scream. The old mare I rode lifted her head in alarm, but Irish Jewel shied sideways so hard Jase was almost unseated.

"It's just deer," he said once he regained control of Jewel. "A little herd bedded down for the night. We scared them more than they scared us, yeah?"

"That's debatable."

For about a half-hour, we followed a sandy white trail that stretched through the woods. Off to one side, I occasionally spotted the glint of reflected moonlight.

"That looks like water over there," I said.

"It is. This trail follows Sand River. Though I'd say it's more of a creek."

Silently, we continued riding through the woods like ghosts, listening to the sounds of the night forest. We reined in when a skunk stood brazenly in the trail, blocking our path. His white stripes glowed in a shaft of moonlight seeping through the tangle of pine needles.

Skirting him forced us off trail. As I followed Jase, a maze of saplings and brambles tore at my clothes and skin. Instinctively, I dropped my head onto Bally Girl's neck and buried my damaged face in the protection of her thick mane. When I saw her nose was all but glued to Irish Jewel's hind end, I closed my eyes and held on until we cleared the undergrowth.

A while later, we came to a fork where Jase chose a path that headed uphill. Maybe fifteen minutes later, we cleared the woods and reached a post and rail fence enclosing a small pasture. Beyond it was a large, handsome stable with a cupola. Overhead, stars stenciled the sky, and the barn's pale metal roof gleamed in the ambient light.

We rode along the fence rail until we reached a corner and could ride toward the barn.

"This place belongs to your friend, Mark?" I asked in a whisper.

He nodded. "He's got an apartment built into one end of the barn. Lives there in the winter."

"Any horses here now?" I asked, worrying there might be a caretaker to contend with.

"Nope. They're all up north with Mark. Got the whole place to yourself. Lawn service comes in once a week, but that's it."

In the barn, the horses' shod hooves clip-clopped on pavement as we led them into empty stalls. I followed Jase to a heavy door at one end of the barn. He produced a key, opened the door, and we stepped into a mud room that was cooler and less humid.

An alarm system beeped, and he punched a code into the flashing panel by the door. He hit a light switch, revealing a deep sink, racks for boots, and hooks for coats. Above a brass shelf lined with castile soap, boot polish, and Neatsfoot oil, I was surprised to see a fine-looking oil painting of a show horse clearing a high fence. It had an elegant gilt frame and the matting was professionally done. That it hung in a mud room told me the guy had money.

"Don't worry about the August heat. Mark keeps the air on all summer for his paintings and art work."

Passing through the next door, we stepped into Mark's kitchen. It was small but cleverly built. Quiet, good-quality appliances were laid out to make efficient use of space. Maeve would have hated it.

Like the kitchen, the apartment was small, but cozy, with plenty of hidden closet space, and high-dollar leather furniture. The walls were lined with original paintings of show horses, hunt scenes from the woods we'd just ridden through, and a charming seasonal painting of downtown Aiken lit and decorated for Christmas. I was ready to move in. Permanently.

The one-story apartment had high ceilings that made the floor space seem larger. Two bedrooms, and two and a half baths later, Jase followed me into the smaller bedroom where a window gave a view of the pasture. I sat on the room's comfortable king bed and sighed.

For a moment I allowed myself to imagine beating the murder rap, claiming my inheritance, and living in a place like this with horses of my own.

"Quinn, where are you off to?" Jase asked.

"I was just thinking."

"Sometimes, it's better not to, yeah?"

I shrugged a reply.

"I've got to get the horses back to Ballymoor."

"Sure," I said, suddenly dreading the thought of being alone.

"Don't look like that, Quinn. You should be grand here, yeah?"

He walked to where I sat on the bed. I rose but restrained myself from reaching out to him.

"There are neighbors on both sides, close enough to hear if you make too much noise, but not close enough to see your lights. There's food in the freezer and I'll sneak back tomorrow with supplies." His eyes searched my face. "It's not like I'm abandoning you, right?"

"No."

He put his arms around me and despite my best intentions, I clung to him. A moment later, he pushed me away.

"You'd better stop, Quinn, or I won't be able to leave." His face was flushed, and apparently, I'd instigated something behind his pants zipper.

He took a few steps back and thrust a piece of paper at me. "I wrote down the alarm code for you." Without another word, he turned and left.

I made sure the doors and windows were locked, turned the alarm on, and realized I was starving. An inspection of the freezer produced a frozen lasagna dinner, which I shoved into the microwave above the range.

While dinner heated, I investigated the apartment again, found fresh towels and took a fast shower. I spotted hydrogen peroxide and ibuprofen in my bathroom cabinet. After swallowing two of the latter, I disinfected my face and the cut on my leg. I slapped my convenience store bandages on everything and returned to the kitchen.

After scarfing down most of the lasagna, it was almost three a.m. Exhausted, I crawled into bed, and fell asleep.

Later that night, I sat up, wide awake, listening.

There it was again. A wild sound. Moving in the woods, beyond the pasture. The sound was primitive, a combination of shrieks and savage howls. No dog made noises like that, and it frightened me on a visceral level.

Leaving the bed, I hurried to the window and saw nothing. Clouds had moved in since my arrival, and outside my window was a black hole.

The barbaric noise continued, racing through the woods, moving away. As I listened, I heard a yipping sound bringing up the rear.

Pups, I thought, and relaxed slightly. It must be a pack of coyotes. We didn't have anything like that in Tinkers Town. The area was too developed. But I'd heard they ran wild in the woods around Aiken.

Feeling sorry for the coyotes' prey, I climbed back into bed and eventually dozed off. But the hungry animals had disturbed me, and my sleep was restless, with dreams of wrecked cars, horrible fire, and Deputy Tyler staring up at me from the road.

The intense image of his eyes startled me awake. I may have saved his life, but as soon as he was able, Tyler would hunt me down.

43

In the morning, I awakened to a leaden sky. Rivulets of rain slid down the glass outside my bedroom windows.

A trip to the kitchen uncovered a single-serving coffee maker and little sealed containers of coffee. I made a cup and after putting a teaspoon of sugar in, I shrugged and drank it without milk.

Using my burner, I called Paddy.

"Quinn, darlin' are ya all right?"

"I am."

"Jaysus, girl, that car wreck put the heart crossways in me! Mary and I want to see you, but we can't go two feet without stumbling over a garda hiding in the bushes."

This last image made me grin for the first time in what seemed like ages.

"The garda know I helped you in prison," he said, "opening your comissary account, hiring Sanders."

"Paddy, you and Mary were the only ones who helped me, and I will always thank you for that. But I'm safely below the radar now, and just wanted you to know I'm okay."

"I'm relieved to hear it."

"Paddy, have you talked to Sanders? Has he turned in the sapphire? Is he working on a defense for me? Has he got the name of a lawyer familiar with defending murder cases?"

"I have a call into him. You were only arrested yesterday. Probably your escape put a wrench in things. I'm sure he'll get back to me soon."

Would he? I had doubts about Sanders I couldn't logically explain, so I kept them to myself.

"I know you'll work on him, Paddy, and I bless you for that. Listen, I should go."

"Quinn, wait. Mary saw the damnedest thing two days ago. Maeve was with DuPriest, in Augusta."

"What? Lara saw them together a few weeks back, but I thought it might be happenstance."

Mary says DuPriest handed over an envelope, and when Maeve opened it, it appeared to be a check. Mary says the satisfied look on Maeve's face suggested it was for a large amount. What do you suppose that's about?"

"Nothing that will help me."

Paddy made a scoffing noise. "And now DuPriest's wife just 'happens' to be dead? I wouldn't put anything past that bitch Maeve."

I struggled to make sense of it. "You think she's screwing DuPriest? Maybe has something to do with Sylvie's death?"

"Our Maeve is a crafty one. DuPriest's wealthy, and Maeve would want the money, wouldn't she? We'd better find out what's up with her. For all we know, they murdered DuPriest's wife and set you up."

"Somebody set me up. Paddy, I should go. People can listen in, maybe track my location through your phone or something."

"You might be right. Call me when it's safe, darlin'. I'll see what I can find out and track down Sanders for you."

I spent the rest of the morning feeling powerless. I wandered through the apartment, staring nervously out the windows, thinking about my conversation with Paddy, wondering what the hell the deal was with Presto and Maeve. The image of the two of them together was not something pleasant to envision.

Early that afternoon, I was startled by the sound of a vehicle slowly approaching the apartment on the gravel drive outside.

Hurrying to the nearest window, I saw a strange black truck. My sudden panic eased when I recognized the "Roberts & Sons Construction" sign on the side of the truck, the one Jase had used when we'd stolen back the sapphire from Connor. I relaxed even more when I saw Jase behind the wheel in his carpenter's uniform.

"You scared the hell out of me," I said, when I let him in.

"I couldn't exactly drive the Ballymoor farm truck in here, could I? We don't need the neighbors or a stray copper putting the pieces together, do we?"

He was right, of course. It occurred to me a crafty criminal was a marvelous thing.

At the moment, my favorite criminal was carrying a grocery bag and a sack of hot Chinese food from one of Aiken's restaurants. I'd eaten nothing but the remnants of the previous night's lasagna, and the fresh scent of garlic chicken, vegetables, and duck sauce smelled wonderful.

While I scrounged up plates and silverware, he put milk, ham, and eggs into the fridge, before setting a loaf of bread on the counter. I dished the hot spicy food onto the plates and dug in.

While I scarfed down orange chicken and vegetables, he went back to the truck and brought in a bag of my clothes. Another trip later, he'd, retrieved his computer, and a few mysterious components.

"Isn't that your super hacker stuff? Is it safe to bring it here?" I asked.

"Better here than hidden in my closet at Ballymoor, yeah?"

"I guess."

He held up a piece of paper. "Don't lose this, you'll never get any-where without it."

Staring at the paper, I saw he'd written out step by step instruc-tions of how to hack into the court's documents, the sheriff's depart-ment, and several other government agencies I knew nothing about.

"But this is illegal," I said.

"Are you daft? You're wanted for murder and you're worried hacking is illegal?"

We stared at each other, then burst out laughing. Overcome with the absurdity of my comment, Jase collapsed in the chair near his food, and soon, our hilarity reached the table pounding stage.

"Oh, I needed that," I finally stammered, wiping a tear from my eye." Damn, this man could make me happy.

Jase glanced at the kitchen clock and plowed into his meal. "I have to finish this," he said between mouthfuls. "Get back before I'm missed. I'll set the computer up in the study, give you a brief lesson and then I have to go, yeah?"

"I understand." But I wished he could stay.

Reading me easily, he said, "Lose the glum look. You've got important stuff to do, like searching to see if Presto has a life insurance policy on Sylvie, yeah?"

It took a moment for his meaning sink in. "Jaysus, I'd forgotten all about that."

"It's not like you haven't had plenty of reason to," Jase said. "Now, look. If you leave here, I'll kill you. But I'm going to give you some cash just in case."

I took the money and counted almost a hundred dollars.

"Thanks. I'll look for that policy this evening," I said, thanking my lucky stars this clever man seemed determined to watch my back.

Late that afternoon, I sat in Mark's office behind his carved wooden desk, enjoying the soft, clarifying glow of the room's recessed lighting. It was still raining and gloomy outside and I switched on a desk lamp designed from a bronze horse statue.

It was finely made, and though a warm gleam reflected off its polished surface, it was a sad reminder of the lovely china statue Sylvie had given me.

Pushing her tragic death from my mind, I forced myself to study the instructions Jase had left me for his computer and add-on components. Thanks to Da, the crook in me was thrilled to know I could hack into various government agencies. My mother's genes seemed more concerned with finding answers.

I pressed the keyboard, and the machine lit up. An hour or so later, I knew there was no life insurance policy on Sylvie payable to

Presto DuPriest or anyone else but me. Damning evidence for the prosecution.

As disappointed as I'd been to learn this, I was still very curious about an anomaly that had popped up when I searched for a policy payable to Delbert. I could find no record of a Delbert DuPriest that matched the man I'd seen with Presto. There were a number of Delbert DuPriests but their driver's license photos and locations were wrong. I'd even been able to check Department of Defense records and found no trace of Presto's Delbert.

So, who the hell was this guy?

Though Jase had showed me how, I couldn't open bank records to discover if any peculiar payments or deposits had been made by Presto, Maeve, Connor, or Sylvie before her death. I was especially curious about the check Presto had given Maeve. And I wanted to check Sanders. I had an uneasy feeling I couldn't be too careful or thorough with anyone.

Jase had said he'd return the following evening and I'd have to wait until then to dig into the bank records. Calling him on his cell to ask was way too dangerous.

Feeling stonewalled and anxious, I walked to Mark's living room and considered his bar. Spotting an open bottle of something called Bailey's Irish Cream, I twisted off the cap and sniffed. *Irresistible.*

I poured some into a wine glass. As the warmth of the cream whisky hit me, so did the realization I could use Jason's equipment to search for my mother! My fingers trembled with excitement as I began a new hunt for Jennifer Smith or Jennifer O'Neill. I easily found the things I already knew; that she'd attended the Catholic school, Stone Ridge, in Maryland, obtained her undergraduate and master's degree from Cornell, and nailed her doctorate in anthropology at Yale.

There were only two new discoveries. Papers she'd written had been published in several anthropology journals, and I was able to read two of her published works. I was fascinated by her use of language and how she framed her ideas and formed her opinions. It was startlingly familiar.

I also learned that when she'd graduated from Cornell and Yale she'd done so with honors. No wonder some of the Travellers in Tinkers Town had been threatened by her. She came from old and honest money and had enjoyed a privileged lifestyle. Until she married Da.

I'd already known her parents were deceased and that she'd been an only child. But even with Jase's computer and software, from the time of her marriage forward, I found no record of my mother. Either she'd changed her identity, or she was dead. And if she had died, her death certificate was filed under an alias.

Feeling helpless and disappointed, I gave up the search and stared out the window beyond the desk. Though the sun was still bright, the shadows were lengthening as the afternoon moved toward evening.

A hard knot of anger formed in my stomach. Why had I wasted time searching for my mother instead of fixing the mess I was in? I was a Traveller, for God's sake. I had my own bag of tricks. Damn it! Instead of sitting in a stranger's home waiting for someone to rescue me, I should save myself.

But I thought of Jase and hesitated. He was risking a lot for me. The last thing I wanted to do was get him in trouble. But realizing I was hesitating yet again, only increased my annoyance. I hoped he'd understand.

What would Da have done in my situation? I felt my lips curve up realizing Da would have laughed and blithely charged ahead, as if obstacles were only imaginary. If I stayed in this house doing nothing, I would surely go mad. I would clear my own hurdles.

And there was no time like the present.

44

Scooting my chair away from the desk, I sped through the apartment and entered the barn through the mudroom. I located an office midway down the center aisle, and inside, noticed a second door. It opened into a garage.

Bingo! A new black-and-white Jeep Wrangler and a red Corvette were parked inside. The stickers on the tags were up to date and the Jeep's gas tank was full. It also had dark tinted windows and an elaborate in-dash infotainment system I could use. I ran back the way I'd come to the kitchen and found two sets of keys conveniently sitting on hooks. Score!

I rushed into Mark's bath and rummaged through his vanity drawers until I found a pair of sharp scissors that looked good for cutting hair. I went to work on my long blond mane.

First, I cut bangs, then I leaned over so my head was upside down. After a brisk brushing, I grabbed the whole hunk and stood up. Holding it with one hand I chopped it off. I brushed that out, stared in the mirror, and felt like crying. What had I done?

Keep going, Quinn.

Being as careful as I could, I trimmed until it was short and more layered. Opening another drawer, I found hair gel, and smoothed my hair back. From Mark's bedroom closet I grabbed a ball cap, a large, blue long-sleeved tee shirt and a matching pair of cotton sweat pants.

Using several safety pins, I secured a bath towel around my waist and pulled on the clothes. I rolled the waist band on the sweat pants until they were short enough to walk in. After perching the hat on my head, I snatched up a pair of Mark's designer sunglasses, stared in the mirror and burst out laughing.

I had transformed myself into an overweight mess. *Perfect.*

Back in the kitchen, I grabbed the Jeep's keys. Dashing back to the garage, I turned the key in the Wrangler. It roared to life and

bathed me in the wonderful scent of new car leather. I found the re-
mote on the sun visor, opened the garage, and rolled out.

Mark's road was dirt, and following it slowly through the rain, I
came to an intersection with a slightly larger dirt road. Eventually I
was able to turn onto a paved road called Dibble, and once I found
myself on the Hitchcock Parkway, I knew how to get to the Walmart
Super Store on 78. After parking, I quickly disappeared into a throng
of people and shopping carts.

I made a beeline for the hair care products and picked up a box
of Clairol hair dye in "dark brown nutmeg." I grabbed a tube of extra
hold gel, and after paying cash, I forced myself to walk leisurely back
to the Jeep and drive the speed limit to Hitchcock Parkway.

A light ahead of me turned yellow, and I eased to a stop. In my
rearview mirror I saw a sheriff's deputy ease up behind me. God,
every cop in Aiken was looking for me! I was certain he was staring,
and panic surged through me.

Rather than staring back at him in the mirror, I pretended to fid-
get with the radio. After what seemed like an hour, the light turned
green. When I reached Dibble Road, I put on my blinker and turned
left. My heart seemed to have lodged itself in my mouth, and my
hands were damp on the steering wheel.

Instead of following behind me, the cop went straight. I hadn't
realized I'd been holding my breath and exhaled with a gasp.

As I'd prayed, my short hair, dark glasses, and Mark's Jeep were
not on his radar.

After I drove into Mark's garage and shut the bay door, I sat in
the car decompressing. I was grateful that both going and coming,
I'd seen no cars on the dirt roads. Probably the rain was keeping people inside. Still, I'd taken a big risk and been very lucky. Jase and Paddy would probably be furious if they knew what I'd done, but I was
through waiting on other people.

In the bathroom I ripped off Mark's clothing and the towel padding. Then, I mixed the two bottles of color products according to directions and sat in the tub to avoid coloring the bathroom with splotches of dye. Twenty-five minutes after applying the product, I rinsed the stuff out, worked in the seal-and-gloss tube, then hit my hair with the dryer.

In the mirror, a pixie stared back at me. The anxiety of the past few days had caused me to lose weight and I looked like a waif, although a cute waif. It was such a different look, I couldn't stop staring in the mirror.

"Boo!" I said, before leaving the mirror. I threw Mark's things into the wash. I made a mental note to return everything exactly where I'd found it.

By now, it was growing dark outside and I decided to finish off the Chinese food, try to get some sleep and leave very early the next morning. I used the computer to study a map of South Carolina, then searched for places I might need along the way. I hadn't formulated an exact plan for the next day, but I was a Traveller and had learned a lot from my Da.

And I was damn well going to do something!

45

I went to bed early that night but lay awake, my brain racing fast as a runaway Gypsy Vanner. Who had killed Sylvie? Certainly, Presto was a suspect. Especially if he'd latched onto Maeve. But why not just have an affair? Sylvie gave him whatever he wanted, and homicide was such a huge risk.

I felt sure Maeve was capable of murdering Sylvie, so she'd have Presto *and* the money. But was she certain Presto would stay with her after something so violent and drastic as murder? Presto's brother, Delbert, had nothing to gain, did he? There was no advantage for Carl or Timmy to kill Sylvie, unless someone had paid them. And there was no way it could be Jase, right?

Clearly, on paper, I had the most to gain. I rolled over and punched my pillow. I hit it again then wrapped myself around it in the fetal position, forcing myself to think about the horses at Ballymoor. I imagined scooping grain into feed buckets and finally fell asleep, only to wake up at one a.m. Damn, I needed sleep. I got up, heated a cup of milk, added a tablespoon of Baileys and sipped it in bed.

Next thing I knew, it was 4:20 a.m., the rain had stopped, and it was time to get up. I slipped into some of the clothes Jase had brought from Ballymoor and padded into the kitchen.

Skipping breakfast would be foolish, so I made toast, cooked ham and eggs, and poured coffee with milk. I made a ham sandwich for the road, stuffed it in a storage bag, and cleaned up the kitchen.

I poured more coffee and milk into a travel mug, grabbed the keys, and climbed into the Jeep Wrangler. Before long I was back on the road and merging onto I-20. At 5:10 a.m., the highway was already filling up. It got more crowded as I neared Augusta.

I continued west on I-20, careful to drive neither too fast nor too slowly. I motored safely through a speed trap with gritted teeth and hands clenched on the steering wheel, then I kept on rolling.

Three hours later, when I reached the far west outskirts of Atlanta, I pulled off at an exit sign indicating food and gas were available. I preferred to be lost in a crowd, and fortunately, the exit led to a series of strip malls instead of a lone convenience store. I cruised by the usual fast food and chain restaurants, several gas stations, a laundromat, and the entrance to a big box store.

What to do next? Between the dark glasses, ball cap and new hair, I was unrecognizable. I didn't care so much if I was picked up on film, but I didn't have a supply of fake tags, so the Jeep was another matter. If somehow, I was recognized, it would be disastrous if the Jeep's tag numbers, make and model were caught on film with me. Besides, I didn't fancy stealing another vehicle.

Scanning the area, I spotted a small grassy lot with a convenient mud puddle. Pulling onto the lot's edge, I collected enough mud in my travel mug to cover most of the Jeep's license plate numbers. Connor wasn't the only master of confusion and illusion.

Next, I drove until I located a dry cleaner with no discernible video cameras and parked the Jeep behind it.

From there, I walked to the box store. A breeze came up, and I was surprised at how much cooler the air was becoming as September drew closer. Inside, I grabbed a small grocery cart, a box of baby wipes, and three five-gallon gas containers with filler hoses.

After paying, I rolled the shopping cart into the lot. I kept going until I reached the Jeep, hidden behind the dry cleaners.

I stuffed everything into the back, including the small cart. As I climbed into the driver's seat, it occurred to me that only Jase knew where I'd been staying, and even though he didn't know where I was currently, he was the only one who could betray me. I was betting *everything* on him.

With my bottom lip pressed hard between my teeth, I started the engine, slowing a few blocks later near an older, seedy-looking filling station. After parking, I walked over, and seeing no CCTV cameras, I hopped into the Jeep and drove in. Minutes later, the Wrangler and three jugs were filled with gas. But it had taken more cash than I wanted.

Next, I walked across several parking lots to a shiny new convenience store. There, I used the facilities and washed the gasoline stink off my hands. I bought a large cup of soda, cheese-and-peanut butter crackers, and two more burner phones.

Finally, I used the baby wipes to clean the mud off the license plates. Muddied plates on a shiny new Jeep with dark tinted windows might arouse suspicion.

Soon, I was on the road, continuing west toward Alabama. With one of the new burners plugged in and charging, I ate my crackers and drank my soda. Sailing along the interstate I realized how much I enjoyed being on my own. After the last few months, it was a heady and freeing experience, and I loved that nobody knew where I was.

I'd thought my trip was about safe phone calls and leaving a false trail. But it was also about a need for freedom and control.

I hit the edge of Birmingham, Alabama around 11:30 a.m. I'd been on the road for six hours, and it was time to stop. I wanted to use my burner somewhere I wouldn't be noticed. With the Jeep's info system, I located the University of Alabama Hospital on 16th Street and programmed in the address.

About twenty minutes later, I pulled into the hospital parking lot, pleased it was mobbed with parked cars. Nothing like hiding in plain sight. I found a spot, parked, fired up the burner, and called Jase.

"It's me," I said.

"I'm where you're supposed to be, Quinn. I see you took a car. Where the hell are you?"

He sounded like he was ready to strangle me.

"Jase, I had to get out of there. Don't worry, I'm on a new burner. I need to get more cash, and information."

"You're daft if you plan to use your bank card!"

"Jase, I'm not stupid! I know what I'm doing!" *At least I hoped I did.*

"Your picture's all over the news! What if someone sees you?"

"I don't want to talk about that," I said, knowing his phone could be bugged. I wasn't about to state that I'd changed my appearance.

"Listen, Jase, I couldn't see the bank accounts for Presto or Maeve. We need to know about that check Presto gave her. I'd really like to know if anything significant pops up on Connor's account, too, and even on my lawyer's, Sandy Sanders. For that matter, what about Carl and Timmy?"

"What about them?"

At this point, I hoped the whole world was listening. "Could one of them have been paid to murder Sylvie?"

"Anything's possible," Jase said, his tone softening.

"Since you've got the hacking stuff, can you check for me?"

"Yeah, but you shouldn't stay on the phone, my cell probably has as many open lines as Waterloo Station, yeah?"

"I have another disposable. I'll call you back."

"Do what you must. It's not like I can stop you, is it?"

"Nope," I said and disconnected.

A wailing siren startled me until I remembered I was in a hospital parking lot and it was only an ambulance and not a police squad car. I was so tired of being afraid.

Get a grip, Quinn. Keep going.

I plugged in the second phone to charge, then considered my options. After a few moments cogitating, I remembered the Mississippi Travellers, a branch of our clan that lived outside Memphis. Thinking I could use them to embellish a false trail, I called Paddy.

"Are ya all right, lass?" he asked, when he heard my voice.

"Yes. Any news for me?"

"Sorry, lass, I have none. Only that Maeve has met with Sanders a few times, but then he is her lawyer, so . . ."

"It probably doesn't mean anything," I said.

"It's a fine mess you've gotten yourself into, Quinn O'Neill."

"Especially since I'm the only suspect the cops are looking at. I've got to find out who killed Sylvie, Paddy. And while I do that, the garda mustn't find me. If they do, I'll be in for life."

Through the airwaves, his sigh came long and sad. "What can I do to help?"

"Don't you have a cousin with the Mississippi Travellers?"

"That would be Paddy O'Rourke," he said. "What do you want with him."

"His phone number. Can you get it for me?"

"You're in luck, I'm home. Hold on."

A moment later he was back with the number. After giving it, he said, "Are you going to Memphis?"

"Probably," I said, for the benefit of any ears that might be listening. "Thanks, Paddy. I have to go now." With that, I ended the call.

The Memphis Travellers would probably hide me if I asked them to. But I wasn't going to find out who murdered Sylvie if I holed up next to the Mississippi River.

Still, I called the number, got O'Rourke's voice mail and left a message saying who I was, that I was coming to Memphis for a visit, and hoped to look him up.

Subterfuge is my middle name.

"And now," I said out loud, "I need to get some cash."

Using the Jeep's info system, I found a nearby branch of my bank and was about to head that way when there was a news bulletin on the radio.

"Birmingham state police indicate a search for Quinn O'Neill, of North Augusta, South Carolina, has broadened to include North Carolina, Georgia and Alabama. O'Neill, wanted for questioning in the murder of Aiken resident Sylvie DuPriest, escaped custody two days ago. Anyone with information on the whereabouts of this individual should call–"

Trembling, I shut the radio off, took a deep breath, and drove from the hospital lot. I was almost to the bank when I spotted a beauty shop. On display in the storefront window, was a long blond wig. I parked, went inside, and studied the wig. It resembled the hair I'd chopped off the night before.

At the counter I tried it on and purchased it.

The purple haired woman behind the register gave me a quizzical look and a smile.

"You wanna wear that outta here?"

"I'd like to," I said.

"Lemme put some of this gel on your hair. Flatten it back so it won't show."

"That's great," I said. "Thanks."

She did her thing, I put on the wig, and managed to almost look like my former self. From the shop I walked the three blocks to the bank's indoor ATM machine without my dark glasses or ball cap. After pulling out my card I withdrew the maximum allowable amount–fifteen hundred dollars.

Now the entire police force knew I was in Birmingham. But they didn't know what I was driving, except CTV cams could trace me back to the Jeep. I walked to a strip mall across the street and stepped into a music shop. At the counter, a bearded guy stood before a wall hung with used guitars for sale.

"Hey," I said, trying to look anxious. "Some guy I don't know is following me. You got a back way out of here?"

His eyes slid to the storefront window, probably looking for my bad guy. "Yeah, sure. Come on."

I followed him through the shop to a door that opened into a storage room with a rear door.

"I'd go over there," he said, pointing to the rear of the shops across the alley. "That red door is always open cause they got security and like to let their customers come in and out the back when they want."

My kind of place. "Thank you for your help," I said, and made a beeline for the red door.

It opened into a dress shop, where I found a gaudy, flowered purple tunic, something I wouldn't ordinarily wear. I grabbed it and a black pair of leggings and I tried them on. When the sales girl came to the dressing room curtain to ask how they fit, I said, "Perfect."

At the counter, I paid for them, then told the sales girl I wanted to wear the clothes out. She cut the tags off, and I zipped back to the dressing room and drew the curtain closed. Removing the blond wig, I fluffed up my short hair and retrieved the ball cap and dark-glasses from my tote bag. Peeking out the curtain, I waited until the sales girl went to help a customer near the front of the store before zipping out the back.

A short time later, I was heading out of the city to where the road split, giving me a choice of taking 65 due north to Nashville, or 22 northwest to Memphis and the Mississippi River. I took 22, and a few miles later when I crossed over a small river, I threw the burner out the window and into the water. Then, I ate my ham sandwich while listening to rock music on Sirius Radio.

As a murder suspect, my name and photo were probably in the hands of the Alabama, Mississippi, and Tennessee State Police. No doubt, the cops were probably listening to Paddy's phone calls and had seen the hit on my bank account in Birmingham.

Outside Tupelo Mississippi, a highway sign proclaimed the city to be the birthplace of Elvis Presley. How could I not stop? At first, I was amused. But just inside the city, I was confronted by a life-sized statue of Elvis that bore an unnerving resemblance to Presto.

By now, I'd been on the road almost eight hours and I craved a proper meal. I was tired, almost out of gas, and spooked by a statue. It was time to end the trail.

As I had in Atlanta and Birmingham, I cruised the area quickly discovering it was not what you'd call a bustling metropolis, although it did have a lot of churches.

Driving through a Kentucky Fried Chicken, I picked up half a chicken, three biscuits, a large order of coleslaw, and a soda. From there, I slipped into a grocery store parking lot and devoured my food. I'd chosen the lot for its location–two blocks down and across the street from a service station.

Inside my tinted windows, I removed the ball cap and dark glasses, smoothed my hair and put the wig back on. Walking to the rear of the Jeep, I dipped the last biscuit in the remains of my soda and smeared the resulting mush over the license plate. After pulling out the gas jugs, I heaved them into the grocery cart, then drained them into the Jeep.

With the empty jugs back in the cart, I rolled everything across and down the street. Three lights later, I was in the service station. When I swiped my credit card, the pump refused to accept it.

Inside the station, a lanky guy behind the counter with a pompadour and Elvis sideburns, told me the card was no good.

"Really?" I said, handing him four twenty-dollar bills. "Guess I hit my limit." I smiled like it was no big deal that my account was frozen. I wasn't surprised the law had shut me down. It was why I'd withdrawn the maximum amount in Birmingham. Besides, there were ways to get more cash from Paddy and Lara.

The main thing was the cops would see a hit on my card and believe I was still on my way to Memphis. I filled the jugs and rolled them back to the Jeep, praying I wasn't being tracked by CTV cameras. Though the plate was unreadable, a shiny new black-and-white Wrangler was way more noticeable than I liked.

Ten minutes later, I was parked outside a Walmart, next to a MacDonald's, with my fingers gripping my second burner. I took a breath and made my last and most nerve-racking call.

46

A part of me hoped Sanders wouldn't be in his office and I could just leave a vague message. But that was dumb. I needed to know what he knew, or if anything else had happened.

He was in his office and picked up as soon as I gave his secretary my name.

"Quinn, where are you?"

"I'm not going to tell you that."

"You don't trust me?"

"Sandy, I don't trust anyone! Besides your phone could be bugged."

"It isn't! We sweep this place several times a week."

"Look, I know lawyers don't need to believe their client is innocent to defend them, but without knowing who killed Sylvie, how can you possibly help me? Without that information, I'm finished."

"I've been working on that, Quinn."

"What exactly have you been working on, Sandy?"

"Finding another suspect. We need one to establish reasonable doubt."

"That's not good enough," I said.

"Look, Quinn, I don't know where you are, but if you leave South Carolina things will only get worse for you. Interstate flight to avoid prosecution could bring in the FBI. You've got to give yourself up. The longer you're out there the worse it looks for you."

I didn't respond. The smell of French fries and greasy burgers had seeped into the Jeep and after the recent biscuits and Kentucky Fried chicken it made me nauseous.

Sandy had paused a moment. His tone grew more gentle. "The *accident*. I saw the car. It was gruesome. They say the one deputy died on impact, a blessing really, since his body was incinerated. How badly were you hurt?"

"I'm fine," I said. "How's Tyler?"

"Who? You mean the other deputy? He's okay. You two were incredibly lucky. But you can't keep running, Quinn. Every officer in South Carolina and beyond is on the alert for you. Sooner or later they'll catch you, and it could get ugly. Please, turn yourself in!"

I ignored his outburst. "So, do you have a suspect?"

"Maybe."

"Who?"

"Quinn, I'm not going to tell you unless you come in."

I didn't like the sound of that. "Look, I've got to go. I'll call you again to see if you've made progress with your suspect. I didn't kill Sylvie, and I'm not coming in until we know who did."

"Quinn, wait—"

"Bye, Sandy."

I sat staring at the silent phone for a moment before driving behind the Walmart looking for a Dumpster. I found one with the lid partially open and threw the phone in. After scraping the hardened mush from the license plate, I left Tupelo and headed southeast on 22 back toward Alabama.

I drove until I was beyond Birmingham and pulled into a rest stop, where I parked between two darkened eighteen wheelers, closed my eyes, and fell asleep.

Four hours later, armed with caffeine and a candy bar, I was back on the highway. I kept going until I was almost to Atlanta where, feeling relatively safe in my new short and dark hair, I stopped for gas at a Love's station. After using cash to fill the Jeep and buy two new burners, I drove straight through to Mark's place, rolling the Jeep into the garage a little after 1:00 a.m.

First, I checked Mark's study. The desk chair was not where I'd left it, and a pad of paper lay on the desk top. The top page had been torn off, and holding the remaining page to the light, I could see a vague impression of what looked like names and numbers.

Jase had to have been there checking the bank accounts. Knowing he'd kept his promise filled me with relief and a sense that I wasn't alone.

I took a quick shower, letting the hot water beat onto my neck and shoulders to ease the tension and pain from the long road trip. I changed into dark jeans and a black tee, made another ham sandwich and drank a glass of milk.

It was almost two, but instead of going to bed, I drove the Jeep to the grounds of the Aiken Training Track, parked next to two pickup trucks, and walked down the deserted dirt streets to Ballymore.

Creeping into the barn, I breathed in the comforting scents of molasses, hay, and horses. I longed to visit Irish Jewel, but instead, walked to Jase's door, where I slipped through his foyer and into his bedroom.

In the soft glow of a nightlight, he lay on his side, sleeping beneath a sheet. His tousled blond hair curled across one cheek. The man was beautiful. As I stared at him, a protective feeling and desire welled up in me. It took my breath away.

I swallowed, then whispered, "Jase. Jase, it's Quinn, wake up."

He opened one eye but appeared to still be half asleep. "Mm, Quinn. Care to join me?"

He stretched under the covers, a lazy smile on his lips, before suddenly sitting bolt upright.

"Quinn! Are you okay? Where the hell did you go? What did you do to your hair?"

I briefly thought about sitting on the edge of his bed, but my fingers seemed to have a mind of their own and longed to stretch out and touch him. I remained standing.

"Let me put my jeans on," he said. "I sleep in the nude, so turn around, yeah?"

I looked away, heard him rise from the bed and take a step toward his closet. I was too tired for willpower. With a quick glance,

I caught the profile of his tight butt and . . . oh my God. My cheeks filled with heat and a mixture of desire and trepidation filled my core. Turning, I forced myself to stare at one of the photos of him in show clothes sailing over a jump on a handsome bay horse.

"It's safe now," he said. Wearing a tee-shirt, jeans, and a mischievous grin, he sat on the edge of the bed near his pillows, gestured to the far end, and said, "Sit, and explain yourself."

I did, and when I was finished, he said, "So everyone thinks you're hiding out near Memphis?"

"I hope so."

"Sounds like you were careful enough to keep the Jeep off the grid. It may have worked. Anyway, it should buy you some time."

His scent that wafted to me from the rumpled bed was surprisingly familiar and pleasing.

His eyes grew more intense as he looked at me. "You know, if you hadn't told me it was you, I might have thought a strange woman had come to my room to ravish me."

"You wish."

"I do," he said, as if stating a simple fact. "I like you better as a blonde, but you look pretty cute this way, too."

"Um," I mumbled, searching for something clever to say, and failing. "I'm trying to figure out what I should do now."

"Now? I tell you what *I* found out."

The hair on the back of my neck prickled. "I'm listening."

"First off, I found this to be a tad dodgy. DuPriest keeps *his* money with First National Trust of Tupelo Mississippi?"

"You got to be kidding me!" I said, still being careful to whisper. "Tupelo is the birthplace of Elvis Presley."

"That's really where Presley was born?" Jase asked, apparently thinking I was joking.

When I nodded, he said, "Our Presto, he's a real nutter, yeah?"

"Pretty much. Ridiculous to have an out of state bank just so he can feel closer to Elvis. He doesn't have another account here?"

"Oh, yeah, he has an account here. A joint account with Sylvie, soon to be in his name only. Then there's a big fat Merrill Lynch brokerage account in both their names. It's worth more than a hundred million. There are also properties and holdings in England."

The amounts made my head spin. I couldn't imagine such wealth, but it raised a question.

"So, what's up with this Tupelo account?" I asked.

This is where it gets interesting. From everything I can see, the Tupelo account is Presto's little secret. He has a PO Box in Aiken, and any correspondence from the Mississippi bank goes there, not to Ballymoor."

In the distance, I heard a muffled snort from one of the horses. We both listened a moment, but all was quiet.

"Does Presto have much money in that account?" I asked.

"Gets even more interesting. He's had the account for years, since before he married Sylvie. Back then, there wasn't much in it. Only what I'd expect an Elvis impersonator to earn. Then," he continued, with a lift of both brows, "he marries Sylvie."

He paused as if waiting for a drum roll.

"And *what?* Don't tease, Jase, I'm not in the mood."

"Okay," he said, holding up both palms. "Don't get your knickers in a twist. So, as soon as he got the ring on his finger, he started bleeding Sylvie. Over the years, he cashed checks on their joint account, then bought money orders from the Aiken Post office, sent directly to his Tupelo bank. Always small amounts, under ten thousand, but never less than a thousand."

"He's a snake," I said. "I bet he got tired of collecting eggs from his golden goose. I bet he killed her!"

"Could have. But let's not jump to the obvious conclusion. That check for Maeve? He wrote a Tupelo bank check for twenty thousand the day before your Aunt Mary saw him give it to Maeve."

"You should have been a detective," I said.

"Thieves make more money."

The amusement that danced in his eyes reminded me of Da. "So," I said, getting back to the subject, "Maeve did it or had someone do it."

"Or he wanted her to buy something nice for herself because he's been shagging her."

"Ugh."

"I'm not done, Quinn. There was a five-thousand-dollar check cashed not long ago. Right about then Carl comes to the barn with a new pair of expensive boots and a nice collection of single malt scotch."

"Carl? No, he's the nice one. Timmy with those tattoos seems more likely."

"Look," he said. "Boots and scotch may not mean a bloody thing. I was just saying because you asked me to look."

He'd given me a lot of information. But what good was it? It hardly spelled out who killed Sylvie. We were both silent a minute. Jase yawned.

"I should let you get back to sleep, Jase. It won't be that long before you have to get up."

He nodded, and I stood. I started to leave, then turned back. "What about the guy who isn't really Delbert?" I asked.

"Oh, him. You were right. Delbert DuPriest doesn't exist. *Anywhere*. I intend to dig deeper. He's been staying with Presto ever since Sylvie died. He's here tonight. God knows the mansion is big enough for ten Delberts." He paused a moment and rubbed his eyes. "I know you wanted me to look at Sanders, too, and I will. I haven't had enough time"

"Hey," I said, "There's only so many hours in a day, right?"

He yawned again, and I left him to sleep.

In the barn, I paused to soak in the horsey smells that hung sweet in the air. Then I crept upstairs to my room. I retrieved my set of lock picks. No self-respecting Traveller is without a means of breaking in, and my O'Neill genes had persuaded me to bring them with me to Ballymoor. Before leaving, I stuffed a lightweight pair of gloves in my pants pocket.

I was almost out the door, when I stopped to stare at the statue of the palomino and the girl who so resembled me. How I wished Sylvie had given me only that, and not the million-dollar life insurance policy naming me as beneficiary. The policy still made no sense to me.

Moments later, I stole from the barn into the cool, night air. As far as I was concerned, the night was still young. The four hours of sleep I'd snatched on the highway were enough to keep going.

I *had* to keep going.

47

In the distance, Presto's mansion loomed, large and dark. I wondered if Sylvie's restless spirit hung about in the unlit house. The thought creeped me out, and I shuddered.

Stop it, Quinn. This is no time to be silly.

As I walked quietly along the drive, a damp breeze kicked up, rattling the massive limbs of the closest live oak. September had just arrived at midnight, and on the Jeep radio, the news had warned of a severe hurricane forming in the Gulf. I could almost sense it.

The house drew me like a magnet. I had an urgent sense that answers lay within, answers that could save me. Maybe I was crazy, but I'd never know if I didn't try.

Doubtless, Presto had some sort of elaborate alarm system, but sometimes you get lucky. I walked around the perimeter looking for that luck and found it. In the den, where I'd seen Presto watching TV with Delbert what seemed like eons ago, someone had left a window open.

It was time to slip on my gloves. The sill was about level with my chin and using the muscles I'd gained working that summer, I put my hands on it, sprung up, and managed to swing a leg over the ledge.

With no discernible chair or table in my path, I allowed myself to fall gently and silently into the room. I landed on a soft carpet, and I lay still, listening.

The house was silent. Rising to my feet, I looked around the den. Tiny lights from the room's audio video equipment allowed me to see the area was only for entertainment. But I wanted information, and for that, I needed an office.

As I tiptoed silently through the den, the hair on my arms rose, and my ears strained for sound. The room opened into a large living area. Though it was unlit, the ambient light coming through tall windows allowed me to negotiate my way through without crashing into tables or chairs. In the darkened room, it seemed like there were acres of furniture.

I smelled roses and saw the reflection off a crystal vase filled with something dark. Presto must have his gardener maintaining Sylvie's tradition, which seemed kind of nice.

A large archway led into the main hall. I stood on the threshold listening, but the house remained silent. Across the hall was another living area, much like the one I'd just come through. Beyond it, I could make out another room, like a match mate to the den. Thinking it might be an office, I crept toward it. In the doorway, the dusty smell of books stopped me dead. *Sylvie's library.*

I backed up and turned around. I wasn't about to go back in the room where I'd seen her head lying in a pool of blood. No way. Retracing my steps, I inched along the main hall, freezing in place when I heard a loud rattling sound. When I heard a whirring and the sound of water drawing, I realized it must be the kitchen's icemaker.

I forced myself to relax, remembering to breathe.

Near the end of the hall a huge double staircase rose out of sight. If the kitchen was ahead on my right, maybe an office would materialize on my left. As I crept forward, I spotted a room on the left and moved through its doorway.

Bingo, an office! There were no windows in this room, so after shutting the door, I felt around and found a switch. It flooded the room with light, painful as it hit my widened pupils. Seeing a desk lamp, I turned it on and doused the overheads.

Presto's desk was massive and ornate. I would have expected no less. I rifled through every drawer, finding the usual stuff I'd expect, except Presto was a neatnik. Numerous built-in compartments held pens, sorted by color, sharpened pencils, paper clips in different colors that were also neatly sorted, adhesive tape in different widths, and note pads with the name Elvis Presley imprinted at the top. *Really?*

In a deeper drawer, there were files related to the horses, payroll for the help, and other information, but nothing nefarious. The last drawer was locked. I got out my picks and had it open in about thirty seconds.

Staring at the contents, my blood ticked up. My fingers closed on two passports and withdrew them. Sylvie's, Presto's. Opening them, everything seemed in order.

A locked steel document box was at the bottom of the drawer. I retrieved my picks and worked on its lock. It took me a few minutes to get it open. Presto had wanted to secure whatever was inside.

Lifting the lid, I found another passport for someone named Ransdale D. Nelson, except the laminated picture inside was of Delbert DuPriest.

Just you wait until I run your name through Jase's computer, Ransdale whoever you are!

Then the obvious hit me like a ton of bricks. This guy was not Presto's brother. If not his brother, then who?

Searching through the contents at the bottom of the box, I found a Liberty Life Insurance policy. It was the one Sylvia had bought naming me as beneficiary. Why was it in *Presto's* lock box? I stared at her signature. Would it match the handwriting on the note she'd given me with the palomino horse statue?

There was nothing else of interest in the lock box. I folded the policy, put it and the passport in my pocket, and left the room.

I should take what I'd found and get out, but that same sense of urgency pulled me like a magnet and drew me to the large double staircase. I dropped my palms to the first step and climbed the stair with my palms and feet, keeping a low profile and a steady climb with no risk of stumbling. I could also feel each step for the kind of give that would turn into a creak with my full weight.

My climb was punctuated with pauses to listen. The house remained still. When I reached the top, I slowly rose and stepped onto the landing. In the wide hall before me, an antique pier table stood against a tall gilded mirror. A bronze lamp with a low wattage bulb acted as a night light, dimly illuminating the area.

Pausing to get my bearings, I headed toward an open door that should lead to a room over the main entrance to the mansion. If it were me, I'd want my bedroom to overlook my stable and carriage house and have them be the first thing I'd see each morning when I rose.

At the threshold to this room, I froze. The area was large. An opulent and massive four poster bed was centered between two tall windows. Pale light shone in from a setting moon that had fallen below the cloud bank promising rain. The silver light reflected on a tangle of white sheets, arms and legs. I could just make out Presto's pompadour where he lay on his back.

This was Sylvie's bed, and the son of a bitch already had a woman in his dead wife's bed? I crept forward. It had to be Maeve. But it wasn't Maeve. It wasn't even a woman.

For a moment I was unable to move and then, already knowing what I'd find, I crept forward. To make sure.

Delbert lay across Presto, his head on his lover's chest, a hand on his lover's leg. I could smell their sweat and something sour. I backed away from them. I'd seen enough and only wanted to run from the house.

48

AS QUICKLY AS POSSIBLE I tiptoed from the bedroom, walked through the hall and began to descend the staircase with my thoughts spinning. Had Presto or his lover murdered Sylvie so they'd be free to be together?

The thought hit hard and distracted me from caution. My foot slipped off one step plate and I grabbed for the banister and came down hard on the next plate. The banister creaked loudly and the stair step all but shrieked in protest.

Hearing mumbling and rustling in the bedroom, I froze. A shadow filled the bedroom doorway.

"Who's out there? Damn it, who's there?" Presto's voice.

I heard a soft click and a flashlight beam began its search for me. There was nothing to do but run. As I flew down the staircase, an alarm siren began shrieking and all the overhead lights came on at once.

"It's a woman, Randy," Presto shouted, apparently using his lover's nickname. "Come on!"

As I reached the main hall, I could hear them thundering down the stairs behind me. Presto would have been smarter to keep the lights off and use his flashlight. With the illumination, I had no problem racing through the huge furniture-filled living room, into the den, and out the window.

I dropped into the driveway and ran as fast as I could for the main gate.

Behind me someone yelled, "She's gone through the window. Hurry!"

The outside lights on the estate blinked on. Ignoring them, I kept running, thanking God I'd had the sense to cut my hair short and dye it dark. They couldn't identify me unless they caught me. As I pounded through the gate and onto the dirt street beyond, I thought my lungs would burst.

Keep going, Quinn.

I slipped through a fence into a neighboring yard thick with hollies, magnolias and box bushes. As I sprinted through that yard, the low hanging moon lit my way. Sliding through the next perimeter fence, I raced behind a large magnolia and stopped, my hands clutching my knees as I gasped for air. When my breathing quieted, I listened.

The only commotion or light seemed to be coming from Ballymoor. I heard distant raised male voices. Probably Carl, Timmy and Jase had joined the hunt. But around me, it was dead quiet. And without a knowledgeable tracker or dog, it was unlikely they'd find me.

Once I caught my breath, I walked as quietly and quickly as possible until I could see the Jeep. I stilled, using all my senses. I was alone. I raced to the car, cranked the engine and drove away, not using my headlights. I never saw a headlight behind me or even in the distance. Luck had been with me again that night.

At Mark's house, I powered up the computer and searched for Ransdale D. Nelson. An easy find, now that I had his name. In no time I learned he'd also been an Elvis impersonator and had been born in a tiny town south of Tupelo, Mississippi, called Verona. He'd left Verona with a high school degree and little job experience.

Considering that he was now living at Ballymoor, he'd come a long way. He'd worked Elvis gigs in Las Vegas and Reno, probably where he and Presto had met. He was younger than Presto. And both were a lot younger than poor Sylvie.

I leaned back in the office chair and closed my eyes. It was almost dawn and the promised rain started pattering outside the window. I had no problem with two men or two women loving each other.

It was the cheating, the duplicity, and probable murder I couldn't stomach.

I didn't want to think anymore. Pushing away from the desk, I walked to the bedroom, took another hot shower and crawled under the covers. I went out like a light.

I awoke at ten that morning, grateful I'd been able to sleep after my narrow escape the night before. Feeling groggy and disoriented, I slogged my way into the kitchen for a strong dose of caffeine. The rich coffee, sugar and milk tasted like heaven. I tossed it down and made another cup. Fully awake, I made ham and eggs, and after devouring that, I took a third cup of coffee with me to Mark's study.

Outside, only a light rain was falling, but the trees and bushes swayed in a stiff breeze. I remembered the report of an impending hurricane working up through the Gulf and hoped it wouldn't be hitting Aiken.

Checking the weather, they predicted a storm with hurricane force winds should make landfall at Gulfport, Mississippi, then head northeast through Alabama and on up into Tennessee, so Aiken should be fine.

A sudden ping sounded on Jase's speaker, and a pop-up message showed me that I, or rather Mark, had an email from Irish Jewel. Jase must have set up accounts in both Mark's and the horse's name figuring I'd know it came from him.

How he'd managed to have an email to Mark arrive on his own computer, I didn't know. Like me, he had his own bag of tricks. I opened the message and read it.

"Hey, Mark. You okay?"

"Yes," I typed. "I've got something for you."

"Great. See you later."

"Later," I typed, signed it Mark, and closed the message.

Jase arrived at the apartment at a time suggesting he'd just finished his late afternoon chores at Ballymoor. Once again, he spooked me by driving up in a strange car. Once I saw his face through the window near the front door, I breathed a relieved and grateful sigh and let him in. He came bearing the gift of a takeout box that smelled hot and rich with garlic and tomato sauce. Hard not to love a man that brings you food.

When I asked him about the change in vehicles, he told me he'd borrowed it from a mate who worked at Bruce's Field, the fancy showgrounds on Powderhouse Road.

"But didn't this guy want to know what was wrong with the farm truck?" I asked.

"Not a problem. I walked over there, told him ours was in the shop. And no, I didn't let anyone follow me here. I'm not dumb, am I?

"Sorry," I said. "I'm just nervous."

"After last night's kerfuffle, I'm not surprised. What happened over there?"

I related my exploits from the previous night, then pulled Ransdale's passport from the desk drawer. "Look at this."

He stared at the name and the photo, slowly comprehending what he was seeing. His eyes widened.

"They got a dodgy deal going on there, don't they? I think you may have found a touch of reasonable doubt, yeah?"

"I hope so."

"Quinn, I've got some news, too." My face must have tensed, for he said, "Relax, it's good—well, at least, useful."

"What?"

"I wormed into some of our friends' emails." He paused a moment before continuing. "Didn't you tell me you were depending on Carl to back you up about Presto handing you the wrench?"

"Yes," I said. "*Why?*"

"There's an email from Carl to your lawyer, Sanders. Apparently, Sanders had asked him about testifying on your behalf. Carl's saying that he knows nothing about the wrench. He insists you're making it up."

"That bastard," I said. "The five-thousand dollar check you told me Presto cashed? The money must have gone to Carl. He's been paid to lie!"

"But there's no paper trail with cash, is there? We'd need a photo of the payoff between them and it's too late for that."

By now, Jase's gift of Italian food was growing cool. I put the box in the microwave to warm and glancing at him, I could see Jase looked as glum as I felt. With every new discovery that moved me toward vindication, the next one pushed me back.

Across the room, the microwave whirred efficiently while I fired mental blanks about what to do next.

Jase sat, stretched his hand across the table and closed it over mine. "While you were on your travels toward the great Mississippi, did you call Sanders?"

I realized we hadn't talked about my call to Sandy the night before. The sight of Jase lying in bed had not been conducive to clear thought.

"I did call him. He said he was looking for a suspect that would cause reasonable doubt. I told him that wasn't good enough and I wouldn't come in until we knew who killed Sylvie."

"Then Presto's affair with Ransdale is your lucky card," Jase said. "Those two have doubled the motivation. Money and lust. They're odds on for guilty. You need to get the word to Sanders."

"Yeah, I do."

With the rain and a breeze still blowing outside the kitchen windows, Jase's company and the scent of dinner warming made the room very cozy. I didn't want him to leave but didn't voice the thought. Things were complicated enough.

"Tell you what," Jase said. "After I get back to Ballymoor, I'll call that traveller mate of Paddy's in Memphis. I'll get him to phone me back so there'll be a record and then I'll call Sanders, tell him I spoke to you and you found Ransdale's passport earlier."

"No good," I said. "If I had, I would have told him about it when I called him yesterday."

"Right. Then I'll tell him I had my suspicions about those two, found the passport, and nicked it for you. I'll tell him I did it because I believe you about the wrench and I'm convinced you're innocent."

We were both silent a moment as we thought it through, looking for a flaw.

"All right," I said. "We'd better eat so you can get going."

In the end, though it smelled delicious, we only picked at the chicken cacciatore in the takeout carton. We were too preoccupied with an uneasy sense that things were about to come to a head.

Jase gave me a tight hug, kissed me on the cheek, and left. When he was gone, I felt as lonely and cold as the cacciatore I'd put in the refrigerator.

I had trouble sleeping that night. The breeze was just strong enough that a few untrimmed branches leaned against my bedroom windows occasionally emitting a scraping noise that startled me.

The rain that came in fits and spurts was not enough to deter the coyote pack from running in the woods beyond the horse paddock. Long after their yowling faded into the distance, I lay awake waiting for whatever was coming next.

Finally, near dawn, the wind eased. The rain had become more of a drizzle, and I thought the storm must be ending. The sluicing of water in the drain pipes and the gurgling in the gutters eventually lulled me to sleep.

49

I slept late, but once my conscious brain woke up, it darted to the obvious question. Had Jase reached Sanders the night before? Throwing off the covers, I rushed to Mark's office to check for an email.

There was no message. I tried to shake off my frustration and the dismal mood of the previous night with caffeine. When that failed, I watched the news on the computer to see if there was an update on the murder of Sylvie DuPriest. But the broadcast was all about the weather.

Although the hurricane was still headed for the Gulf Coast, it had made an unexpected and sudden right turn. The storm had already made landfall in Panama City, Florida, and was heading northeast through Albany, Georgia. One computer model showed it with dead aim on Augusta and Aiken.

Oh, for God's sake. What else could go wrong? Still, I was even more anxious to know what had transpired between Jase and Sanders.

Though I probably shouldn't risk an email to "Irish Treasure," I needed the information too much to resist. After asking Jase for an update, and clicking send, I was informed the email had failed, that there was no such address.

Of course, he had removed it. Jase probably knew how to permanently scrub anything from the internet. I'd have to wait until he showed up. It was all I could do not to race to the Jeep and drive to Ballymore, but common sense prevailed.

To keep from going mad, I tuned in a movie on Netflix, and pretended to watch it while I waited.

Outside, the wind was picking up and the rain had come back, only now it was blowing sideways. I almost didn't hear the Ballymoor farm truck over the noise of the approaching storm, but when I did, I dashed to the front window, relieved to see Jase climbing out.

He sprinted through the rain to the house and came in. His Outback raincoat and black leather hat dripped water on the floor until it pooled at his feet. Running to the laundry room, I grabbed a towel before scurrying back and tossing it on the floor by his boots.

He stepped on the towel. "Thanks."

I wished he'd shed the coat and hold me, but his focus seemed to have turned inward.

"So, tell me," I said, "what happened when you spoke to Sanders?"

"A lot."

"Like what?"

"He says he can prove that Presto paid Carl to murder Sylvie."

I could feel my eyes widen. "Carl? I don't believe it! How does Sanders know this?"

"Maeve."

"What does she have to do with it?"

"Sanders is her lawyer. She's confided in him. Apparently, she's gotten friendly with Presto. He did give her that big check, yeah?"

"But how does that figure in?" I asked. Something was wrong with this story. "If he's gay, he's not giving her money because they're having an affair. And, why would he admit to her that he paid Carl. It doesn't make sense. I'm supposed to believe Presto made a mistake like that?"

"But it fits, Quinn. Say Presto had too much to drink or the guilt thing got to him. If he did spill what he'd done, the twenty thousand could have been to keep Maeve quiet."

"Then he's twice a fool if he thinks she won't want more."

"That's Presto's problem, not ours," Jase said. "The main thing is, Maeve is willing to testify that Presto said he'd paid Carl to do it."

I shook my head, finding it hard to believe any of this. Maeve would never want to help me. "Jase, do you believe Sanders?"

"Actually, I do. He sounded very earnest, Quinn. It was obvious to me that he believes Maeve. And he was quite chuffed about Delbert's false identity. He says it means Presto had more to gain from Sylvie's death than you do. Like you said, it was a way to be with his lover *and* have the money."

I stared at him a long moment, hoping he was right.

"Look, we should go," he said. "I couldn't let Sanders know you're hiding here, so I told him I'd bring you to his office. He wants to go over the details with you and make an airtight defense before you turn yourself in."

"Turn myself in?" I didn't like the sound of that. I'd been through so much, I didn't trust anyone anymore.

Jase sighed and placed his wet hands on my shoulders. "Look, you need to get this bloody mess behind you. You said you'd come in once there's proof, and now there is, yeah?"

He paused a moment, as if thinking. "Oh, and I almost forgot, he and your Uncle Paddy have lined up a criminal defense attorney who specializes in murder trials. Paddy says this new guy is tops. Apparently, he met with Sanders yesterday."

"Does Paddy believe this story," I asked.

"He does."

A sudden gust of wind drove rain against the window by the front door. A small branch smacked the glass before disappearing sideways. Fear seemed to ride that wind, and it blew through me until I shuddered.

When I took a step back from Jase and wrapped my arms around my waist, he took a step closer.

"I hate that this is happening to you. You know I'll do anything I can to help you, Quinn."

I nodded but continued to hug myself as if it could somehow protect me.

"Look, Quinn, it's time to see Sanders. What other choice do you have?"

"I could run."

"With what? You won't see a dime of your inheritance if you do that. You'll never survive."

I closed my eyes and exhaled a long breath. "All right."

"You're a brave soldier, Quinn O'Neill. You've got Delbert's passport, right?"

I nodded.

"Good. Make sure you take it with you and this is a copy of the bank records."

I took the sheets of paper from him, folded them and slid them into my tote where I'd already placed the passport. Jase moved to the front closet and opened it. It was a walk-in filled with coats, boots, riding hats and gloves.

"Mark doesn't wear all that stuff, does he?" I asked.

"Keeps it for guests." Jase leaned in and pulled out a long oilskin riding coat and a matching hat. These should fit."

They did, but when we were almost out the door, I remembered to get my burner phone. In my room, I snatched up the phone, tossed it into my tote bag and started to walk out, but something made me hesitate.

Moving to the dresser, I grabbed my lock picks and slid them into my jeans pocket. Having them made me feel more secure. Besides, I could almost feel Da's smile of approval.

As I buttoned the long coat against the weather outside, I felt a sudden surge of courage. Where it came from, I couldn't imagine. But I knew I wanted to beat this thing. I wanted my life back, and I wanted . . . I wanted Jase.

Sandy's office was a rectangular brick building off Park Avenue. As Jase and I splashed up the office sidewalk, the building's gutters sang and overflowed with water, causing us to duck quickly under its green awning to avoid the deluge.

We entered a large room with a waiting area and two desks, probably for secretaries. Except no one sat there. The room smelled faintly of mint. The scent grew stronger as Sandy appeared through a doorway.

With his height and long legs, he swallowed the distance between us in two strides. He offered a hand to shake, and when I extended mine, he grasped it in both of his.

"I'm so glad you've come in. I know this is scary, Quinn, but we've got the evidence on Presto and Carl. It's all going to work out. You can trust me on that." He smiled and released my hand.

What is it about a man who always insists you can trust him?

I glanced at Jase, but he looked confident. I needed to stop being paranoid. Sandy was trying to help me. He appeared to have been under a strain. The ever-increasing dark shadows and lines beneath his eyes told the tale. As did the strong smell of mint mouthwash that failed to hide the alcohol on his breath.

Sandy glanced at Jase. "Thanks for getting her here." As he continued to stare at Jase, his lips compressed into a tight line. "Look, son, the meeting we're going to have needs to be confidential. You should leave. You understand, right?"

"No," I said. "Jase stays, or I leave with him."

Sandy's eyes narrowed, and he looked away for a moment. Then he smiled and said, "As you wish."

His smile appeared forced as if hiding annoyance. Well, wasn't that just too bad.

Jase glanced at me and then at Sandy. "He's right, Quinn. I shouldn't be privy to your plans. The more I know the more chance I could let something slip. I live surrounded by the enemy, yeah?"

Sandy hurried to press the point. "That's right. If anyone finds out our strategy it wouldn't be good. Trust me when I tell you that.

Resigned, I said, "All right."

Jase gave me a one-armed hug and pushed through the entrance door into the rain. Watching him through the office window as he ran through the downpour to his truck, I felt forlorn, almost abandoned.

"Come on through, then," Sandy said, indicating a long hall punctuated by closed doors.

I followed him into a conference room where several files were spread open on the table. I took a seat next to them.

"The girls got a new espresso machine," Sandy said. "I wouldn't mind a cup in this gloomy weather. Can I get you one?"

I nodded.

What I really wanted was for this whole thing to end. My mouth was dry, and my arms had wound their way around my middle again. Would my life ever be normal? If the deputies were going to come and take me in, and I assumed they were, I just wanted to get it over with.

The loud hiss of Sandy's espresso machine brought me back to the present. Moments later he came in with a foaming mug and a tray of creamer and sweeteners.

"This is good stuff," he said. "Drink up, and I'll be right back with mine."

It was good and I drank most of it down, liking the swift kick that came with the caffeine. It would probably be the last time I tasted good coffee for a while.

He returned with his mug and sat. He seemed to take forever to doctor it with creamer and sweetener. Finally, he took a sip and slid his glance to me.

"Do you have Delbert's passport and the bank records with you?"

"Yes." I leaned over and pulled the items from my tote bag on the floor. When I sat up, I felt slightly dizzy. Too much stress.

I handed the material to Sandy and he opened the passport.

"This is good," he said. "This is very good." He unfolded the bank records and studied them. His voice was jovial. Did evidence really make him this happy?

The room seemed to shift. I stared at my mug and the remains of the espresso. Was I getting sick?

"How're you doing there, kid?" Sandy asked. His stare seemed too intense. "If you ever want a job as a detective for the defense, just let me know." He laughed as if he'd told a terrific joke, but a private one I wasn't privy to.

I glanced at him. The smile on his mouth loomed large and nasty. Behind me, the door opened. With difficulty, I managed to turn and look. Were Presto and Delbert entering the room or was my imagination imploding?

I thought I should ask Sandy something, except I couldn't think what it was. The table lurched up and smacked my forehead. After that, nothing.

50

Slowly, I became aware of my surroundings. I lay on a carpet. I knew this because I was on my back and my fingers felt its woven texture before I raised my hand to touch my head.

An inadvertent moan escaped me as I brushed my forehead. It was so sore. My whole head ached, and I had no idea why. Carefully, I opened my eyes. Thankfully the room was dim, and there were no windows with blinding shafts of light.

As I became more alert, I realized I had no idea where I was or how I'd gotten there. Then I saw the desk. Massive and ornate. I'd seen it before.

Presto's desk in his office, where I'd found Delbert's passport. There was something about the two names together that tried to stir a memory, but nothing would come.

I rolled to my hands and knees and pushed myself into a sitting position. My rain coat was gone. There was no sign of my tote bag which meant I had no phone, no ID, and no money. No aspirin or ibuprofen either.

What had happened to bring me here? I took a breath and thought back. Jase had come. I'd been with Sanders. Coffee, he'd given me coffee and that was the last thing I could remember.

"He drugged me," I whispered.

Bracing my hands on the floor, I rose carefully, scanning the room. A dim lamp glowed from the depths of a bookcase. I walked to the nearby desk lamp and switched it on. The desk surface was devoid of clues, nothing to tell me what had happened. I walked to the door. It was locked. Gingerly, I pressed my ear to the painted wood and listened. I could hear muffled voices but was unable to make out the words.

I was in a locked room with no windows. If I'd had a screwdriver, I could have undone the hinges and opened the door that way. Perhaps a letter opener? But the desk divulged no tools and no phone. This time I was out of luck.

Frantic, I searched every drawer and cubbyhole in the room, praying I'd find a cell phone, an iPad, anything that would get me out of that room or allow me to contact Jase, Paddy, or at this point, even the police. Did Jase know where I was? Did anyone?

I found nothing. They, or whoever was outside that door, meant to keep me their prisoner. I sank into the office desk chair. As I leaned forward to put my elbows on the wood surface, something hard pressed into my butt. I slid inquisitive fingers into the pocket.

My picks!

Moments later, I had picked the lock open. After carefully turning the brass knob, I cracked the door an inch. An eye to the space showed the hall to be dim and empty. The voices were clearer and seemed to come from the living room. The one I'd fled through two nights earlier.

After slipping into the hall, I closed the door quietly behind me. From beyond the kitchen I heard a generator running. I remembered the hurricane. The power must be out with only a few outlets providing electricity. Tiptoeing along the wall, I skirted a large wooden chest and headed for the archway to the living room.

The hall was humid from the rain and the smell of damp earth seemed to seep inside from beneath the front door. Ahead, the long narrow windows and fan light that encased it almost shivered beneath a barrage of wind-driven rain that beat against the glass.

Only a terrible storm could drive the rain underneath the large portico outside. And terrible people inside. Over the noise of the hurricane, I heard multiple voices. Who and how many were involved?

Inching forward, I was grateful that the weather drowned the sound of my footsteps. My heart was hammering, my breathing ragged as my fingers touched the molding surrounding the arch. Light flooded from the living room into the gloomy hallway.

I eased one eye beyond the edge of the molding and scanned the room inside. It looked like an effing party in there.

Five people sat among a grouping of two couches and armchairs. Side tables held drinks. A pitcher of ice with a green tinged liquid sat on the coffee table.

Maeve sat next to Sanders on a beige couch, wearing her signature scanty animal print clothing. She leaned against his shoulder, looked up at him adoringly before leaning toward the coffee table.

"Darling, can I get you another gimlet?"

"Please," he said, one long finger tracing her bare shoulder.

God, had it been those two all along? Of course, it had! But what were they planning?

Facing them Presto and Ransdale, formerly known as Delbert, were in comfortable armchairs, well-fortified with their own gimlets. No surprise there, but I was startled to see Connor lolling in an armchair close to his mother.

I pulled my head back out of site. I knew the voices. Listening would suffice.

"Why do we have to *kill* her?" Presto's voice.

His words unleashed a wave of horror inside me as he continued.

"I thought putting her in jail for life met everyone's needs. I don't cotton to murder."

I almost choked on his last comment. He didn't *cotton* to murder. What did he think happened to Sylvie? As their intention sunk in, my heart pounded so fast I thought it would fly from my chest.

"This is not something I want to be involved in, either." Ransdale's voice.

I had to get out. Maybe through the kitchen? I took a step, but suddenly, even louder than the storm, was the sound of someone rapping the brass knocker at the front door.

"What the hell?" someone said.

"I'll see who it is." Connor's voice grew closer.

I flattened against the wall, then turned, thinking to hide behind the chest. It was too late. Connor entered the dim hallway, but his attention was focused on the front door and he didn't see me pressed against the wall.

When he opened it, Jase stood there, dripping water from his oil-skin coat.

"I need to talk to Mr. DuPriest. A tree's down on the barn. We've got horses loose."

Connor gestured toward the living room. "He's in there."

Connor didn't appear to recognize Jase from our sapphire retrieval. Jase started for the living room, but suddenly his eyes widened as he caught me in his peripheral vision. Connor followed his gaze.

"Shit! The bitch is loose. She's out here!"

Jase stilled as Presto shouted and sprinted into the hall. Presto ran at me but Connor was already on me like a rabid dog, lunging, hitting the back of my shoulders and knocking me to the floor as I vainly tried to race to the kitchen. I scratched and kicked. Did my best to reach his eyes with my fingers, but Presto grabbed my arms, and Connor smacked my head with a fist.

The walls around me spun crazily and I went limp, afraid I'd pass out if I kept fighting. When my senses settled, I realized Jase was standing over me, his face expressionless.

"Jase," Presto said, "help us get her up. Take her in there," he said waving at the living room, "and don't let her go!"

"Yes sir," Jase said. He helped them drag me into the living room where they slammed me into an un-upholstered, wooden armchair.

Presto and Connor held my wrists tight to the chair arms, and Jase never looked at me. His face was closed, unreadable. Not so Maeve. The satisfied smirk on her face made me wish I could slap her.

"Ransdale," Presto said, "get that duct tape in the kitchen. We need to tie her to this chair, and you," he said, glaring at Jase, "you work for me, remember?"

"Yes sir, of course." Under the circumstances, Jase's voice was strangely quiet and steady.

"Look, son," Sanders said, "you'd do well to remember that. There's a lot of ways we can send you back to jail. Trust me, it would be easy."

"There's no problem," Jase said. "I work for Mr. DuPriest and will do whatever he says. It's not like I need trouble, is it?"

His words stunned me. I'd never felt so abandoned, so stranded. Was I hearing him right? But suddenly, I remembered how quick he'd been to agree to Sanders' request that he leave the office. He'd had no problem leaving me alone with Sanders. Maybe he was just playing along with these men. Or maybe his support for me had always been a sham.

I caught his eye. "They're going to kill me, Jase."

His face remained impassive. "That's their business," he said, and turned his gaze to Presto. "Look, Carl and Timmy are trying to get the horses in, but we could use a fourth man. I need to get back to the barn and hammer some boards over the gap. Can you help?"

Before Presto could answer, Ransdale came in with the duct tape. "Ransdale," Presto said, "help Connor fasten Quinn to that chair."

Ransdale tore off a long strip and wound it around one of my wrists and the wooden arm of the chair.

"You go see about buttoning up the barn," Presto said to Jase. "I'll be along to help catch those horses as soon as I get my rain gear."

I couldn't take my eyes off Jase. Would he turn to look at me, give me a sign? But he simply nodded at Presto and turned to go. A moment later, I heard the storm raging through the opened front door. My last hope left with him as surely as the sound of the door slamming shut.

51

The living room windows trembled as the storm waged war against the house. Jase was out there, and he'd left behind an emotional tempest that ripped at my heart. Had he abandoned me so easily?

A shuddering sensation in the floor boards followed a loud crash from outside. A huge tree must have come down near the house. I stared at the ceiling, afraid I'd see water dripping through, but whatever had smashed to the ground must have left this part of the house unscathed.

"I'll tell ya," Presto said, "I have never seen a storm like this. Randy, could you see if there's any damage inside the house?"

Ransdale, who'd finished taping my right side to the chair, nodded, and left the room. Connor, however, was enjoying himself too much to finish. He kept giggling as he used yards of duct tape to fasten me to the chair's other side.

Maeve egged him on, saying, "She doesn't look so high and mighty now, does she?"

"She ain't nothing," he said. His bonds were much tighter than Ransdale's, and I was relieved that when he finished his work, he didn't double his tape over Ransdale's.

With her fake smile, Maeve cuddled against Sanders. "How about I make sandwiches for everyone and refresh this pitcher of gimlets?"

Connor rose from where he'd just settled on the couch. "I'll go with you. I'm starving."

"I'll make the gimlets," Sanders said, and with that the three of them left the room, leaving me alone with Presto.

A blast of wind and another crash caused him to stare out the window. I pulled against Ransdale's tape and it gave a little. I tried again, using all my strength, but was unable to make more headway.

When Presto turned back to me, he was breathing hard and mumbling to himself. He stared blindly at the floor as if frightened by something inside himself. Maybe he didn't like seeing his world crash around him any more than I did mine.

Gazing out the window once more, he spoke words almost too soft to hear.

"Lord, I always wanted to be the kind of man who wouldn't offend you. And I am truly sorry about Sylvie. But Randy, he would have his way. I couldn't lose him, Lord, I just couldn't. Her life in exchange for our life together. I'm sorry, but it was the only way."

I was surprised he sounded so torn. Maybe it was hard to watch the disintegration of the good-man image he'd constructed for himself. And now, he was about to destroy what was left of it. I almost laughed. He had me in *his* house, strapped to a chair, about to be murdered.

His mumbling to the Lord ceased as people filtered back. Maeve bore a platter of sandwiches, Connor was already stuffing one in his mouth, and Sanders carried the refreshed pitcher of gimlets. The three of them sat on the beige couch before the coffee table laden with food and vodka.

Sanders had seated himself before the tall window that rattled from the onslaught of the storm. Maeve sat between him and Connor.

In the gloom outside the glass, I could make out the massive form of one of the ancient live oaks. Its leaves shook and its branches swayed alarmingly.

Inside, the smell of ham and cheese sandwiches on top of whatever drug I'd been given made me nauseous. The strong sweet-and-sour scent of lime juice wasn't helping either.

Ransdale finally trailed into the room behind the others. "Nothing has broken through to the house," he said. Then his gaze turned to me. "I don't like what you people intend to do to this young woman."

"Don't be a wuss," Connor said, his mouth crammed with ham and cheese.

Maeve swallowed a slug of vodka. "Ransdale, you just don't get it, do you? *She* knows too much. She's got to go."

Maeve's hand moved to the sandwich platter where a long-bladed knife lay. She grasped its large handle and stroked the side of the blade with a finger. She and Connor exchanged a look and smiled.

"No offense meant, Maeve," Sanders said, "but since she's a Traveller and already wanted for murder, no one will care if she winds up dead."

Maeve grinned. "No offense taken, sweetheart. Your plan is so delicious, I think it calls for another drink."

Her lovey-dovey tone sickened me. It was the same false flattery she'd used on Da. Didn't Sanders realize she'd stick a knife in him if it paid her money? Obviously not. Smiling, Maeve lay the knife down and poured herself another gimlet. How could they still be sitting up straight with the amount of vodka they'd consumed?

"Presto, I know you have doubts, too," Sanders said. "But trust me, it will be easy to convince law enforcement she broke in here and tried to kill you when you caught her robbing your safe."

"And," Maeve's syrupy voice added," as executor of Rory's estate, Sandy and I get all his money, and Presto, you get Sylvie's without any questions asked. If Quinn's dead, she can't talk."

"That's right," Connor said, "and guess what? I'll be happy to get rid of her for you. You chicken shits won't do it. None of you has the guts, except Mom. You think we're dumb enough to let Quinn live to write a will? She'd leave everything to Uncle Paddy."

Connor swallowed the last of his sandwich and rose from the couch. His voice grew louder until he was shouting, "I had to kill your stupid wife, Presto! Remember, I got proof! You wrote a twenty-thousand-dollar check so I'd do it. So stop whining and enjoy the ride. I know I will."

Ransdale's eyes widened in shock. He hadn't moved since he'd entered the room, apparently rooted to the spot by the acrimony that spewed around him. His horrified gaze flew to Presto.

"*You?* You had Sylvie killed. You told me it was her!" he shrieked, pointing at me. "You *lied* to me!"

Presto rushed to him. "Randy, I did it for you. For us!"

Ransdale held up his hands. "Stop it! Just stop." He backed away from Presto and for a moment, there was shocked silence.

Connor had killed Sylvie? My bound hands clenched into fists. I wanted to hurt him, really hurt him. But I was powerless. These people and their plotting had tied my hands since the day I was arrested for the sapphire. I wanted to scream.

Connor's laughter broke the silence. "Trouble in paradise for you boys? You queers are too much."

"Shut up, Connor," Sanders said. "You're not helping!"

Maeve scowled at Sanders while Presto hurried to the pitcher of gimlets and topped off everyone's glasses with more vodka. Everyone except Ransdale.

For Ransdale, Presto poured a fresh glass and held it out to his friend. "Calm down sweetheart. We'll talk about this, okay?"

When Ransdale refused to look at him or take the glass, Presto's lips compressed in an angry line. He tossed down the vodka, slipped into his rain gear, and headed for the front door. Moments later he was gone, leaving behind a damp, chilling draft.

Maeve and Sanders were arguing about Connor, who ignored their bickering by slurping down more liquor. Maybe he'd pass out.

Glancing at the three of them, Ransdale moved close to me and whispered, "I'll help you if I can."

I was stunned and felt a momentary flash of relief. But what could he do against Presto, Sanders, Connor and Maeve, and for that matter, maybe even Jase?

A thunderous cracking and ripping sounded as a huge oak limb crashed through the window behind Sanders. Wind and rain hit my face as the tree struck Sanders' head, twisting his neck into an impossible position. His eyes widened with surprise. Maeve screamed, and as I stared at Sanders, the light left his eyes. I was sure he was dead.

Ransdale pulled a small utility knife from his pocket and began to cut away the tape that held me.

Maeve and Connor, apparently stunned by Sanders' death, and distracted by the rain, wind, and debris that surged through the broken window, were oblivious to Ransdale's movements.

I pulled against my restraints, the tension making it easier for Ransdale to slice through. He got my hands loose enough that I could rip at the tape while he squatted on the floor and released my legs.

"Run!" he hissed. "For God's sake, run!"

I sprinted to the front door, opened it, and plunged into the storm.

52

When I left the shelter of Ballymoor's portico, a sideways gust almost knocked me to my knees. Turning my back to the wind, I let it drive me away from the house and toward the entrance gate.

In seconds, I was drenched to the skin. Rain poured down my face, and my clothes grew heavy with water. The smell of wet earth and sodden vegetation layered the air rushing past me.

I could barely make out the darkened barn through the rain and the wind. Was Jase there? I longed to find him. Maybe he'd only pretended to be unconcerned about my fate. But I was a fool to think it. I couldn't trust him.

The glance I threw back at the house only increased my desperation. Maeve and Connor were running behind me and closing in. My only hope was to outrun them. I set my sights on the main gate, praying I might find first responders in the neighborhood.

Something heavy thwacked my shoulder blades. It knocked me to my knees and then to the ground. A desperate look showed that a short, broken limb, maybe four or five inches thick, had struck me. Behind me Connor was in mid lunge and about to nail me where I lay.

Grabbing the limb, I twisted it upright. Connor's chest landed on its sharp, broken end. His mouth opened but I couldn't hear his cry over the storm's blast. An electrical charge of anger jolted through me. I jerked the limb out from under him and hit his head as hard as I could.

I could hear Maeve's anguished scream of rage over the storm's roar. She held the long-bladed knife and thrust it at me where I knelt over Connor's crumpled form. I tried to twist away, but her knife plunged into my upper arm.

But her attack had left her off balance. With arms flailing, she tumbled to the ground. Gritting my teeth, I pulled the knife from my arm, crawled to her, and pressed the sharp blade to her neck.

Her eyes showed terror. "You wouldn't!"

"Sure, I would."

"Quinn, don't!" Jase had emerged from the storm and was leaning over us.

"Do I have to fight you, too?" I shouted.

"No Quinn, no. I've called the cops. They're coming. I had to say what I did. I'd never have gotten out to get help. You know that."

His eyes begged me to believe him, but I continued to press the cold steel to Maeve's neck. Jase could still be lying.

A new sound mingled with the shriek of the wind. Flashing blue and red lights sped through the entrance gate, and the sound of the squad car's siren became clear.

The world shifted and became familiar again, like coming home after a long journey. My eyes burned with tears. Jase hadn't lied.

53

A month later, I sat with Jase and Lara in Mark's apartment, eating deli sandwiches and drinking sodas.

It was good to see Lara again. Today, I even liked her super bleached blond hair and black makeup. I hadn't seen her since she'd sped me into the barn at Ballymoor so Jase could hide me in his secret closet. It seemed a lifetime ago.

I'd seen Paddy and Mary often since the night of the hurricane, but today they were at a Travellers' party. Mark, who I was beginning to think I'd never meet, had decided to live in England during the coming winter. It was a stroke of luck, as he'd agreed to let me stay in his barn apartment until I got a place of my own.

The three of us were sitting at his kitchen table when Lara gave me an inquisitive look.

"So, as of yesterday, the grand jury basically decided that the evidence against you for Connor's death is no good? That is so cool!"

"I think instead of 'no good,' the expression is 'not prosecutable,'" I said.

"*Whatever.* But you're in the clear with no criminal record, right?"

I could feel myself grinning. "I still can't believe it!"

"The thing that gets me," Jase said, "is how dumb I was to believe Sanders' story that Maeve would testify against Presto, that she'd swear in court Presto had paid Carl to murder his wife."

"Don't feel bad," I said. "Sanders knew we were desperate and naïve enough to believe his lie. And face it, we were."

Lara made a slight grimace. "Those bastards really played you, Quinn."

"That they did," Jase said.

I glanced at her. "Did you hear about Sylvie's life insurance policy? The one that supposedly named me as beneficiary?"

"I heard it was fake or something."

"Exactly," Jase said, "Presto and Sanders set the whole thing up just to make Quinn the prime suspect. They even faked an ID showing Quinn was a relative of Sylvie's. That's how they were able to get the policy written."

"Wait, don't tell me," Lara said, "They planned to get rid of you, right? So, there was never a risk their insurance fraud would be discovered?"

"That's about it," I said.

Lara tucked one long white-blond lock behind an ear. "And Presto and Maeve?"

"In jail awaiting their trials," I said. "My new lawyer assures me they'll be in prison for a long time. Anyway, I don't want to talk about them. I am glad, though, that no charges were brought against Ransdale."

"So, Quinn," Lara asked, "what's next?"

"Get the money Da left me from my new lawyer, put it in the bank, and buy a place to live in Aiken."

"So, you're done with Tinkers Town?"

"That she is," Jase said.

"I want to get some horses and a little land. Maybe raise Gypsy Vanners."

"I think I heard a 'but' in there," Lara said.

I stared through the window into the distance. "My mother. If she's still out there, I want to find her."

Nobody said anything for a moment. Then Lara put her hands on the table, her gaze on me intense. "I hope you're not opening a can of worms."

"Why would she be?" Jase said. "She's hiring a private detective, she'll find her mother, and take it from there."

"Maybe it's the gypsy in me," Lara said, "but I feel like you should leave it alone."

"I can't. I have to find her."

"Lara, don't worry," Jase said. "Quinn will take that journey with me." His eyes held mine for a moment. "We'll travel together, yeah?"

"That's the plan," I said.

Acknowledgements

FROM SOUTH CAROLINA and Georgia law enforcement, I wish to thank:

Aiken criminal defense attorney, P. Andrew Anderson.

Jeffrey Buerstatte: Former Undercover Narcotics Agent, Washington State. Former Special Agent and Agent in Charge, Bureau of Alcohol, Tobacco and Firearms, Portland, Oregon, Miami & Ft Lauderdale, FL; Former Assistant U.S. Attorney, U.S. Attorney's Office, Southern District of Georgia, and currently, Attorney in Private Practice, Brunswick, GA.

Judge Doyet A. (Jack) Early, III, Judge for the Second Judicial Circuit in South Carolina, with jurisdiction in Aiken, Barnwell, and Bamberg counties. He was kind enough to let me interview him in his chambers during recess. I was glad he removed his black robe as he was much less intimidating in a suit!

Thanks also go to Capt. Nick Gallam, Jail Administrator with the Aiken County Sheriff's Office Detention Division, who kindly spent his time giving me a lengthy tour of the Aiken Detention center.

And my appreciation goes to Liz Godard, Clerk of Court, Aiken Judicial Center[1];

Lt. Mahoney, Aiken Public Safety Public Information Officer.

---

1.   https://www.aikencountysc.gov/DspLoc.php?qLocID=JC

Mariane Parker, paralegal for the Aiken Solicitor. She was extremely helpful in finding the right people for my questions regarding this book. She was also extremely knowledgeable regarding all court matters.

And finally, as always, huge thanks to my critique group, "The Assassins Guild." Couldn't have done it without you guys!

I love to hear from my readers!

Please visit me at SasscerHill.com.

If you enjoyed this book please leave a review.

Want more? Read on for a preview of *SHOOTING STAR*, the fifth "Nikki Latrelle" mystery.

SHOOTING STAR
Chapter 1

LIKE A HUNGRY BIRD of prey, the dark eye of the movie camera raced beside us as I galloped my horse along the sandy dirt of Santa Anita's backstretch.

Knowing the camera, a Panavision Genesis, recorded my every move and facial expression intimidated the hell out of me. So did the truck and crew rolling dangerously close to our side.

Maybe movie stars like Tom Cruise, who loved to do his own stunt work, get used to this stuff. But me, I was glad I was only an extra, used by the director of photography, or DP, to work out his blueprint for shooting scenes in *The Final Furlong*, a horse racing movie about to be filmed at Santa Anita Park.

Somebody in the truck yelled, "Cut!" The vehicle fell back, and I stood in the stirrups and eased my horse, Daisy Dan. It was the third time we'd shot this scene, and Daisy Dan was tired. The DP, Gabriel Dubois, might be French, stylish, and handsome, but he didn't know a horse from a hamster.

"Okay, Nikki," Gabriel yelled, "that's a wrap. You can take the horse back."

I sketched a wave and patted the horse's sweaty neck, relieved he was done for the day. As I held him to a slow jog, he rounded the far turn of the mile-long oval, before I pointed him toward the gap that would lead us off the track.

The GMC camera truck sped past us, with Dave, the assistant camera man at the wheel. The pickup had a crane bolted to its bed. It held the Genesis camera, remotely controlled by Gabriel from the passenger seat.

Dave stopped to let Gabriel out by the grandstand. He was probably going to see his contact at Santa Anita's special projects office. As Gabriel walked away, Dave circled the vehicle back toward me. Glancing at his profile, he once again struck me as a nervous loner with secrets to hide. He wasn't the friendliest guy in the movie crew.

Keeping Daisy Dan to a walk, we passed through the gap in the rail, soon leaving the dirt path behind and stepping onto the dirt and gravel of the parking lot. Nearby, Dave rolled in, heading for the base camp, a parking area track management had allotted the studio. The dozen or so trailers for actors, wardrobe, makeup, catering, and camera crew had turned this space into a luxury trailer park.

The air was clear and cool, a dry seventy degrees in February in Arcadia, California. In the distance, the Santa Gabriel mountains rose to meet the golden-blue skyline. No wonder so many people loved living in this state. Except the Arcadia summers were hot and dry, and when the wind blew off the mountains, the forest fires started. I wouldn't want to be around then.

I rode toward the private gate that allowed us into the limited stable area we'd been given. Nearby, Dave paralleled my path, heading his truck for his parking spot by the trailers.

I'd only been with the company for a few days and being late afternoon, and my scene the last of the day, most of the movie people had left or were in their trailers behind closed doors and curtains.

Since it was a "dark," or non-racing day, the backstretch was quiet. Grooms would reappear closer to five p.m. to give the horses their evening feed, water, and hay. Now, the area was all but deserted.

Sensing a change in the air, I glanced at the mountains. A gray cloud bank had built behind them, and its gloomy presence crept toward me and Dave who'd parked about a hundred yards away.

A muffled, but sharp pop zinged past me. I flinched as my gaze shot to the sound of shattering glass where Dave sat in the camera truck. Horrified, I stared as blood blossomed from the side of his head. Red gore splattered and spread across the inside of the passenger window. Dave's form slumped and slid sideways toward the passenger door, finally disappearing from my sight.

I knew what I'd seen but couldn't believe it. I forced myself to breathe slowly. Once my nerves steadied to where I could think, I pulled Daisy Dan to a stop, whipped out my phone, and tried to hit a speed dial connection. My hands shook so badly, it took two attempts.

My boss and former fellow jockey, Will Marshall, answered on the first ring.

"Yeah, Nikki, what's up?"

"The camera man, Dave, was just shot. I think he's dead!" Beneath me, my horse shifted uneasily as my emotions traveled through the reins like electricity.

"Where are you?"

I told him.

"Be there in two minutes."

"This is so bizarre," I gasped. "I'll– I'll call the cops and track security." By now, my horse was alternately backing up lifting both front legs in little half rears. I had to get him moving forward before he exploded. Gathering my reins, I booted him toward the gate and tried to still my trembling hands.

Twenty minutes later, I stood at the murder site next to Will. Around us, the scene was mobbed with police and emergency services. The report of gunfire had brought two fire trucks. They'd flashed in, big, bright and red, with sirens screaming. They were parked now, but their diesel engines still idled noisily.

The dozens of green, wooden barns on Santa Anita's backstretch were flammable enough. The stalls filled with wood shavings and straw bedding were a pyromaniac's delight. Even though we didn't need the fire brigade, I was glad they'd come. Better safe than sorry.

A crowd of gawkers had formed, and cops were all over the place, along with the medical examiner, crime scene investigators, and the ambulance to take Dave's body away.

Two medics wheeled a gurney with what was left of Dave zipped in a black body bag. I had to look away. He might not have been my favorite person but what had driven someone to *murder* him? What could he have done to deserve this?

Mentally I tried to shut out my surroundings and glanced at Will. Now that he wasn't riding, he'd gained a few pounds, and they hadn't hurt his looks. In the past, constant dieting to maintain jockey weight had given his face a honed, almost aesthetic look, enhanced by intense green eyes. When I'd first met him, I'd thought him quiet and a bit introverted until I discovered his wicked sense of humor, part of why I'd fallen for him.

He caught my eye. "You've been here what, four days? And we've already had a murder? What is it about you Nikki? Trouble *loves* you." He managed to keep a straight face, but his lips compressed a little with the effort.

"It's not funny," I protested.

"Sorry, you're right. But it's so typical of what happens when you're around." By now his eyes were bright with amusement and he'd lost his fight not to grin.

I knew Will so well. We'd both seen our share of murder victims and I didn't blame him for seeking refuge in humor.

For a time, we'd been an item. When I was twenty-three, Will was the first man I ever slept with. The relationship hadn't survived.

I'd never gotten over how he'd hidden his part-time undercover work from me.

He'd been a subcontractor to the Thoroughbred Racing Protective Bureau when I'd been involved with some bad people at Florida's Gulfstream Park. He'd spied on me, using me to get information back to the TRPB and the DEA. Hard to be certain if he'd come after me as a woman he was falling in love with, one he initially believed was a criminal, or simply a commodity he could use to further his ambition to become an agent for the TRPB.

He'd realized his goal and secured the job. Now, for a short while, I was a subcontractor for the bureau, like he'd been four years earlier. I guess what goes around comes around.

We shared a lot of history and remained friends who respected each other. He'd gotten me the job working for Estrella Studio's movie as an exercise rider and occasional jockey for the race scenes they'd be shooting.

Just then, a man I suspected was a homicide detective for the Arcadia PD peeled away from a group of cops and first responders and headed for us. He looked like so many cops. A cheap suit and hard eyes.

Glancing at Will, he said, "Are you the TRPB agent?"

When Will said he was, the cop thrust out a hand. "Detective Ernesto Garcia." Glancing at me, he said, "Could you excuse us, Miss?"

"Sure," I said, turning on my heel and heading for our backstretch gate. Though I'd turned Daisy Dan over to a groom, I wanted to go back and check on him. I needed to know he was cooling out okay, getting his legs done up properly, and that he seemed comfortable.

The entire string of *Final Furlong* racehorses were older Thoroughbreds. Some of the ones the film company had collected had been running as cheap claimers. As for the rest, who knew where they'd come from or if the movie could succeed at convincing an audience they were top notch racehorses.

One of my undercover jobs was to keep Will informed of the condition and treatment of these animals. Since the mission of the TRPB is to protect the integrity and image or American horseracing, the bureau wanted to avoid the kind of troubles that occurred with the ill-fated HBO racing series, *Luck*. The show had been cancelled after public outcry due to the deaths of several horses on their set.

Since Will wasn't undercover, and I was, I should avoid the appearance of working *with* him. I could be his friend, as long as no one thought I was feeding him information. Remembering the crowd at the murder scene, I wasn't worried about the short time I'd stood next to him. But I'd be careful in the future. My job might depend on it.

Santa Anita management had made it clear to the movie's Panamanian director, Frank Zalaya, that all cast and crew must stay inside the temporary fence surrounding our area. We'd been given a nice thirty-stall barn with wide dirt paths edged with evergreens. I liked the weeping Australian willows and especially the silver green eucalyptus trees with their fresh, citrus sent. We were forbidden to go beyond the fence. There were too many star trainers at Santa Anita, like Bob Baffert, who'd be very unhappy to have a bunch of ignorant movie people near their barns and horses.

I walked past the Australian willow tree, that along with the movie's security guard, stood sentry by our gate. By now the guy recognized me, and I strode past without having to show ID. Following the dirt path into the backside, I passed beneath a queen palm before stepping onto our shedrow.

Stan Gabrino, the washed-up trainer the production company had hired to manage the horses, stopped me.

"What the hell's going on out there?"

When I told him, I wasn't surprised at his reaction. A quiet sigh and an increased droop in his shoulders were his only comment. Somewhere in his late sixties or early seventies, his wrinkled face and tired eyes were crowned with wispy gray hair.

"Did our string behave themselves today?"

He was referring to the horses. "Yeah, but they pushed Daisy Dan too hard and too long."

With another sigh, he stepped away from me. Sadly, his most prominent feature was a bad limp where his leg had been broken and crushed by a runaway horse. I suspected he desperately needed the job he'd been given and would simply go along to get along.

"Okay, then, Nikki. I'll see you in the morning."

He turned away and hobbled down the shedrow. The guy was useless. Maybe the production company wanted him like that. Turning away from his receding figure, I called to Orlando, who was walking Daisy Dan.

"Hey, how's he doing?"

Orlando shrugged. "He tired. And *el director de fotografía*? He not know what he doing."

"That's why he's the director," I said.

When Orlando led the horse past me, his double gold earrings sparkled, and his teeth flashed white beneath his long, carefully groomed moustache. "*Exactamente!*"

We grinned, and Orlando led Daisy Dan down the aisle before disappearing around the corner of the barn. I'd met Orlando four years earlier when I'd been at Gulfstream Park racetrack. He was a competent groom and I was glad we'd been able to hire him back for this job.

But when things got rough, it was Will I'd trust to watch my back. Orlando, though a cocky little rooster, would run shrieking to the hen house at the first sign of trouble.

But we probably wouldn't have any more trouble, right?

About Sasscer Hill

AUTHOR SASSCER HILL was involved in horse racing as an amateur jockey and racehorse breeder for most of her life. She sets her novels against a background of big money, gambling, and horse racing. Her mystery and suspense thrillers have won the Dr. Tony Ryan Best in Racing Literature Award (Flamingo Road) and the Carrie McCray Award (The Dark Side of Town). Her books have also received multiple award nominations for Agatha, Macavity and Claymore Awards.

Her most recent novel, "Travels of Quinn" a stand-alone mystery-thriller based on the con artists known as Irish American Travelers.

Sasscer lives in Aiken, South Carolina horse country, with her husband, a dog, and a cat.

Don't miss out!

Visit the website below and you can sign up to receive emails whenever Sasscer Hill publishes a new book. There's no charge and no obligation.

https://books2read.com/r/B-A-RLYC-VOXCB

BOOKS 2 READ

Connecting independent readers to independent writers.

Made in the USA
Columbia, SC
21 June 2021

40364462R00174